THE GOBLINS OF BELLWATER

MOLLY RINGLE

central
avenue
publishing

2017

This is a work of fiction. Names, characters, places and incidents either are the
product of the author's imagination or are used fictitiously and any resemblance to
actual persons, living or dead, business establishments, events or locales is entirely
coincidental.

Published by Central Avenue Publishing, an imprint of Central Avenue Marketing Ltd.
www.centralavenuepublishing.com

THE GOBLINS OF BELLWATER

Trade Paperback: 978-1-77168-117-9
Epub: 978-1-77168-118-6
Mobi: 978-1-77168-119-3

Published in Canada
Printed in United States of America

1. FICTION/Mythology   2. FICTION/Romance - Paranormal

Dedicated to my sisters,
both the biological and the honorary.

"Hug me, kiss me, suck my juices
Squeez'd from goblin fruits for you,
Goblin pulp and goblin dew.
Eat me, drink me, love me;
Laura, make much of me;
For your sake I have braved the glen
And had to do with goblin merchant men."

CHRISTINA ROSSETTI, "GOBLIN MARKET"

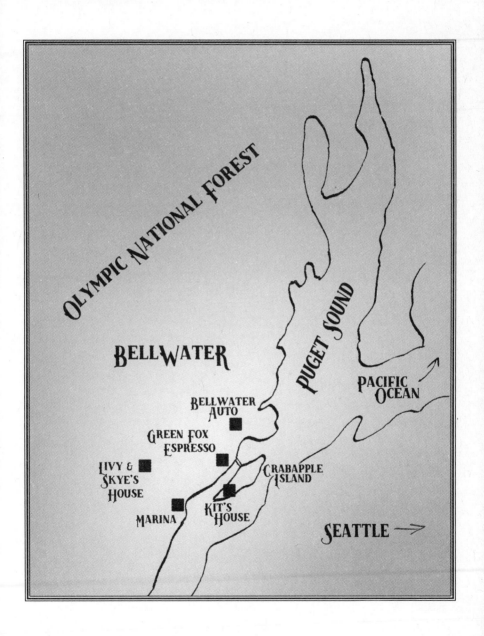

CHAPTER ONE

WITH NOT QUITE ENOUGH GOLD IN HIS POCK-
ET, KIT SYLVAIN TRUDGED THROUGH THE UNDERBRUSH, TRAMPLING SA-
lal and fern under his hiking boots. The sun had set, and the light was
fading. Not that there had been much light to begin with. It was a
Wednesday in early December, and here on the western side of Puget
Sound, clouds generally socked everything in for the whole winter, and
a good deal of fall and spring too. Tonight the sky hung pewter gray between the swaying fir branches high above, and on the forest floor the
colors were washed out to a greenish black.

Kit couldn't see the rising full moon what with the thick forest and
all the clouds, but he knew it was there.

By now he didn't even bother with a flashlight. He knew where to
go. He wouldn't recommend anyone else wander out here alone after
dark, though.

He weaseled between close-growing trunks and stopped in a tiny
clearing wedged in by six thick trees. Only dead fir needles lay under his
feet here; no other plants could take the constant lack of sunlight. Except
mushrooms, of course. Never any shortage of mushrooms.

Kit ran his hand through his hair and pulled the slim gold necklace
from the pocket of his leather jacket. Another full moon, another offering.

He lifted his face toward the treetops and whistled a few notes of one
of the tribe's songs. None were tunes you'd hear on the radio, though Kit

would have sworn one of them had stolen riffs from a Bowie song. No surprise. Goblins stole stuff every chance they got.

In answer to his whistle, a few notes on a pipe floated down from the trees. Then someone blew a raspberry from a hundred feet up, and someone else cackled.

Immature buttheads. God.

"Guys." Kit held up the chain. Three little gold hearts dangled from it. "It's me."

"Kiiiit. Daaaarling." The cooing voice sank closer to the ground.

At the base of the trees, something light caught his eye. Several puffy white mushrooms had arranged themselves into a row. The line trailed out between two of the trees, through a space that hadn't been there a minute earlier.

He gritted his teeth and walked forward, following the mushroom trail. The goblins wouldn't show their faces unless you accepted their invitation and followed their path. But he hated doing it, every time.

Soon he reached a spot where the mushrooms formed a circle. They glowed, casting a bluish-white light on the ferns and roots. Kit stood in the ring and waited. Within seconds, an arm shot out of the darkness, brown and gnarled like a twig, and grabbed the necklace away from him. In the same moment someone else tweaked a fingerful of his hair from behind and tugged it, then let go.

He grunted in pain, though not in surprise. "You're welcome," he muttered.

The creature who had taken the necklace coalesced into view, shifting into a larger shape as if borrowing material from the shadows and soil. Kit always found it fascinating, and somewhat wished he could see it in broad daylight so he could see how the transformation worked. But then, you weren't ever going to meet these guys in broad daylight.

Redring stood in front of him, a few inches taller than Kit. Always had to make herself bigger than whoever she was menacing. In the glimpses he'd caught, she and the other goblins ordinarily looked like porcupine-sized gargoyles carved out of driftwood and decorated with shells and ugly jewelry. When they interacted with humans, though, they took on a human-ish form. Kit attached the "ish" in his mind because any human would see they weren't quite right.

Redring, for example, looked like a chubby woman around fifty, with big fluffy hair in a bottled shade of orange. Every time he saw her take this form, she wore the same thing: a knee-length brown sweater or maybe bathrobe that tied around the waist, over what looked like pale pink pajamas and alligator-skin slippers. You'd glance twice at anyone standing around in the woods like that at night, and when you did glance again, you'd notice the weird smoothness to her skin and the sharp points on every one of her teeth.

The goblins rarely told him what he wanted to know, at least not in a straightforward fashion. Since inheriting this job seven years ago, at age seventeen, he had worked out a lot about them, like how they were named after the first item they'd stolen.

This tradition did mean that a lot of goblins these days should rightly be named "iPhone" or "Honda key." But they generally found ways to make unique nicknames out of those, such as the goblin called "Slide," named after the "slide to unlock" injunction on old iPhone screens.

On a filthy string around her neck, Redring wore a silver ring with a large, opaque red stone. She'd said it had belonged to a traveler a long time ago. From his ancestors' records Kit knew Redring had been around for hundreds of years, and had worn the ring the whole time, so that theft had taken place before he was born; the victim was no one he knew. This didn't make him feel better.

If the ring had been gold instead of silver, Kit knew she wouldn't be wearing it as a keepsake. They'd have used it immediately, turned the gold into whatever new thing they coveted. Redring was already holding the new gold chain up to her eye and running it through her fingers to calculate its weight. Kit shifted uneasily.

"This is all?" Redring's voice didn't go with her matronly look. She sounded more like someone who had inhaled helium.

"For now. I'll bring more later. I ordered some gold forks and stuff two weeks ago, but they're not here yet. Give it a couple days, all right?"

"*This* won't get us our milk steamer." Lately they were into making espresso drinks, partly to lure people in with the scent, but also because they constantly lusted after new tastes and possessions for themselves.

"Or even our milk," chimed in a voice from the darkness, behind Kit's shoulder.

He glanced back, but saw no one. Still, someone licked his ear, then cackled. He shuddered and scrubbed at it with his palm.

"Get your own milk," he said.

He got another hair-tweak for his attitude, but hell, they lived for stealing, so they ought to enjoy it. Then again, there were weird magical rules they had to follow, and if they broke those rules, they got some kind of smackdown from "the locals." As far as Kit could tell, the locals were other fae. Kit, like his ancestors, never saw these locals, probably because the goblins' taint on him kept the rest away.

The goblins stole stuff off hikers and other people in the woods by inviting them in. If you followed paths that mysteriously appeared while you were alone in the forest between dusk and dawn, then you were accepting their invitation. They'd appear, mug you, and jumble your memory so you couldn't recall what happened.

If you were lucky, they'd leave it at that.

Kit, at least, had immunity from those antics. To a degree. Kind of.

"I'll try to get you the milk steamer," he said. "But listen. Tonight I also want to invoke protection for someone."

"Ooooh," chorused the voices.

"Is Kit in love?" one said.

"No. It's family." He glared past the grinning Redring into the darkness, then returned his attention to her. "My cousin's coming to live with me a while. His name's Grady. Last name Sylvain, like mine." He took out his phone and brought up the photo of Grady from a social network profile: messy dark hair, goofball grin, jug-handle ears and all. He showed it to Redring. "He's twenty-one. About five foot eleven..."

Redring waved away the phone, though her long pink nails scraped it as if she was tempted to snatch it. "We don't need pictures. If he's cousin to you, we will smell him."

It sounded like an insult, but it wasn't actually. They could smell all kinds of information off people.

"Then you'll leave him alone?" he said. "Don't care if he's by himself out here, don't care what kind of glowing paths or trails of cookies he follows into the woods, you'll still leave him alone. I invoke protection." He used the formal phrase, hoping it might carry extra magical weight.

Redring scowled, while the others in the shadows continued cackling and improvising crude love songs. "Fine, he is protected." She flapped the gold necklace in his face. "But you must bring us more than this. Tomorrow. You've come up short this month."

"I can't just conjure up gold. You know that. It's expensive, and it generally belongs to other people, and—"

"You have our magical sanction to steal." Redring used what she probably supposed to be a sweetly coaxing voice. It was about as appealing as a blob of congealed jam stuck to the underside of a table.

Yes, his arrangement made it so he could steal for them and not get caught. Sounded like a dream come true, on paper. But in reality...

He looked down and ground a mushroom into obliteration under the heel of his boot. "I hate doing that to people."

"But if you don't, we get hungry, and..." She spread her fat faux-human hands in a *What you gonna do?* gesture.

"Hungry," with them, could mean all kinds of things beyond merely hungry. Could mean bored. Lustful. Violent. And it often meant willing to take their knocks from "the locals" and lash out anyway just to wreak havoc.

The frustration strangled Kit. "Don't. Just…wait, all right? Please."

"More gold tomorrow?"

"I can't promise tomorrow! How about a week. Give me a week." Maybe he could drive to Tacoma or Seattle, drop in on some chain store he didn't feel *quite* as terrible swiping stuff from, or at least it was better than lifting things from the small-town folks who lived around here…

Redring folded her arms. "Four days."

"Okay, all *right*. Four days. Goodbye."

He spun and stomped off, his shoulders knocking tree trunks. Wet boughs swiped his forehead, and goblin cackles blended into the whisper of the wind behind him and then washed out into silence.

They could wait a full fucking week for their loot, and if he heard of them acting out in any way because of the delay, he'd… Well, there wasn't a lot he could do, was there. That was the trouble.

CHAPTER TWO

SKYE DARWEN STEPPED OUT OF GREEN FOX ESPRESSO AND BREATHED IN THE FRESH AIR. AFTER BEING ENCASED IN coffee steam for six hours, she found the crisp chill a relief. Though it was only a little after five p.m., the daylight had vanished, since this was Bellwater, Washington, in December. But tonight wasn't as gloomy as most evenings had been during the past month. The low blanket of clouds had blown away, stars twinkled, and the air was calm.

Skye smelled salt water: the shore of Puget Sound was only a matter of yards away, on the other side of the cafe. A walk along the quiet beach before returning home tempted her.

Then a breeze arose, sweeping over her from inland, carrying the smell of the forest: wet mossy ground, logs, mushrooms, dirt, the Christmas-tree aroma of firs. The evergreen scent hardly changed all year, and the forest was always there for you, cool on hot summer days, calm in blustery winter.

If there was anything Skye loved more than art, it was the forest. She smiled, jogged across the street, and hiked up the sloping road toward the trees.

Skye was twenty-three, and still lived with her sister Livy in the house they'd grown up in. She had earned a bachelor's degree in art at University of Puget Sound last year, and had been gainfully employed as a barista here in her tiny hometown ever since. The cafe used her art skills when they could—she decorated the menu chalkboards every day, and vacationers and local regulars complimented her designs. Some of her drawings and paintings hung on the walls for sale, and occasionally someone even bought one. She also sold prints and T-shirts from her Etsy store, though not at a rate that would let her quit her day job.

Meanwhile she kept scouting ads for graphic-design jobs in the Puget Sound area, and her email inquiries had gotten a few promising responses lately. So life might be about to change.

Entering the forest, Skye released her dark hair from its chopstick-held bun, shook it behind her shoulders, and smiled up at the looming trees. "I'd miss you guys if I moved to the city," she told them. "But I'd still come visit, don't worry."

Branches swayed in a breeze, whispering in response. At least, she liked to think of it as response.

She had always felt the aliveness of the woods. Not just the nature: the ferns and vine maples and huckleberries, the tree frogs and deer and coyotes. She appreciated all that, with an instinctual comfort that came from having lived under these branches all her life. But she had also always felt there was something else alive in here, something more on the…imaginary side.

She'd have sworn it wasn't always her imagination, though. She wasn't sure what to call it. Spirits maybe, or Teeny-tinies, the name she and her older sister, Livy, had given them when they were kids. This being the Northwest, some would suggest calling it Sasquatch. But it didn't strike her as a Sasquatch type of presence. This was less like a big animal, and more like…well, she'd never admit this out loud, but if this were Scotland or Ireland or something, they'd probably be called the good people. Faeries. The fae.

A few times, inexplicable stuff had happened to her out here. It was only ever when she came alone into the woods, which was inconvenient, since she would have appreciated some witnesses.

One spring evening when she was eight, trotting back to the house through the woods at sunset, a sweet scent stopped her. It was the smell of cookies—vanilla-rich sugar cookies, as if someone was baking them a few feet away. She'd been saying to Livy that very afternoon, as they walked through the forest, that sugar cookies were her favorite food. (Livy told her she'd die of malnutrition if she didn't come up with some healthier other favorite foods.) Skye looked around, and saw a skinny path winding off through a clump of red huckleberry bushes. The path was just wide enough for one of her feet at a time, and she was sure no path had ever been there before. She'd have known if it had. Though it twisted back into the forest, away from home, she followed it. As she walked, the scent of cookies grew stronger. Then a scratchy, tinny voice called, from high above her head, "Little girl. Do you want a treat?"

She stopped and stared up into the trees in the fading light.

Her mother called for her, sounding strangely far off. Skye whirled and called back, "I'm out here!" and a noise scurried in the trees like a squirrel dashing away. Then Skye found herself in the middle of the forest, surrounded by red huckleberries, with no path to guide her back. She followed her mom's voice and got home, and by dinnertime a few minutes later had reckoned she had probably been imagining things.

When she was twelve, tromping around the woods one October afternoon, she heard music and followed it. It wasn't beats from someone's car stereo; it was otherworldly music, like if you took cricket chirps, frog croaks, breaking twigs, and river gurgles, and set them to a rhythm. That time, a friend of Livy's soon appeared on her way through the woods, and waved to Skye. Skye turned to join her, and the music died away.

When she was fourteen, a glowing line of mushrooms at dusk—actually glowing—led her a few yards off the trail before she got spooked and ran home.

And when she was twenty, lying on her back with her eyes closed on a fallen log in the forest at sunset, listening to hip-hop through her earbuds, she suddenly smelled coffee. It was strong enough that she figured someone had to be standing next to her with a steaming cup in hand, but when she opened her eyes no one was there. Instead she found another of those paths that hadn't been there before, this time a line of rocks, alternating gray and white. She took the earbuds out and followed it, her heart pounding. The smell of coffee clung to her like a cloud. Then came the voice. She heard it for sure this time; she was no little kid anymore. From overhead it said, in an eerie, squeaky tone, "Freshly brewed coffee, pretty lady?"

She looked all around, trembling, then nearly screamed when her phone jangled. It was a text from her boyfriend, asking where she was. She darted back to the log where she'd started, and sure enough, when she looked again, there was no line of rocks. With the next breeze, the coffee smell blew away and vanished.

All those phenomena had taken place around nightfall. She was almost never in the woods during actual night; it was too dark and there was no reason to be there. But dusk, twilight, when you could still see a little, she'd been here then, admiring the way the forest transformed into something mysterious and sinister in the dark.

As a kid she'd tried telling Livy about the sugar-cookie voice and the strange music. Livy had gotten excited and told her she'd seen or heard similar stuff. But then, she and Livy liked making up Teeny-tiny stories for each other, along with ghost stories and monster stories and alien stories and time-travel stories, so neither of them quite believed the other, was the impression Skye got. She even began to doubt her own memory of those uncanny events. She didn't try telling anyone at all about the coffee-scent incident from a few years ago; it would sound crazy, and probably she had just been tired and half-dreaming.

But now, at twilight, alone in the woods, her curiosity flared to life. She fancied herself brave and open-minded, no longer as easily-freaked as in childhood. She looked around at the darkening forest, and said aloud, "You out here, Teeny-tinies? Making your coffee or cookies? Playing your tunes? Come on. Show yourselves."

And someone, or something, cackled.

The laugh came from the shadows, higher up, as if the person or thing was in a tree. Skye squinted to look, but the trees had all become featureless black trunks with bits of dusk-blue sky caught between their fingers. Someone could be messing with her, or maybe she just happened to hear a bit of conversation from a person approaching on the path...

Then she smelled dessert. Not a mere whiff, but a wave of scent that made her mouth water. Fruity this time, a berry pastry perhaps—not sugar cookies, but pie or other baked goods. Where could that be coming from? The few restaurants in town were behind her, downwind, and the scattered country-road houses in the forest were nearly a mile away.

Her gaze dropped to the underbrush to seek a way through, and she blinked in surprise. Hundreds of flat white mushrooms grew low on the tree trunks, sticking out like rounded shelves. That she already knew; she saw them every day. But they didn't usually line up in a perfect row the way they were currently doing, striping around one tree trunk and continuing onto the next and the next, like a dotted line pointing the way into the woods. There were two such lines, in fact, one on each side of a thin space between the trees, delineating a path.

The path hadn't been there a minute ago. Skye would have bet all her colored pencils on it.

Her fingers tingling in excitement, she pulled out her phone and snapped a photo of the mushrooms. When she looked at the picture, it was hard to see the lined-up pattern that was so obvious in real life, and in any case the darkness made everything grainy.

She considered trying again, then the mouth-watering smell gusted stronger. Someone above whistled a sing-song call, three notes, low to high to middle. Someone else emitted a stifled giggle.

Skye stepped onto the path between the mushrooms and walked

forward. Her shoulders brushed wet tree branches. Moss and soggy fir needles squelched under her rain boots. She considered switching on the flashlight bulb on her phone, but soon her eyes adjusted to the darkness—and besides, the mushrooms had started glowing. Now they looked more blue than white, and when she knelt to touch one, blue light spilled across her hand and cast a shadow from one finger onto another.

"Pretty la-dy," a voice sang.

She snapped her gaze up, still crouching by the mushrooms.

A dark shape moved among the bare branches of a tree.

"Who's there?" she asked.

"Blackberry tart for the pretty lady? Fresh and sweet."

Blackberry was her favorite variety of pie, tart, or jam. And it did smell maddeningly enticing, which was a beyond-weird thing to be distracted by right now. This had to be a hoax, maybe pulled off by people she'd gone to school with. And yet...

"I've heard your voice before." She stood slowly, scanning the darkness, trying to pin down the shifting shadows. "Or voices like yours. When I was a kid."

"Did she?" The new voice, higher than the other, sounded delighted.

"Has the lady been looking for us?" the first said.

"I have." Her heart thudded in her throat. "Who are you?"

"I think the lady means *what* are you."

Holy shit. Skye swallowed. "We've called you the Teeny-tinies, my sister and me. But we don't know what you'd call yourselves."

Many voices laughed now, in pleasure, it sounded like.

"Lady wants to see us?"

"Skye. My name's Skye. Yes, I would. Please."

"We are not so teeny tiny. Though we can be if we want." The shadow took shape as it crept head-first down the trunk of the tree, into the range of the blue mushroom light.

A chill skittered up Skye's flesh. The creature reminded her of a giant spider, dark and spindly-legged. But she counted only four limbs, and two eyes gleaming at her, so, more like Gollum than a spider. Still creepy.

If it was Gollum, though, it was a Gollum made of twisted sticks and clumps of lichen, or some kind of natural camouflage that had evolved to look like that. She and Livy had pictured the Teeny-tinies as truly tiny, little enough to stand on the palm of your hand. This creature, while still smaller than her, certainly outsized that imaginary being. It was almost as big as Skye had been herself as a child.

Others approached too, descending trees and crawling across the ground. Her feet felt rooted to the earth, and her breath came shallow and fast. She looked behind her, and a new rush of fear dizzied her. The lights of Bellwater's streets, shops, and docks, modest in number though they were, should have been visible through the trees. Instead only a dark forest stood there, stretching away into the indigo night. Shadows moved toward her, and fuzzy lights floated in the air or bobbed across the ground. Decidedly not the lights of Bellwater. No lightbulbs behaved like that.

"You see us. You like us?"

Skye pivoted to face the closest creature. A tarnished ring glinted on a string around its neck, and a few small, white shells dangled from its thin hair. Those touches of human-like decoration gave her hope. Anyway, as they'd pointed out, she had come looking for them. She had been curious, and still was.

She nodded. "What are you, then?"

"We have many names. Most commonly 'goblin.'" The creature, the goblin, smiled, and Skye tried not to shudder. Its teeth were pointed and long.

"Goblin." She cleared her throat. "Well then, sure. I've heard of you."

Another goblin emerged from the shadows on a trunk on her left, at face level like the first. "She is a keeper."

"Oh yes," the first said. "We would like her. We like someone new once in a while." The goblin pulled a pastry from a dirt-colored sack hanging around its body. It extended the pastry toward Skye. "Blackberry tart?"

Despite its disgusting storage location, the tart looked luscious, its crust golden, its scent warm and buttery and so pungent that Skye could nearly taste the flaky shell, could almost feel the sweet cooked berries melting on her tongue.

She closed her teeth with a deliberate click. Magic. Had to be. Everyone knew you shouldn't go biting into fruit offered to you by magical creatures in the woods, even if you'd thought until just five minutes ago that such stories were, you know, only stories.

But her head swam pleasantly, as if she were drunk, and it was hard to say what she meant. "I don't know," she said. "What does it do?"

"It helps you join us." The goblin nudged the tart closer. "Have a little party with us. Fun. Right?"

"I...I'm not..."

But as Skye groped for what she intended to say, someone shoved her head from behind, knocking her forward. Fast as a pouncing cat, the other goblin pushed the blackberry tart into her face. Sticky filling invaded her mouth, so hot it burned her tongue. Juice and crumbs smeared down her chin. Her throat made a muffled scream, but instinctively she swallowed the bite. Her arms flailed, feeling as heavy as if she were swimming. Little hands, rough like twigs, caught hold of her in several places at once.

She fell and never hit the ground. The goblins carried her crowd-surf-style. Everything became a dream; she couldn't respond the way she wanted to.

Afterward she still remembered what she saw and what they did before releasing her. Even though she couldn't speak of it.

CHAPTER THREE

KIT TROMPED INTO THE FOREST. IT WAS DRIZ-
ZLING, TURNING THE EVENING DARK EVEN EARLIER THAN USUAL, AND HE
wore a rain parka over his leather jacket and flannel shirt. The large box
under his arm had a spare parka over it to keep it dry. Inside the box was
a milk steamer, stolen from a home goods store in Olympia with the
blessing of his magical immunity. He would have bought it, but seven
years of scrounging gold and other junk for the goblins had cleaned him
out. A small-town auto repairer and part-time chainsaw-carving artist
didn't make all that much cash. If only their magic could have topped up
his bank account instead of granting him license to steal.

He had at least left a five-dollar bill on the shelf in the store, where
the milk steamer had sat. He always tried to offer what he could.

He whistled in the darkness of the woods. They whistled back. A
path appeared: broken oyster shells on the ground this time, their pure
white glowing in the gloom.

When Redring dropped down and morphed into her bathrobe-and-
pajama-clad form, Kit removed the spare parka from the box. "Here.
Your milk steamer."

She seized the box and sniffed it. "You said four days. It's been a week."

"Well, I have a life. Now you can have lattes. There. Can I go?"

"Don't you worry we might get up to mischief when you take so long?"

A few others giggled in the trees.

Kit narrowed his eyes. "Should I worry?" He'd heard nothing in town about anyone being attacked in the woods, but then, people didn't always say anything right away. In fact, in the few past cases he'd heard about, people had been enchanted in such a way that they *couldn't* say anything about it.

"Oh no, we are angels," Redring assured.

The others cackled.

Kit turned halfway to go, but pointed at her. "I better not hear of anything. You're getting what you want, you just leave everyone else the hell alone."

"But we always want new things." Redring's tone started as a wheedle, then turned sinister. "You aren't our boss, Sylvain. Only our liaison."

Too furious to say another word, he glowered and stalked away. He'd have heard if anyone got hurt. It was probably nothing. They were just trying to get to him.

But long, slow pieces of mischief that unfolded over months—or generations—were another of their many specialties. He knew that firsthand.

Livy Darwen's kayak glided noiselessly through the water. Puget Sound was glassy smooth this morning, clear and dark, a color between seaweed green and black. Wisps of mist drifted atop the surface, and Livy's breath joined them in tiny clouds. It was the last day of December, and the town dock had been slick with frost when she launched her boat.

Today, she thought, probably belonged to Water. Although perhaps Air; something in the frozen, scentless quiet of winter tended to suggest Air to her. She was an environmental scientist and had therefore taken more than enough organic chemistry to know that nature contained far more than four elements, but the traditional Earth-Air-Fire-Water system of organization still appealed to her. There was something human and emotionally real about looking at nature that way, and she often found herself categorizing the feel of each day under one of the four.

Working for the Forest Service as she did, the importance of those elements was especially obvious. Understanding the forest meant understanding the soil, air, and water, and, much as they unnerved her, the wildfires.

At least winter had been good and soaked, free of forest fires, the way she preferred life. Dealing with a fire season on top of Skye's problems would be altogether too much.

She frowned at something crinkled and silver marring the water's surface. She steered the kayak toward it, jabbed the blade of her paddle at it, and fished it out.

"Fuck you, Mylar balloon," she told it, and dumped it into the boat between her feet.

Lately she addressed too many inanimate objects that way. Used to be she would fish garbage out of the water and declare in triumph, "Haha, potato chip bag! No Pacific trash vortex for you."

Now she swore at it. Same with the invasive plants she pulled out of the forest when she was working. Instead of her old, "There you go, trees, bet you can breathe easier now," it had become, "Fuck you, ivy. Fuck you, knotweed. Fuck you, blackberries." It had been like this ever since Skye fell ill.

Or depressed. Or whatever she was, exactly. Two weeks now, and the three doctors they'd seen weren't sure what the problem was. A sudden-onset depression was their best guess, and they'd treated her accordingly—some pills, some therapy. Nothing was helping yet. Skye still barely spoke or ate, and looked unhappy all the time. She continued to work at the cafe, but not as many hours, and she didn't draw or paint as much as she used to.

Livy let the paddle go still, resting it across the edges of the kayak's cockpit. Why would Skye be depressed? It was such an abrupt change. Up until now Skye had been a resilient, happy person with so much going for her and plenty to look forward to. And lately Livy would have sworn she detected trauma in Skye's eyes, as if something had happened to her. But then why wouldn't Skye tell her? She knew she could tell Livy anything.

A scraping sound coasted across the water. Livy looked toward shore. She floated a hundred yards off the northern point of Crabapple Island, one of the many small islands stranded in the middle of their long inlet of Puget Sound. On the island's rocky shore, a man was trying to haul a waist-high chunk of driftwood up the slope toward his truck.

Livy grimaced, swung the bow of her kayak toward shore, and paddled forward. The curt reminder about taking driftwood from public beaches withered on her tongue, though, when he stopped and jerked upright as if in pain, hands planted on his lower back.

Her kayak slid onto the beach. Its fiberglass hull scraped against the rocks, and the man turned. As she expected: Kit Sylvain. Scruffy dusting of beard, shaggy brown hair sticking out from under a ball cap, teeth flashing in a wincing smile as he spotted her.

"Here. Let me help you." She shipped the paddle and climbed out of the boat, stepping into the shallows in her knee-high rubber boots. She dragged the kayak higher onto shore where the tide wouldn't pull it away. Small round rocks slid under her feet as she plodded up toward Kit. "Bad back?"

"Yeah. Tweaked it the other day when I was moving a Mustang engine."

"Ouch." She took hold of two of the twisted protuberances on the driftwood stump. "I'll take this side."

"Thanks." He grasped the other side, and together they hefted the stump to his truck, and shoved it into the open tailgate.

"That's a big guy," Livy said, breathing hard. She ran her fingers down the stump's bumpy surface, chaotically striped in all colors of brown. "Cedar, I think."

"I think so too. Should be a good one."

"Going to carve something with it?"

"Yep." He grinned. "Guess you recognize me, then."

"Course I do. Small town. I'm Livy Darwen, though, if you didn't recognize me."

"Course I did. Small town." He thumped the tailgate shut, then gave her another smile-wince. "It's illegal to take driftwood, isn't it?"

"From a beach that isn't yours, yeah. Technically. But I'm not going to bust you."

"Really? I thought you worked for the state or something."

"Forest Service. But I've got to admit, I like seeing your carvings when I drive in and out of town."

"Thanks." He patted the stump. The wind gusted and she caught the comfortable scent of his battered brown leather jacket. "Would've brought my cousin to help me carry it, but he's busy at the auto shop."

"You have a cousin in town? I hadn't heard that."

"Yep." He smiled at her. And for a second, despite her numb hands and wounded soul, she remembered why girls in school always used to gaze at Kit Sylvain, and why grown women surely still did. "His name's Grady," Kit said. "A little younger than me, twenty-one. His branch of the family lives out in Moses Lake, but Grady loves it over here on the Sound. So I'm letting him stay with me till he finds somewhere afford-able in Seattle."

"Could be a long wait. City's getting expensive."

"Sure is."

An awkward silence fell between them.

"Well hey, can I buy you coffee?" Kit said after a few seconds, and Livy was so startled she stared at him. "I owe you for this." He slapped the driftwood with the flat of his hand. "And for not busting me."

"Oh. Thanks, but—" She flipped her thumb toward her boat. "I've got the kayak. Have to get it back to the dock in town, where I parked."

"I can fit it in here." He nodded toward the truck bed. "Plenty of room."

She was tempted for a second, which was bizarre. Kit was so not her usual type—her usual type being older guys with a couple of college degrees and a tranquil love of science. Not that those had been working out so well. In school, Kit had belonged to one of the years between Livy's and Skye's classes. She remembered him as a rebel with torn jeans who didn't talk to people much, but who could sometimes be seen making out with a girl in his truck cab in the high school parking lot. Which, she had to admit, always inspired some curiosity in her, but she and Skye had both kept their distance from him.

Maybe that had been snotty of them. Maybe she ought to give him a chance, now that they were older.

Then she thought of Skye back home, of the doctor appointments she had to take her to, the symptoms and treatments she had to Google, the way her life had a pall thrown over it lately. She was only twenty-six, but these days she felt old and tired.

Livy shook her head. "I just got started. I ought to finish the paddle, get the exercise."

"You sure?"

She nodded.

"Okay, well." He jingled his keys in a pocket. "Come find me at the garage if you want a raincheck. I'd be happy to, anytime."

"All right. Thanks."

"Happy New Year."

"You too."

She walked down the beach as he went around to the driver's side of the truck. Automatically she picked up a juice-box straw lying in the tide line of sticks and seaweed.

His truck door squeaked open. She frowned at the straw as if it were of deep significance. A few seconds after the engine revved to life, she dared a glance up. His eyes met hers in the side mirror, and he splayed his fingers in a wave. She returned a weak wave with her numb hand. The engine revved and Kit drove away, the cedar stump bouncing in the bed as if excited about its new journey.

Kit glanced again in the rearview mirror. Livy's form descended toward her kayak, reduced by distance to a collection of items and muted colors: navy baseball cap, green rain jacket, brown boots. Nothing fancy. She was still cute, though; always had been, even chilled and without makeup. But then, she'd never been the nail polish and hairspray type, as far as he could remember. They'd never been classmates, but their school was small, so he'd seen her around plenty. To his mind she was a babe with a nice rack and blondish hair that curled in a way he liked, and sweet pouty lips.

To her mind, he was evidently not worth accepting coffee for. Kit smirked, coming to a half-stop before steering onto the island's loop road. Oh well. A guy in his position couldn't get tied down in a relationship anyhow.

That didn't stop him from casual dating. Ordinarily he let the women do the asking, which happened often enough in the form of vacationers coming through town and needing cars repaired, or stopping to delight in his chainsaw carvings. But by December, he usually had been going a couple of months without many vacationers around. So when fate threw him together with a fellow local, he thought he'd give it a shot.

Or get shot down. Whichever.

Could be she was seeing someone, though. Maybe nothing personal.

He glanced at the hunk of driftwood in the mirror, and told it, "She was nice, anyway. Gave me a hand."

Deciding he'd make Grady help him haul the stump out of the bed later, he drove off to get coffee. Alone, for now.

CHAPTER FOUR

HELP, I'M UNDER A SPELL PUT ON ME BY
GOBLINS IN THE WOODS. THE WORDS WERE SIMPLE ENOUGH. THERE WAS
even the outside chance Skye could find someone who'd believe them.
But when she tried to speak them, her voice vanished in her throat. It
felt blocked, like the times in dreams when you try to scream but can't
make a sound.

She had tried writing the words as well. That was equally useless.
They turned into the wrong words, different each time.

Today, while Livy was out for her Saturday morning paddle, Skye
picked up a sharpened graphite art pencil in her left hand and stared at
the blank white journal page as if challenging it to a duel from which
only one of them would emerge alive. She began writing.

Holly around a scroll with a jellyfish in the woods.

"Argh," she said, teeth clenched.

She smacked her palm down on the page, intending to rip it out.
Then she let her muscles wilt in resignation, and uncovered the page and
gazed at it. She leaned her temple on her right hand, and sketched the
strange picture the words described: a holly bush growing around a parch-
ment scroll flaking at the edges and tied with a limp ribbon, with a jellyfish drifting through the air like a strange butterfly. In the background she
added the tall trunks of fir trees and their interlaced canopy of branches.

Her words remained in a white space at the top, like a title for this bizarre piece. She *should* tear it out, and stuff it deep in the recycling bin. Anyone who saw it would be convinced she was insane.

And wasn't she, in a sense? She added flourishes of pencil to the trunks in the picture, deepening their bark texture, growing little broken limbs upon them. The exercise felt like the obsession that had consumed her when she was a teenager and sketched the faces of her crushes. She lifted her head to gaze out the window at the real deal: the dark green, pointy-topped forest on the hill above town. Her heart yearned for it; her feet shifted under the little kitchen table, restless to push her out into its mossy arms again.

That was what she hated most about this spell, sometimes. The goblins had taken her love of the forest and tainted it, bound it up with their magic.

They had carried Skye up, up, up the trunks into a fantastically weird bunch of cobbled-together houses and bridges and mismatched dim electric lights that they had built all around a huge swath of evergreens. A treetop village, but its surfaces slimier and its inhabitants more disgusting than any of the fantasy faerylands Skye used to envision. Somehow she understood she could only see the place because she had taken their path and eaten the blackberry tart. She also understood that although she had only been carried a few hundred yards off the road, she was now almost totally out of reach of regular humans.

"You love these trees, yes?" their leader had said. Skye gathered her name was Redring.

"Yes." Skye couldn't lie, her tongue answering as if under some honesty potion. She still lay in the arms of half a dozen goblins, their prickly hands clamped all over her body.

"And you wanted to see us. You accepted our invitation. We are so flattered, darling one." Redring leaned closer, her foul breath spilling across Skye's face. "Some we would simply steal from, and leave to fall apart, but not you. You we would like to keep."

"Me. I want her," another goblin said, bulling his way in against Redring's shoulder. Or at least, Skye assumed it was a he. His voice was deeper and his gaze upon Skye more lustful—it made her shudder, but all she could do was avert her eyes.

Redring shoved him. "Be patient, Slide!" She grinned at Skye again and softened her voice. "You see, there is a procedure for this. You will go home again, but eventually you will come to us."

Someone shoved another sticky bite of food into Skye's mouth: orange marmalade. She grimaced, but her obedient enchanted mouth chewed and swallowed it.

"You will want to," Redring continued.

A different goblin crammed what tasted like musty mince pie into her mouth. She swallowed that too.

"You will lose your way in the human world."

Another stuffed her mouth with stale cake with raspberry filling, gelatinous and with too many seeds. Tears of despair ran down her temples, yet she ate it.

"You will come to the woods and choose your mate."

"Me!" the gruff goblin shouted, while someone smashed a handful of candied cherries into Skye's mouth.

"Shut up!" Redring told him, and the others cackled. "She called to us, so she gets to choose. Besides, it's more fun, watching to see who she picks." She turned to Skye again. "And when you have withered enough among the humans, you will join us here. You will become goblin."

Skye shuddered, alone at home over her weird holly-and-jellyfish art. She picked up her mug of coffee. It was three-quarters gone and the remainder was cold and stale, but she swilled the rest anyway, welcoming the bitterness. Anything to rinse away the memory of those sticky, horrible fruits.

That first night, back at home, after she'd climbed into bed shivering with a fever, Livy had brought her some mint tea and offered to make toast. "With blackberry jam?" Livy had suggested, and reeled back in shock when Skye had abruptly found her voice and shouted, "No!"

Skye flipped back a few pages in her sketchbook, and glowered at the pencil drawings there. The day after the assault, she had drawn Redring from memory, along with the goblins' treetop dwellings. Apparently she could do that much. But so what? She'd shoved the drawings in front of Livy, who had dutifully examined them and said, "Huh. Those are really cool. Trying something new?"

The spell wouldn't let Skye say anything about the connection between her silence and these drawings. She couldn't even pantomime it. All she could do was gaze at Livy in burning frustration.

No one would get it. Of course they wouldn't. Why would they, if they hadn't seen what she'd seen?

She should have been tearing things apart in her fury over how little she could communicate. Her former self would have, the Skye who had walked into the forest that night, the Skye from every day of her life before that. But when the doctors said she'd been hit with a sudden depression, they weren't entirely wrong. The spell brought with it a lack of desire to do much at all, an inability to care strongly about anything. Or at least, anything beyond following the dictates of the spell: feel the pull of the woods, retreat from human life, come and choose your mate...

She did want to fight it, ached to tell Livy or someone. But the fight in her was as dampened as her voice. Even drawing this unsuccessful sketch had proven exhausting.

The front door opened. Livy peeked into the kitchen, tugging off her rubber boots. "Hey."

Skye closed the sketchbook. "Hey." She could echo words well enough, usually. It was coming up with her own that had become challenging.

Livy had grown accustomed to it and kept up more of the conversation alone than she used to. Which was also pretty damn depressing.

"Cold out, but the water's nice and smooth today." Livy took off her baseball cap, tugged the ponytail holder out of her hair, and shook the curls loose. They had gotten frizzier in the damp outdoor air. Skye had always wanted tighter curls like those, and Livy's blonder color, rather than her own dark brown, sort-of-wavy, sort-of-straight combo. She'd told Livy so in the past. She wished she could compliment her again today.

"Nice," Skye echoed instead. Goddamn magic.

Livy peeled off her raincoat and hung it over the back of a chair. "Also, I caught Kit Sylvain stealing driftwood."

Skye lifted her eyebrows.

Livy gave a one-note chuckle. "I didn't bust him. I helped him put it in his truck. We all know he does it. I mean, how else would he carve that stuff? He's part of the local color; we can't mess with it." She wandered to the coffee machine, sniffed at the remaining brew, wrinkled her nose, and dumped it in the sink.

Skye looked down at her sketchbook with a sigh. It would be useful to tell Livy what other sorts of local color existed around here.

"He kind of asked me out, too." Livy rinsed the pot under the tap. "Offered to buy me coffee. I took a raincheck."

She leaned sideways against the counter, her curves hugged by her faded jeans and dusty-pink hoodie. She looked so solemn and lovely with her downcast eyelashes and full lips. Men *should* ask her sister out, and Livy should go out and have fun. Skye hadn't wanted much lately except the goblins and the woods, and at the same time to be free of the goblins and the woods, but she wanted this.

This desire helped her rebel against her spell long enough to push two encouraging words to the surface.

"He's cute."

Livy looked at her in astonishment. The water filling the pot overflowed and ran down her hand. She shut it off, then sent a grin at Skye. "It's true. He is, damn it." She set the pot on the counter and shook off her wet hand. "Suppose I could take him up on that raincheck." She glanced at the clock. "But not today. Got to do some work, even though it's Saturday. You're working too, right?"

Skye nodded. Her hopes sank back down into their usual mire as she envisioned another afternoon of trying to serve customers at the cafe without being able to converse freely, nor even smile. God, why did they have to make the spell so she couldn't smile? That was a diabolical touch. The fever had gone away after one day, but the rest of the magical symptoms were only getting worse by the week.

She glanced up to find Livy chewing her lip as she regarded Skye. "Might want to…wash your hair?" Livy cringed in apology.

Skye lowered her face again. Not giving a shit what she looked like: another side effect. She scooped up her notebook and shuffled off to the shower.

CHAPTER FIVE

SKYE SAYING "HE'S CUTE" ABOUT KIT WAS UN-
USUAL ENOUGH, IN SKYE'S LIMITED COMMUNICATION LATELY, THAT IT
made Livy think all week about how she probably *should* go find him
and have coffee. After all, Skye seemed to think she should. So maybe,
somehow, it would improve Skye's well-being if she did—which made
no sense. But the thought wouldn't stop pestering Livy, and by the end
of the week she'd decided to act on it.

Saturday she took the kayak out for a paddle again, and circled Crabapple Island as before. She knew he lived somewhere on it, though she
wasn't sure which house. But today she saw no one on the gray shore except a woman walking a golden retriever.

That afternoon Livy stopped by the drugstore, right across the street
from the garage. *Bellwater Auto*, the old red-lettered sign shouted at
her through the windows as she picked up deodorant, conditioner, and
dental floss. The auto shop's neighboring garden of chainsaw carvings
drew her eye too: bears, Sasquatches, orcas, and gnomes all seeming to
watch her.

After emerging from the drugstore, she set the bag of purchases in
her trunk, then glanced up and down the two-lane street. No traffic
coming. She shut the trunk and crossed the street. She paused at the edge
of the sculpture garden, looking up at the wind chimes that hung from
the high crossbars of the fence posts. On chains of all styles and colors

swung miscellaneous bits of metal and plastic: silverware, switchplates, jar lids, gears, doorknobs, bottle openers, washers, rusty bells, oarlocks. They jingled with surprising musicality in the cold wind. She closed her fingers around the sparkly streamers fluttering off one wind chime, and identified them with a smile as strips of Mylar balloon.

When I pick this stuff up I swear at it and throw it away, she thought. *He turns it into art.*

"Car trouble?"

Kit strolled out of the garage, wiping his hands on a black-stained towel. He was dressed for work in zipped-up gray jacket, industrial-thickness jeans, and steel-toed boots.

Livy let go of the Mylar strips, suddenly feeling absurd for showing up like this. "Nope. I was just nearby, and got curious what you used the cedar stump for."

"Ah." He lifted his chin in invitation. "Come see."

He beckoned her forward and she followed, as if they were old friends rather than quasi-neighbors who hardly ever spoke to one another. He led her through the tiny office with a cash register that, as far as she could tell, served both garage and art sales, then out the back door. They emerged into an open-air work space with a roof covering it. Cyclone fencing topped with barbed wire protected its sides. Sawdust coated the concrete floor, and heavy, sharp-edged tools and hunks of wood stood all around.

"Here she is so far." Kit swept his hand toward the partially-carved driftwood stump. "What do you think she's going to be?"

Livy skirted the teeth of the chainsaw lying dormant on the ground, and drew close to the sculpture. "A woman?" With her forefinger she touched the long waving hair of the figure, and found it still gritty with fine sawdust.

Kit stood rocking back on his heels, arms folded. "Sort of."

Livy moved around it, studying the head and shoulders, which were all that had taken shape so far; the body melted back into its natural stump shape below that. "I can't tell yet, but she's nice-looking."

"My plan is mermaid," Kit said. "Cheesy, I know, but people dig mermaids. They buy stuff like that. And look." He bent to point to a thick upward-curving section at the lower back of the stump. "This'll make a perfect tail."

Livy tilted her head. "You're right. That's so cool. How do you see things like that?"

"I spend a lot of time thinking up weird stuff, what can I say."

Livy examined the serene face. "She kind of looks like my sister."

"Yeah?"

"Skye. If you've bought coffee at Green Fox, you've probably seen her." Livy heard the melancholy note in her own voice, though she hadn't intended to let the emotion show.

Kit apparently noticed. He took a couple of seconds to answer. "Ah. Sure, I remember her from school, anyway. I don't get down to Green Fox much. Carol next door keeps us fixed for coffee. She'd get jealous if we went anywhere else."

Carol's Diner had been Bellwater's staple greasy-spoon for thirty years. Everyone knew Carol by sight. "I haven't eaten there in a while," Livy said. "We used to get milkshakes at Carol's in high school."

"As did we all. Hey, I still owe you coffee. Or milkshake, if you'd rather. I'll treat you if you've got time."

Given that was what she'd walked over here to claim, Livy felt silly for hesitating. She nodded after a moment. "Of course, yeah. Let's."

"Come on. I'll tell Grady where we're going." He strode back into the office, and she followed. This time they veered off to the left, into the garage. It was small, probably fitting no more than three cars at a time. Today it only held one maroon SUV. Livy smelled motor oil and heard the repeated clang of a metal tool hitting some car part. "Grady!" Kit said.

The clanging stopped, and a few seconds later a young man's head popped into view above the SUV. He had dark hair with bits sticking up here and there, protruding ears, cheerful eyes, and full lips. "Yeah?"

"Livy and I are going to grab some coffee."

"Milkshake," Livy corrected, on impulse.

Kit sent her a grin. "Right, milkshake. I owe her. She's the one who didn't bust me for picking up that cedar piece."

Grady's smile turned his face handsome. "You helped carry that? Dude, that thing was heavy. You must be strong."

"I shove logs around now and then," she said. "Part of the job."

"Right on." Grady lifted a wrench in farewell. "Have fun. Nice to meet you!" He vanished behind the SUV again.

"He seems nice," Livy said as they walked out the front of the shop.

"He's all right. Barely knows what he's doing in the garage, but he's learning."

He glanced attentively at Livy as they turned toward Carol's. "So is it just you and Skye? Any other siblings?"

"Nope, just the two of us."

Kit opened the glass door of the diner for her. "I don't have any brothers or sisters. Always wished I did. Someone to share the load."

"What's this, Sylvain, now you're bringing dates?" Carol's voice boomed. "Hoo boy, and a Darwen girl, too, you lucky stiff." She strolled over to them, a purple apron stretched around her wide form, and ensnared them in town gossip for a few minutes.

Carol settled them into a window booth and took their milkshake order: French vanilla for Livy, salted caramel for Kit. A minute later she brought them the shakes, then strolled back to the kitchen.

Kit pulled the long spoon from his shake and sucked it clean. "So you work mostly out of town?"

Livy nodded, stirring the whipped cream with her red straw. "The office is in Quilcene. But I'm only there about half the time. I do a lot of driving around to forests, checking out one problem or another."

He laid the spoon on a napkin. "Not much time spent here in town, then?"

"Well, more lately."

He lifted his brown eyes to her in curiosity, and she realized she had to explain after saying that.

She pulled out her spoon too, watching it drip onto the mound of whipped cream. "My sister's been sort of sick lately. Well. Not sick exactly, but…depressed, I guess."

"That counts as sick." Kit sounded sympathetic.

"I don't want to leave her by herself too much, just because…I don't know. She hasn't been herself. We're still trying to figure it out. Mom lives with her boyfriend in Portland now, so she's down there, even though she comes to see us when she can. So, anyway, it's mostly fallen to me, looking after Skye." She pulled in a breath and forced a smile at him. "Jeez, sorry. T.M.I."

He looked thoughtful, brushing the scruff on his cheek with one knuckle. "Nah, believe me, I get it. Do they think it's seasonal affective disorder, or…"

"Could be. I mean, it's winter, and it's only been going on for a few weeks. It's just…this is so not like her. Winter never bothered her before. Still, she's getting to the point of finding a serious career, and I think maybe it's hitting her hard, becoming a grown-up and all that. She's an artist, so, moody temperament."

"Oh yeah. We're practically unstable." He smiled.

She laughed, abashed. "I forgot you're one too. Sorry again."

He shrugged, rolling the remark away with a casual wrinkle of his nose. "Well, then you've got your hands full."

"Yeah." She sucked up a sip of vanilla shake. "Hoping one of the medications will finally work. And she's seeing a therapist, but that's not a lot of use either when she'll hardly talk. Or maybe when spring approaches she'll get better. I don't know."

"Sounds like you're the one who knows her best."

"I suppose. Probably."

"Then I bet you'll get her through it. Whatever it is."

He didn't say it in a fake encouraging tone, the way too many people did when trying to make Livy believe everything was going to be fine. Even their mother used that tone; she was still in denial. Instead Kit sounded grave but sincere. She lifted her gaze to him. His eyes were a tea-brown with depth and clarity to them, shaded by thick brown eyebrows, the same shade as his facial hair, which in turn was a tint lighter than his hair...

Yep, he was cute, but he was only treating her to milkshakes out of obligation, and he surely wouldn't be interested in her now that she'd spewed her family mental health problems onto the table. Nor was she in the best place in life to start dating someone.

She averted her eyes to the counter, watching Carol's back as she moved around and fetched plates. "Thanks. I hope so." She looked at him with the brightest smile she could manage. "So, what's Grady going to do around here? Is he looking to become a mechanic?"

Kit smirked. "No way. He only does it because I can pay him some, and there's not a lot else to do in this town. Really, though, he wants to be a chef."

"A chef?"

"For real. He's taken community college classes and worked in restaurants and everything, just not, you know, the serious certification the fancy restaurants in Seattle would want."

"Does he cook for you, then?"

He nodded, swallowing a sip of shake. "All the time. Oh my God, he makes crazy shit. I never in my life thought I would like kale chips or—what the hell was it last week?—coconut curry soup, that was it. With broccoli in it, I'm serious. But he actually made it good." Kit's eyes widened, as if he were still not over the shock.

Livy laughed. "Wow. Those sound awesome. I'll be happy to take the leftovers if you have any."

"For sure. Come out to the island and try them sometime." The low, lazy way he said it, and the way his gaze held hers—suddenly her face grew hot with a blush.

All that un-sexy talk about Skye's problems, and her own general awkwardness, and he was still hitting on her? The guy was a pro. Or not very particular. Or both.

She took another slurp of shake through the straw. "So how did you get into chainsaw carving?"

He told her about picking up the skill from an old guy who used to live on the island, with whom he used to do side jobs cutting down loose branches or slicing up trees that had fallen on roads. But Kit didn't like climbing up in the trees like that, so he stuck to making art with the wood and being a mechanic like his late dad instead. Those topics carried them until they'd finished their shakes, plus another ten or fifteen minutes beyond.

Finally, Livy pulled out her phone to check the time, and declared she'd better get back home—though truthfully she was liking it a hell of a lot, sitting here in a bacon-scented diner with steam on the windows, riding a sugar rush and talking with a handsome guy. Imagine that.

Outside, on the weedy gravel between the diner and the sculpture garden, she stuck her hand out to him. "This was fun. Thanks."

Rather than shake her hand, Kit took it, bent over it, and kissed it. He didn't make it cheesy; no lingering or smacking. He pulled it off with perfect courtier grace. She felt only a tickle of lips and beard, then he let go and slipped his hands in his jeans pockets, smiling. "I enjoyed it. Stop by again. Or hey, I'll track you down if Grady makes something awesome to share."

"You'd better." She smiled too, and turned toward her car.

CHAPTER SIX

KIT CHEWED ON HIS THOUGHTS ALL AFTER-
NOON, THROUGH SCHOOLING GRADY ON SPARK PLUGS AND BRINGING IN
the wind chimes before closing for the day. Livy's sister had been "not
herself" for about a month, and it was about a month ago Kit had ticked
off the goblins by not getting them enough gold on time, and had to
make it up to them with the milk steamer. He had suspected them of
messing with someone in retaliation, though hadn't been able to find any
proof. Could it have been Skye?

Then again, he suspected the goblins every time something bad happened to anyone in town. Car accident, health trouble, tree falling on a
house, didn't matter, his first thought was always goblins, and his second
was always whether he could have prevented it by somehow appeasing
them better.

Trouble was, he usually couldn't prove it *wasn't* them. They didn't
always fess up to their mischief, and only sometimes boasted about their
crimes.

The worst case, as far as Kit knew, was the man who died of hypothermia two years ago. Kit hadn't known him, really; he was a fisherman
in his fifties and lived alone. Spent most of his time on his boat, the
neighbors said. Then one icy morning a hiker found him dead of exposure in the forest, wearing just a single layer of clothes, insufficient for the
cold weather. Why he'd gone out there at night without a coat or hat, no

one could say. He hadn't been drunk or anything. His neighbors did say, after the death, that he hadn't been himself lately. Just like Livy's sister.

Kit knew the goblins were responsible for the man's death because Redring casually told him so, several weeks later. They had met the fisherman a while back, lured him onto a path, enchanted him, gotten him to hand over all the gold and valuables around his house, then lost interest in him and allowed him to pine away and ultimately wander out into the forest and die. They weren't interested in keeping him, and that was the way they treated those people.

If they wanted to keep someone, though, that was almost worse. Because that meant turning them into a goblin.

The majority of goblins in the tribe had once been humans. Possibly all of them; Kit hadn't unearthed a clear answer on that, nor had his ancestors. Seemed like some of them had been goblins so long they barely remembered where they came from. That, apparently, was the up side, if you could call it that: they couldn't die, or so Redring claimed.

"All fae are pure energy," she had told him once in scorn. "We change shape at will, we heal at will. No, Sylvain, there is no getting rid of *us*."

His ancestors' written records agreed: the goblins couldn't be killed. At best, they could be changed into some other magical form, or so the other liaisons had heard, but that kind of power was beyond human ability. Only other fae could pull it off, and other fae never showed up to talk to Kit, precisely *because* he was the goblin liaison.

Which was exactly why he was out of luck when it came to throwing off this family curse. And whoever came after him would inherit it. That would either be his own offspring if he was dumb enough to have any and subject them to this, or the next of kin, whom the goblins would track down and latch onto. Could be Grady, for example.

They closed the shop and walked out to Kit's truck to go home. Kit glanced in concern at his cousin as Grady hopped into the passenger seat. No one on his uncle's side even knew about the goblins. Kit ached to share the load, but at the same time didn't want to dump this on anyone, especially people who were more or less cool.

Grady gave him an arch little smile.

"What?" Kit said.

"You're so dreamy about your date you're forgetting to turn the truck on."

Kit irritably turned the key in the ignition. "That's not why. I'm just...thinking about stuff."

"She did seem cool. And not bad-looking."

"Not bad-looking at all." Kit's thoughts shifted back to Livy talking to him over milkshakes, her face flushed in the warm diner, her lips shaping each word so deliciously. A more pleasant thing to think about than curses. Not that he should think too fondly about any woman. It'd be inhumane to bring a girlfriend into this lifestyle. Then again, if things got serious between him and some woman, such as Livy, he could always invoke immunity from the goblins for her. However, they might have already enchanted her sister, in which case such a gesture would be too little too late.

"Did I see you kiss her hand?" Grady's question came out innocent enough, though teasing danced plainly behind the words.

Kit backed onto Shore Avenue, the one and only main drag through town, and set the truck forward toward the bridge to Crabapple Island. "Some moves never go out of fashion. I wouldn't expect you to understand."

"Well. I won't expect you to understand tonight's dinner. It involves eggplant."

"God help me."

"You'll like it."

He probably would like it. And Livy's sister probably was just depressed, not goblin-struck. There was even *probably* a way to axe the contract with the goblins and send them packing.

Kit just had no idea what it was.

While Grady sliced up eggplant, tomatoes, and smoked gouda in the kitchen, Kit claimed he'd left his wallet in the shop, and took off.

He brought another scrap of gold from his meager stash at home, this time a spoon from the flatware set that had finally come in the mail, 24-karat gold over stainless steel. Garish, ridiculous-looking stuff. No wonder it had been cheap. But Redring and company would seize it happily.

In the woods, in the cold windy dark, he whistled a few notes. A goblin whistled back, and the path opened to him: a line of hemlock cones this time, dangling from spider-threads, the tip of each cone alight with a blue glow.

As he glanced up, he spotted their dwellings, now that he was in their realm: little lights lined their bridges and roofs in the treetops, a motley collection of stolen electric bulbs and magical glowing stuff. He'd never accepted their invitation to climb up there and check it out up close, and hoped he never would.

"Sylvain, what a sweet surprise." Redring descended to him and morphed into her pink-clad quasi-human form.

He held out the gold spoon. "I'm bringing you this, and I have a question for you that I want you to answer honestly. Please."

She grabbed it, licked it, and stuffed it into her bathrobe pocket. "You can ask." Her tone suggested honesty wasn't promised.

He forced himself to respond as calmly as possible. "Did you invite a young woman recently? Around last month, when you were looking for that milk steamer?"

Smothered laughter rippled through the trees. Lights bobbed and boughs swayed. But then, they laughed at nearly everything he said.

"Kiiiit," Redring reproved. "You think we would steal away your fellow citizens?"

"I *know* you have. That's where most of you came from. You used to be citizens somewhere or other, right?"

Redring flicked her long nails through the air. "Oh, so long ago, who can remember?"

"Did you invite this girl?" he asked again. "Her name is Skye."

"Mine!" someone else shouted above, and others cackled.

Redring looked straight into his eyes, sending a chill along his spine, and said, "Of course not. We know you don't like that. And you're so good to us."

All the other unseen goblins snorted and giggled.

"Look," Kit said, "I can get you two more forks and a butter knife to go with that spoon. But you've got to tell me the truth."

"Do we have to?" Redring tapped her lower lip, and looked over her shoulder as if consulting her minions. "I don't recall that we do."

"You're messing with me, as usual. Fine. But if you could just tell me if there's anyone under a spell, so I have some idea what to expect—"

"I told you we didn't." But she sounded a little too saucy. "We're hurt you would doubt our word."

Hysterical laughter now from above.

He was wasting his time. Maybe, even, they really hadn't done anything to Skye, but if he bugged them enough, they *would* go mess with her, or with someone else.

"Never mind. Forget I showed up."

"Bring us the gold forks!" Redring insisted.

"Yeah, sometime." He turned and walked off.

Why had he even bothered? He had read that some types of fae couldn't lie, but goblins were clearly an exception. They lied all the time. He knew it firsthand, and all the former liaisons had written down the fact. If they'd attacked Skye or anyone else, and if it was like every other crime of theirs, he'd never learn about it until way too late, if at all.

He had to admit, in some ways, he truly did not want to know what they got up to. He might never sleep again if he knew.

CHAPTER SEVEN

YOU WILL COME TO THE WOODS AND CHOOSE YOUR MATE.

The phrase played on repeat in Skye's brain. It was more stomach-turning than any other piece of the spell, even the part about leaving the human world and becoming a goblin. Hanging out in the trees in another form, okay, maybe she could find a way to make peace with that, as long as she were autonomous and got magical powers out of the deal, which seemed likely. But being obliged to choose a mate? From among *them*?

She shuddered.

It was a mild afternoon for January, the temperature almost fifty, and she was wandering in their overgrown backyard for some fresh air. Livy was at work; Skye was home alone. The forest loomed close, just across the railroad tracks. She chewed on a fresh fir needle. It filled her mouth with a sharp green flavor, which combated the taste-memory of saccharine fruit. She prowled back and forth, gaze combing the dark trees. Her feet were chilly in her rubber boots, but at least not wet. She hugged herself for warmth; her black crocheted sweater let too much cool air through its holes, and all she wore under it was a tank top and jeans.

The part of her compelled by the spell that *wanted* to enter those trees and choose a mate was the unnerving thing.

But she didn't have to. She had fought it so far. In the past month she had gone for walks alone, even along the same forest path as before, and had not heard the goblins, nor called out to summon them. Of course, it had been daylight, so they wouldn't have shown even if she had.

It'd be light for at least another hour. Skye could, theoretically, wander into the woods again and come home, and still remain human for one more day.

Livy had come back yesterday from a date at Carol's with Kit Sylvain, smiling and humming. "He's a total womanizer," she'd said to Skye. "He kissed my hand. Can you believe that? It was kind of cute actually… anyway, he's fun to talk to, but I can't imagine anything'll come of it."

Still, she'd been just about glowing.

It made the non-enchanted part of Skye's heart ache with longing. God, to be able to date again. A human guy, not a goblin. To chat, laugh, kiss. Another perfectly normal part of life stolen from her.

She spat the fir needle out of her mouth, unlatched the gate, and strode out. In a minute she was across the weedy grass of the greenway, and up and over the railroad berm with its seldom-used tracks. She trotted down the other side and along the barbed wire fence until reaching the spot where the fence ended and a footpath led into the woods.

She walked down it, the same path where she'd so foolishly accepted the goblins' invitation. Cloudy gray light filtered through the ceiling of branches. Silence wrapped around her. High above, a crow cawed a few times, and a car swooshed by somewhere in town. Her feet squelched through the carpet of needles. She breathed in the familiar wet forest scent that now triggered a combination of intense desire and terror.

I'm defying it, confronting it, not giving in to its draw, she insisted to herself.

She reached the spot where the lines of glowing mushrooms had led her off the path. White shelf-shaped mushrooms did still stick out of the fallen logs, but they grew in no particular pattern now, and she doubted they would glow if she cupped her hands around them to shut out the light. They were just mushrooms. In frustrated defiance, she left the path, stepping over the low branches of evergreen huckleberry that stuck into her way.

After several paces, she stopped and looked around. Still the everyday forest. Another car whooshed past in the distance, and when she craned her neck she spotted the white edge of the railroad signal back on the tracks.

You had to be invited, and accept that invitation, before the forest turned into faeryland. And that had to happen after dusk. She got that now.

Movement caught the corner of her eye, accompanied by a thump of shoes on the ground. She turned her head. Someone was walking down the path, headed toward town. From her partly shielded position in the bushes, Skye watched the newcomer.

He was a young man, around her age. A little lanky, but he had a pretty enough profile and a pleasant thatch of dark hair.

The idea sizzled through her in a second, leaving her hot and trembling. *Come to the woods and choose your mate.*

They never said it had to be a goblin. And even a total stranger, as long as he was human, was better than a goblin.

Maybe this wouldn't even work, wouldn't do a thing to save her. But she felt the magic ricocheting inside her, rising to the ready.

Skye stepped toward the path.

Grady Sylvain stomped through the forest, barely registering the majestic mossy trees he'd been so stoked about on his summer visits to this town.

Another "Sorry, the position's been filled" from a Seattle restaurant this morning when he'd called to follow up on what he'd thought was a promising conversation last week. Then another two hours wasted this afternoon in searching Seattle apartment listings online, and still finding nothing remotely affordable except places that looked like crack houses.

He'd moved to Bellwater after Christmas, three weeks ago. He had expected it to be a step up from Moses Lake out in central Washington, where he grew up. At least he was technically closer to Seattle now, his dream destination. But it turned out Bellwater—an idyllic bayside town in summer, all stand-up paddleboards and ice-cream cones—became a nothing-happening town in winter.

He wasn't even *that* near Seattle. The city was two hours away, one hour of which involved a ferry ride, and he'd only been over there twice to pound the pavement and look for a cooking job. Jobs, like apartments, were being devoured in Seattle ferociously, and employers could afford to be picky. The places he longed to work didn't want some kid from Moses Lake with a community college degree. The places that did offer him a job dispirited him just to be in them, so he had politely said he'd consider them, and left, hoping he'd never be desperate enough to accept those.

Apartment hunting had been equally frustrating: oh, you don't have a job yet? Then no, you can't lease an apartment. And rent prices staggered him, especially for the tiny living spaces they came attached to.

So here he was, stuck in Bellwater, skinning his knuckles on greasy car bolts, cooking for his cousin because there was no one else to appreciate it, and tonight was Friday and that didn't even matter since he had no one to go out with and nowhere to go. Did becoming a grownup and seeking a real job suck this much for everyone?

Something moved at the edge of his vision, out in the trees. He slowed and looked.

A girl stood there, well off the path, just her head and shoulders visible, framed by leafy branches and bare twigs. She stared at him, her eyes imploring. She took a step toward him, then paused.

He came to a full stop and turned toward her. "Hey," he called.

Shadows surrounded her big eyes, and her expression was intent and unsmiling. But she riveted him, reminding him of someone from a spooky beautiful painting, her hair all loose and dark around her pale face, her lips parted like she wanted to say something important.

Grady moved to the edge of the path, closer to her. "Hi. Uh, everything okay?"

"Help me." She whispered the words, seeming to struggle to force them out, as if something were wrong with her tongue. He barely caught the phrase, even in the silent forest.

But he did hear it, and it galvanized him. He threaded between plants and stepped over logs to reach her.

He stood before her, shooting her a glance from head to boots. She didn't look injured or anything. But she breathed shallowly, and kept staring at him with that intensity.

"What's wrong?" he asked. "You need help?"

She grasped the front of his fleece coat. Her knuckles dug into his chest. Grady gazed into her brown eyes in wonder.

"I pick you," she said, again with a peculiarly stilted, numb-sounding vocalization, but she enunciated the words in a deliberate enough manner that the effect was almost formal.

"You what?" he said.

Then she laid one cold hand on the side of his face, and pulled him down toward her.

She couldn't mean to kiss him. That couldn't be about to happen. But she lifted her parted lips as if that was exactly what she had in mind, and though Grady knew the honorable thing, the smart thing, to do was to step away, he felt mesmerized. As her breath touched his face, his common sense fell to shreds. Temptation roped itself around his head, impossible to resist. He *longed* to kiss her all of a sudden, and his mind even supplied a rationale: hadn't he just been wanting something pleasant to happen in his life? Didn't this count, in a weird way?

So although it was beyond crazy, he met her halfway and kissed her. With restraint, like a gentleman. Well, at first.

Through a breath in her parted lips he caught an unusual, enticing flavor, rich and green like the forest itself, and he opened his mouth further to taste it. The kiss locked deeper; their heads tilted. He shut his eyes. Her fingers twined into his hair. The hand clutching his coat relaxed and she slid her arm around his back, snake-like. He wound his arms around her, his fingers penetrating the holes of her loose-knit sweater, clawing at the soft curves and hard bones of her body. As their tongues met, Grady felt like the ground was sinking languorously beneath him. His head buzzed in astonished delight and a fire started in his lower body and crept outward.

She pulled her mouth free. Breathing hard, Grady blinked at her. Some pink had entered her cheeks, making her even more beautiful.

Just as he was about to speak—maybe ask her name—she ripped herself out of his arms and turned and ran into the forest.

"Hey!" Grady lunged after her, and fell on his front. A fallen branch bruised his chest, making him wince. He tried to rise, and found his feet were stuck. Twisting around, he discovered blackberry vines wrapped around his shoes. "Goddammit. How the…hey!" He twisted forward again. "Come back! Please! Who are you?"

He heard her fast footsteps, but only for a few seconds, then they went quiet. By the time he had disentangled his feet from the vines and stood up to look around, she was nowhere in sight.

He called and searched a long while, roving around the forest until the light faded too much to continue. His mystery woman was gone.

It was later than he thought, he realized upon checking his phone. How could it already be nearly dinnertime?

Disheartened, enraptured, and strangely lightheaded, Grady emerged from the trees and walked back through town to the island bridge, his ankles and hands marked up with thorn scratches.

CHAPTER EIGHT

SKYE TORE THROUGH THE FOREST, BREATH-
ING HARD, STUMBLING AND CATCHING HERSELF OVER AND OVER AS SHE
leaped rotting logs and whipped through thickets of young cedars.

What had she done? She didn't know that guy from Adam, and she'd
grabbed him and started kissing him like a strung-out maniac. Even at
parties during college she had at least exchanged names.

It *had* been a wonderful kiss, and a corner of her mind still glowed
with thrilled triumph over having done it. But it was a seriously insane thing to have done, and her mind raced in terror as fast as her feet
bounded across the forest floor. Because, oh God, what were the goblins
going to do to her—or to him—if this did work, and he had now been
tapped as her chosen mate?

The afternoon light was fading. She stopped, panting, and turned
around. She fumbled her phone out and checked the time, and gasped.
It was later than it should've been; somehow she had lost an entire hour.
Part of the enchantment? Could they have stood in that kiss for an *hour*?

Whatever the explanation, twilight had arrived. Which of course
meant...

"Sky-eye..." The rasping voice from above turned her name into
two singsong syllables.

"No," she whispered.

"What have you done, sweet sister?" Redring's voice said, closer. Others chuckled in the background, sinister and low.

Though ninety-five percent of everything in her longed to approach the voice, reach her arms up to the trees, accept the invitation, accept even the fruit, she squeezed her eyes shut and clung to the five percent. That still belonged to herself, to the human world, maybe even partly to the stranger whose warm body she could still feel upon her own.

"No," she said.

"Come in and talk to us."

"No!" She opened her eyes, pivoted, and took off running again, down the slope, back toward town.

"What…have…you…done?" The voice reverberated behind her, furious now.

Skye faltered, turned around like a child seeking her mother, then caught herself and spun toward home again.

"You will weaken. You will be back," Redring called. "And *he* will follow you, and be ours too."

She broke free of the forest, raced over the railroad berm, and sprinted across the grass. She was almost sobbing when she reached her gate, its peeling white boards standing out in the twilight.

"Skye!" It was Livy this time, sounding scared and relieved. Her sister jogged down the concrete steps from the house. The screen door banged shut behind her. "Where were you?"

Skye shot into the garden, shut the gate behind her, and wilted back against it, nearly fainting from exertion. "Walk," she managed.

"You were taking a walk?" Livy planted her hands on her hips. She was breathing fast too, like she was just coming down off a panic. "Are you okay?"

Skye nodded.

"You need to leave a note, or text me or something. Can you at least do that? I was worried."

Skye bowed her head, eyes closed. Her heart still galloped, blood circulating dizzily through her.

"Look, I'm sorry." Livy's hand settled on Skye's arm. "It's fine if you want to go for walks. I just get worried if you don't let me know, all right?"

Skye nodded, not opening her eyes.

"I'm happy to go for walks with you if you want." Livy was making an effort to sound upbeat. "I mean, it's usually dark by the time I get back from work, but hey, we own flashlights, right?"

Skye finally opened her eyes, and focused on Livy's blue and white running shoes. "Right."

"Come on in. It's getting cold. Let's find something for dinner."

Skye let her sister lead her back into the house.

The goblins were right. Someday she'd weaken. She would go back out there, and she wouldn't come back.

She didn't even know yet what fate she might have brought down upon a well-meaning stranger with his whole life ahead of him.

Grady's desire to forge a life in Seattle screeched to a stop. Everything in him concentrated upon the mystery woman. Presumably she was here in Bellwater, but where?

For the next three days, during non-work hours, he walked up and down every one of the few streets in town, and along the shore and around the bobbing docks of the marina, and of course through the forest too. His feet were blistered and the soles of his sneakers starting to peel off at the edges.

The woman was nowhere, vanished like a ghost.

While working at the garage he watched Shore Avenue in distraction, hoping to see her pass.

"What are you looking for?" Kit demanded on the third day.

"Nothing. Just looking."

He couldn't bring himself to ask Kit about her. Obviously he couldn't say, "Hey, I kissed this babe in the forest, but I didn't get her name and then she ran off. Dark hair, medium height, around my age. Any idea who that is?"

He considered altering it to a story about seeing a girl in passing, thinking she looked familiar, and describing her to see if Kit could identify her. But after the way Grady had teased Kit for his milkshake date with Livy, he didn't dare. Kit would razz the hell out of him.

What was her name? He couldn't leave town again without at least learning that much, without seeing her one more time, without asking what exactly had happened in the forest.

Yes, he knew it was crazy to be this obsessed over an encounter that had taken up maybe sixty seconds of his life. (Or had it been an hour and sixty seconds?) But what an encounter. His fingers still felt the bones and flesh through her sweater, his tongue still tasted her mysterious bitter-greens mouth, her voice still haunted him with that whispered *Help me.*

He needed an explanation. He had to know why she needed help. He might very well go insane if he never saw her again.

"CAN I FOLLOW UP WITH YOU A MINUTE?" LIVY
ASKED MORGAN TRAN, SKYE'S THERAPIST.

Skye had just come out of Morgan's office in Olympia after her weekly hour there.

"Sure." Morgan tucked her notebook against her chest. "Skye, make yourself at home. We have some yummy new green tea you can try if you like."

Instead of fixing herself anything from the beverage counter in the clinic lobby, Skye plucked a *Seattle Weekly* from the racks and hunched down into a chair with it.

"I won't be long," Livy promised her.

Skye nodded without looking up from the newspaper. Livy exchanged a glance with the receptionist, who reassured her with a smile. At least the receptionist knew to stop Skye if she tried to wander off. Lord, the things Livy had to worry about these days.

She entered Morgan's office, which was soothingly done up in aquamarine paint and cushions, with a splash of orange in the form of Gerbera daisies in a vase.

"Have a seat." Morgan shut the door and came around to one of the two chairs facing her desk.

Livy sat in the other, appreciating that Morgan joined her there, rather than clinically putting the desk between them.

Livy clutched her hands atop her knees. "Did she talk today?"

"Not much. Still only a few words at a time, mostly just echoing me, though in a way that made sense as an answer. It's like you've said—I think she's present, just inhibited from communicating with us for some reason. Have you come up with any ideas about what might have happened?"

Livy shook her head. "If anyone assaulted her, I haven't seen any proof, and she hasn't said a word. Which isn't like her."

"Well, while we hope it's not that, sometimes a trauma does take a while to surface. Which is unfortunate for the law enforcement side of the issue, where sooner would be better."

Livy curled her knuckles tight inside the opposite palm. "But it *could* just be S.A.D. or other depression?"

"It could. It's a sudden onset and a serious case, but depression works in a lot of different ways. I've seen quite a variety of cases. Were you concerned about any new behavior of hers?"

"Sort of. She went out for a walk a few days ago without leaving a note or anything, and it was dark when she got back. When I got home and she wasn't there, I kind of freaked out. I mean, she seemed mostly okay—tired and winded, like maybe she walked too far. But I feel like I can't even trust her to leave me a note anymore. I feel like she might just wander off and…not come back. If she went out by herself…I guess, do you think she's in a condition where I should worry?"

"Sounds like you live in a small town, not a high-crime region or anything?"

"It is small and relatively safe, but…" Livy uncurled her hands and pressed them flat on her thighs. "We do live right up against the Sound. With a marina and docks and bridges. I mean, is there any chance she'd…"

"You're concerned she might be suicidal?" Ever the professional, Morgan asked even that alarming question gently.

"I would never have suspected it of her before. Not ever. But lately she's just so withdrawn. She doesn't shower unless I remind her. She doesn't eat enough. I think she has nothing but coffee for breakfast and lunch, and only has dinner because I tell her to. She hasn't said or done anything that's clearly…suicidal." Livy had to swallow and collect her strength before saying the word. "But I wanted your opinion."

Morgan nodded, rolling her fingertips across the cover of her notebook. "I haven't seen any clear suicidal tendencies either. I would definitely alert you right away if I did. But you know her best and I trust your instincts, so if you're worried to leave her alone—well, maybe you can ask for help? That way at least you can relax and tend to your own well-being a little more." Morgan smiled in commiseration.

"Our mom visits sometimes, but not a lot. She lives down in Portland now. And Skye's friend Jamie comes by once in a while, but she's got classes and work. Or are you saying we should hire someone? Like a nurse?" Livy winced.

"I wouldn't say she needs a nurse. Some friendly company, though. Someone who can make sure she's all right, maybe remind her to eat."

Livy nodded, though her mind raced desperately through their neighbors and dismissed each one as too busy, too elderly, or too annoying for Skye to want to put up with. There had to be someone.

"I'll think about it," she said.

As Livy and Skye drove back into Bellwater, they had to stop in the middle of Shore Avenue to allow a tow truck to back a pickup into Kit's auto shop. Kit stood near, chatting with a heavy-set guy, presumably the pickup's owner.

Skye's gaze drifted in boredom across the pavement, then snapped to attention upon spotting the young man who stood waving the driver into the space, pointing and shouting to direct him left and right.

Her stranger from the woods. Her mate.

Warmth flooded her. She felt short of breath.

Livy chuckled. "Well, at least we don't have to get under that truck. We're luckier than the Sylvain boys that way."

"Sylvain." Skye leaned forward in her seat for a better look.

The guy jogged out of the way while the driver slotted the truck into the garage.

"Yeah," Livy said. "That's Grady, Kit's cousin. He's in town a while. Apparently he's a really good cook. He's looking for a restaurant job in the city."

Skye watched as he disappeared into the garage to unload the truck. A good cook as well as a good kisser. He sounded nice.

She wondered if the magic would have made a prison inmate sound "nice" to her, however. Because this surely was all due to the spell. *Picked him as your mate? Fine, then here's your mating instinct*, it seemed to be saying.

She longed to see him again. Had he been thinking about her? He must have been, given their extraordinary meeting in the forest.

Kit spotted Livy waiting, and exchanged waves with her. Then the tow truck backed its nose out of the street and their path was clear. Livy drove past.

Skye twisted around to watch the garage as long as she could, until they turned the corner onto their street.

Livy cleared her throat. "Grady doesn't like working at the garage, Kit says. He'd really rather cook. I was thinking it might be nice if I offered him a job, just temporary, like coming over to make us lunch or dinner some days. If he's interested. I mean, if you don't mind him being around while you're there."

Skye examined her. Livy's expression was a little too carefully aloof; she must have guessed at Skye's interest in Grady. Probably from how Skye had been staring.

Livy pulled into their driveway and turned off the engine. "So what do you think? I could ask him."

Skye dragged her black leather purse off the car's floor and onto her lap. She looked down at it, winding her fingers into the strap. His kiss. His kind face. His human warmth. The way he had made her feel good when nothing else had for a month.

"Ask him," she said quietly.

CHAPTER TEN

SKYE DIDN'T NEED A BABYSITTER. LIVY STILL FELT CONVINCED OF THAT, THOUGH IT COULD BE SHE JUST WASN'T READY to face the idea of Skye needing anything resembling a nurse or a nanny. But some friendly company would help, as Morgan had said; especially someone who could cook. Grady's culinary inventions sounded delicious and Livy wanted them in her house. Livy could easily rationalize it that way.

Also, Skye seemed to want him to come. That alone was notable, as she showed so little interest in anything lately. How could Livy *not* ask him?

Livy had taken the morning off to drive Skye to her appointment, and planned to spend the rest of the day working from home, emailing trail-restoration volunteers with the month's plans. But she could put that off another half hour.

She heated up canned soup for lunch, made sure Skye ate some, then told her, "Since I'm here, I'll walk down to the garage and see if Grady's interested. Okay?"

Slouched on the sofa, browsing Netflix by remote, Skye nodded.

"Cool. Back soon."

Livy walked down their sloping street and turned onto the shoulder of Shore Avenue. She told herself her thumping heart was nervousness at asking something kind of weird from someone she didn't really know, and was certainly not excitement about talking to Kit again.

She strode up to the garage. Grady leaned his back against the mud-splattered pickup truck, eating what looked to be some kind of wrap.

As she approached, he swallowed a bite and greeted, "Hey."

"Hey. Is Kit around?"

"Yup. Office." He nodded toward the door.

"Thanks." She paused. "I hear you cook. Is that something you made?"

He nodded and tilted the half-eaten wrap toward her to display it. "Tandoori steak, cucumber, and mint. With romaine."

"Good God. That sounds fantastic."

"Might as well eat something that tastes good, right?"

"You have the right attitude." She sighed, thinking of her woeful can of soup. Best not to even tell him about that. "Talk to you soon."

He waved in the middle of another bite.

She stepped into the office to find Kit behind the counter, frowning over a ledger book. An open Tupperware container sat beside it. The smell of warm Italian herbs mingled with the usual motor-oil scent.

He looked up at her and his scowl cleared to a surprised smile. "Heya. What's up?"

"Hi. I have kind of a weird question for you. Well, an offer. And it isn't really for you, it's more for Grady, but I didn't want to put him on the spot, so I thought I'd ask you."

"I am officially intrigued." Kit rested both hands on the counter's edge, arms straight, and gazed at her.

She interlaced her fingers in front of her chest. "Well…his cooking sounds so amazing, and I suck at it so much myself, that I was thinking it'd be nice to hire him to come over and make us lunch or dinner some days. It'd be mainly hours I'm not around, but Skye would be there, and I think she could use the company, the way she's felt lately. I *know* she could use the good food."

Kit considered, lifting his eyebrows. "He may go for that. I gather he hates working on cars. Only because he tells me daily."

"It's just if you could spare him. Hours could be flexible, so it wouldn't get in the way of his schedule here."

"Eh, just between us, he's not that much help in the shop." Kit picked up a slice of pizza from the Tupperware and held it out on his palm. "This, now, is his superpower. Here, try. You'll see."

"Oh, no, I don't want to take your lunch."

"I got plenty. Seriously, try it."

Livy caved in, took the pizza slice, and bit into it. The flavors blossomed in her mouth, a perfect blend of garlic, basil, crust, and what tasted like the top-quality varieties of pepperoni and mozzarella. "Mmm," she said around the bite. "Okay, yeah. This. We want this."

Kit folded his arms, watching her with satisfaction. "He took pity on me and made me pizza, but of course it's still fancy pizza. Pesto instead of marinara, some kind of leaves on it along with the pepperoni."

Livy tasted the scrap of wilted salad green she had just encountered. "Arugula maybe?"

"Something like that."

"It's awesome. Wow." She ate another bite.

"Then sure, I'll ask him. Would there be any job duties besides cooking?"

"Not really. I mean…I admit it's also that I'd feel better knowing someone was there with her, at least sometimes."

"And this is okay with her? Him being in her space?"

Livy finished the last bite of pizza, and nodded. "She said to ask him. I have the feeling she thinks he's cute."

Kit grinned. "We're playing with fire, then."

"Not necessarily. They could just be friends. Anyway, they're adults. It's their deal."

"Write your number." Kit flipped over a business card and slid it across to her. "I'll let you know what he says."

Cooking at home for two women, one of whom was depressed and needed cheering up with good food—well, it wasn't Grady's dream job, but by now he had to admit in defeat that it was better than what he was currently doing. Sure, he told Kit, he'd be happy to go check it out.

Kit texted Livy to tell her they'd come over after the garage closed. Kit had given Grady a ride to work, so they drove back to the island first, where Grady picked up a sample of his cooking for this Skye woman to taste.

"I'll take you there, show you where it is," Kit said.

"I can probably find it myself. Town's not that big."

"Still, I'll come say hi." Kit sounded too casual, flicking his truck keys between his fingers.

Ah, right, because Livy was the woman whose hand Kit had been kissing the other day. Grady smirked and let him come along.

They parked the truck at the corner of Livy and Skye's dead-end street, and walked up toward the address she'd given.

It was a light blue single-story house at the top of the cul-de-sac, with a sagging wire fence around a garden of robust-looking bushes. The forest loomed behind it, and Grady's thoughts flew to his mystery woman again. But only for a melancholy few seconds, because then Livy came out and strode down the front path.

"Hey, Grady." She beamed. "Thanks for coming."

"No problem." He held up the paper bag. "I brought scones."

"Ooh, that sounds perfect. Wait—no fruit in them?"

He shook his head, puzzled. "They're cheddar."

"Good. Skye's got a weird aversion to fruit lately. I don't know." She glanced back at the house, then lowered her voice as she faced the two men again. "She also doesn't talk a lot these days. So if she's quiet, it's not that she doesn't like you. But she'll listen, and might interact, and…

anyway, you can come in and see if this is something you want to do."

Grady's feet grew cold at those warnings. He was a cook, not a mental health specialist. But he could make excuses and get out of it later if he wanted. For now he'd at least go through with the introductions. "Sure, let's go say hi," he said.

Livy smiled in gratitude and led them up the path. Grady exchanged a guarded, uncertain glance with Kit.

They stepped into the house, which smelled faintly of coffee and perfume, and followed Livy into the kitchen.

"Hey, Skye," she said. "This is Grady."

Grady's curious glance around the kitchen stopped dead as his gaze landed on the young woman sitting at the table, her dark hair in a bun with bits coming loose, her haunted eyes drinking him in.

Her.

He pulled in a rapid breath through his nose, and felt his eyes widen, then mastered his reaction so it didn't show beyond that, even as his heart began hammering like a piston.

He'd considered this younger sister might be his mystery woman, but he hadn't realistically dared hope it. Now here she was, and he was being offered the chance to spend a few hours a day with her *and* get paid for it—okay, he still needed a lot of explanation about that forest kiss, but at the moment, he only thought ecstatically to the Powers That Be, *Oh thank you thank you thank you.*

He gave Skye his best effort at a friendly smile. "How's it going?" He tilted the open paper bag toward her. "Cheddar mini-scone?"

Skye looked gravely at the bag, nodded, and took one of the scones.

"They're good," Kit remarked. "I ate six for breakfast."

"Six?" Livy laughed.

"They're small."

Skye began nibbling the scone. Her gaze kept returning to Grady, and he found it hard to tear his away from her too. As Livy talked to him about the stove, the pantry, and the sorts of things they usually ate, he did his best to pay attention, nodding and studying utensils, feeling like a dork.

"I don't know, if you want to give it a try for a day or two…" Livy concluded after a few minutes.

Grady nodded. "That'd be great." He glanced at Kit, who lounged against the door frame. "Better than getting motor oil in my hair, that's for sure."

Kit smirked.

Skye still watched Grady, not smiling or speaking. But she had eaten the whole mini-scone, at least.

Grady agreed to start tomorrow morning, ten o'clock.

They walked back out to the front yard, and this time Skye got up and wandered along with them.

"Oh, man." Kit squinted across the fence. "Duncan's old Caddy. I haven't seen that running in, what, ten years?" He veered across the garden to get a closer look at the hunk of automotive junk in the neighboring driveway.

"No one has." Livy followed him. "It's been sitting there forever. Look, it's got vines growing through it."

The two of them walked to the fence, talking cars, but Grady stopped paying attention. He looked down at Skye, who hovered in silence at his elbow.

"Good to see you again," he said quietly.

"Good to see you," she murmured back.

"What happened in the woods? What was that? Why'd you kiss me, then why'd you run off? I've been looking everywhere for you."

She hugged herself and looked at her shoes. "I'm sorry," she whispered.

"No—I don't—look, it's okay, I liked it. Don't be sorry. But what *was* it? And why'd you say 'Help me'? Help you with what?"

She cast a miserable look over the roof, toward the forest.

"With…feeling like this?" he guessed, softening his voice. "They said you were feeling down lately. Is that what you meant?"

She looked at the ground again, and shrugged one shoulder.

He shot a glance at Kit and Livy to make sure they were still chatting. "Then I hope it did help," he said.

She didn't answer or look at him, so he added, "Is it actually okay with you, my taking this job?"

She met his eyes again, and nodded.

"You sure? You want me here?"

"Want you," she whispered.

The way she said it, gazing at him, choosing those words to echo— an erotic thrill shivered through him. Which was all messed up in light of, well, everything. His body couldn't forget how that kiss had felt.

"Then I'll come by tomorrow," he said. "We can get acquainted. Maybe I'll even figure out how to help you." He smiled, as if this was a perfectly normal conversation.

She only looked unhappy again, and glanced away.

"Ready, man?" Kit walked back over with Livy.

Grady nodded. "See you tomorrow, then," he said to both women, but his gaze lingered three times as long on Skye.

"Looks like you got a chance to talk to him a little?" Livy said. She and Skye stood on the small concrete front porch, watching Kit and Grady stroll back to the truck.

Skye shivered. The cold outdoor air seemed to invade her body now that he'd left. "A little."

"Nice enough guy. I hope he'll like it, a job doing something he enjoys, even if it's just temporary."

Skye shrugged, distracted. She felt the pull of the forest behind her, hated it and longed for it.

"I think he likes you." Livy smiled as she watched the truck drive away. "Could hardly take his eyes off you."

Skye's eyes filled with tears, her misery uncontainable.

Livy glanced at her, and the smile quickly changed to a look of concern. "Hey, what, what's wrong?"

Skye flopped her hand up and down herself, and ended with a hopeless flourish that pointed back toward the woods. "This."

Livy wrapped an arm around her, and guided her back into the warm house. "I know. It sucks, not being able to talk to people as easily as you used to. But you will again. I know it. You're a strong woman, babe."

In the front hall, Skye sniffled and nodded in acceptance.

Livy patted Skye's shoulder. "How about some chai?"

Skye nodded again. While Livy slipped into the kitchen, Skye wandered across to the back pantry, rested her forehead against the window in the door, and gazed out at the dark treetops.

Grady did seem nice, genuinely so, which tortured her even more. *He will follow you.* She had thrown out a magical hook and ensnared him without thinking of the consequences. She ought to send him away, keep him at a distance, for his own good. But he probably wouldn't go, thanks to the spell that had infected him; and in any case, the magic was working on her too. Just as she longed for the forest out of all proportion, she now longed for him as well, her chosen mate.

She was ruining his life, yet she couldn't bear to let him go. She closed her eyes. She'd thought the spell couldn't get any worse, but it already had.

⁂

Kit had wanted to ask her. God, how tempting it had been to beckon Skye aside and just say those few words: "Hey listen, did goblins have anything to do with this?"

But seven years' worth of keeping this liaison business a secret was too heavy a roadblock to shift. If she *wasn't* enchanted—which, odds were, she wasn't—he'd sound crazy if he asked that. And then she'd tell her lovely, hot sister how insane he was, and he'd never get to enjoy milkshakes or anything else with Livy again. Word might even get out to the rest of the town: what was up with Sylvain, talking about goblins or some shit? Losing his mind like his parents, real shame. Yeah, no. He couldn't ask.

Besides, if she *was* under a spell, there was nothing he could do about it. No method existed for humans to counter goblin magic, or at least none that he or his unlucky ancestors had ever heard of. So, really, he prayed it *was* ordinary depression, much as depression sucked.

Maybe it was, and maybe Grady was about to turn everything around for Skye, just by virtue of being himself, with his good nature and mad cooking skills.

If Grady was honestly up for it.

"Sure you want to do this, bro?" Kit asked him as they drove across the one-lane bridge to Crabapple Island.

Grady gazed out the side window. Bridge railings blurred past. Behind them rippled the expanse of silver-gray water separating the island from the rest of town.

Kit's question seemed to register a few seconds late. "Yeah, of course," Grady said, his eyes still on the water.

"She's pretty," Kit admitted. "I just wonder if, I don't know, she needs more help than you can give. She seemed really…withdrawn. Especially compared to how happy and talkative I remember her being in school."

"She talked to me a little."

"Well. Good." They came off the bridge and curved onto the loop road. Tall conifers took over, interrupted by the occasional mailbox. "Anyway," Kit said, "it's not like helping her is totally down to you. Livy did say she was getting counseling. This is just more like hanging out with her. And feeding her kale or whatever so she's healthier."

Grady finally looked at him. "So she wasn't like this till recently?"

"Yeah, Livy says it came on suddenly, a month or so ago."

"Caused by what?"

"No one's sure. Guess it's not like her at all." Kit pulled the truck into the rutted gravel drive that led to his house.

"Huh." The cabin came into view, with its asymmetrically sloped roof and the sprawling mess of sculptures-in-progress in the yard. "I wonder if something happened."

Kit parked the truck, and frowned out the windshield. "Let me know if you find out."

CHAPTER ELEVEN

GRADY SET HIS ALARM FOR 7:30 THE NEXT MORNING, AND AFTER A SHOWER AND BREAKFAST, HOPPED IN HIS OLD Jeep Cherokee and drove up to Quilcene to buy groceries. While he poured his nervous energy into selecting the nicest-looking produce, his phone rang.

He glanced at the caller ID: Mom. He answered, "Hey," and tucked the phone against his shoulder while he bagged some bell peppers.

"Hello, Grady." She sounded upbeat. "Now what's this about a cooking job?"

He smiled. He'd left his older brother a text about it late last night, knowing that would be all it took to spread the word to both parents and every one of his siblings. "It's nothing much. Just some part-time cooking at home for two women in town."

"Old ladies? Doesn't sound like the kind of thing old ladies would hire someone for."

He wheeled the cart along and inspected the tomatoes. "Actually no, they're in their twenties. Two sisters."

"Oh! Well, even better. What are you going to cook for them?"

"For today, I'm thinking something that'll work as lunch and also leftovers for dinner. I'll bring recipes they can choose between, with ingredients that'll work for both. I'm in Quilcene getting the groceries right now."

"Is Quilcene the one that has the good store?"

"Yeah, or at least, nicer stuff than Bellwater." He picked out four tomatoes. "Bellwater's store is tiny and it's all, like, iceberg lettuce and marshmallows and cans of soup."

"Those poor people. It's a wonder Kit's survived this long."

"That's what I keep telling him."

"Any luck on other job leads?"

Grady rolled the cart toward the dry-goods aisle. "Not really. I'm still looking. Getting kind of demoralizing."

"That's what job hunts are like, hon. Don't give up. But if you do want to give up and move home, we would of course be over the moon to have you back. We miss you."

A twinge of homesickness pinched him. "I miss you guys too. What's new over there?"

While he set groceries into the cart, his mom gave him the rundown, though he'd picked up some of the gossip from texts or emails already: his oldest sister's wedding plans, his older brother's new job, his second-youngest sister's awesome SAT scores, and his freshman sister's scandal-ous flirtation with a senior guy. He could move back to Moses Lake and settle right back into the midst of that happy chaos anytime. They'd wel-come him, and within fifteen minutes everyone would forget he'd ever been gone. He was lucky to have such a comfortable home. Maybe it was insane to be out here looking to live somewhere else.

But...no way was he jumping ship now. Not until he figured out what was up with Skye. Helped her, if that's what she wanted. Generally just hung out with her to soak up her hotness.

He was a little too hooked at the moment to leave Bellwater.

"Well," his mom said as he neared the checkout line, "hang in there on the job front, kiddo. And I'm so glad you've got these two ladies giving you a chance in the meantime. Sounds like they're being good to you."

"Yeah. They've been nice." If by *nice* you meant *grabbing you in the woods and planting the best kiss ever on you.* "I'll let you know how it goes. Bye, Mom."

Grady arrived at the Darwens' house at five minutes before ten. Two canvas bags of groceries weighed down his shoulders. He knocked, his pulse thrumming in his throat.

Livy opened the door and beamed. "Hey. Right on time." She took one of the grocery bags from him. "Listen, I really appreciate you trying this out. I know it's kind of bizarre."

"No no, it's fine. Should be fun."

"Skye appreciates it too, no matter how it seems. Believe me."

He nodded. "Well. I brought a couple options for lunch recipes. I'll let her choose what sounds good."

Livy beckoned him in with a tilt of her head. "Let's get these into the kitchen."

Skye wasn't there. Grady pressed his lips together to keep from asking where she was. He started fitting cheeses, eggs, and vegetables into the fridge.

Livy cleared counter space by putting away mugs and cereal boxes. "Use anything you want—pots, pans, spices, ingredients."

"Okay. Thanks."

"Skye's in the shower. She'll be out soon."

He swallowed, trying to get the picture of her naked and dripping wet out of his head. He wadded up one of the empty canvas bags and stuffed it inside the other. "Okay," he repeated.

"I've got to get to work now," Livy said, "so I'm off. I'll go tell her goodbye."

Grady stood in front of the small kitchen table and smoothed out his two recipe pages with nervously chilled hands. He heard Livy walk down the hallway, knock on a door, and call through, "Hey, Skye, Grady's here, and I'm taking off. I'll text you later, okay?"

He thought he heard a soft "Okay" in response.

Livy appeared again, zipping up her coat, keys jangling. She took a backpack from a hook in the entry, and glanced into the kitchen at Grady. "Call me if you have any questions. Or if you can't find the garlic or whatever."

They had acquired each other's numbers last night through Kit. He smiled. "I will."

"See you." She hoisted the pack onto her shoulder. "Looking forward to the food!"

"Thanks. Bye."

The front door shut. In a minute she started up her car and drove away. Grady slid the papers around, paced across the kitchen to inspect the cookware, and paced back. He took out the set of knives he'd gotten from his parents for Christmas—you always brought your own if you were serious about cooking—and arranged them on the table beside the recipes. From down the hall came the soft thumps of Skye moving around, muffled by the white noise of the bathroom fan.

The fan shut off. The door down the hall squeaked open. He swallowed.

She came into the kitchen, arms folded, dressed in an olive-green hoodie, artfully ripped jeans, and thick gray socks. Her hair was damp and wavy and hanging loose down her back.

"Morning," Grady said.

She wandered up beside him and looked down at the recipes his fingertips lay upon. The smell of shampooed hair drifted into his nose. Her arm leaned against his. The top of her head barely reached his shoulder.

He cleared his throat. "So, yeah. These are your two choices for lunch. Frittata or breakfast burrito—which, despite its name, is awesome as lunch. Or dinner for that matter. Uh, what do you think? Would one of these work?"

Skye examined both recipes, then tapped the breakfast burrito page with her forefinger.

"Good choice. Okay. I'll get that one started. It involves chopping up a lot of vegetables." He paused and looked around the kitchen.

Skye walked to the counter, reached behind the toaster, and slid out a plastic cutting board. She brought it to him.

"Ah. Thank you. Perfect." He set it on the table beside the knives, then turned to fetch the bell peppers, onions, chilies, and tomatoes. While he washed them at the sink, Skye held up a bag of coffee beans, and lifted her eyebrows at him in question.

"Making coffee?" he said. "Sure, sounds great. Thanks."

She opened a drawer and held up a small silver tool with a disk-shaped whisk at the end, and again gave him the questioning eyebrows.

Grady squinted. "Oh, no way, is that a milk frother?"

She nodded.

"You can make a latte or cappuccino or something?"

She nodded.

"Then yeah, for sure, I'll take a latte. Awesome, thanks."

They worked in almost-companionable silence for a few minutes, Grady dicing vegetables and Skye grinding coffee beans and heating milk.

She brought mugs to the table a few minutes later, partially filled with strong black coffee. He paused his chopping to watch as she tipped the frothed milk in from the little saucepan. A few tilts and swirls of the mug, and the white froth formed a feathery shape like a fern against the creamy brown.

"Ah, look at you," he said in admiration. "Are you a barista?"

She nodded, meeting his gaze, and though she still didn't smile, he caught a hint of pride in her posture.

"See, I still can't do that," he said. "The foam, the designs. That takes artistry."

She set the saucepan in the sink, then padded over to the wall beside the table, and touched a framed painting hanging there. She looked straight at him, her fingers lingering on the bottom corner of the painting.

The painting showed a marina, with sailboat masts and board-walks and reflective rippling water, all in crazy bright colors, its paint splashed about in a way that made it look perpetually wet. He leaned closer to read the words inked in the corner in black pen: *Winter is bright in Bellwater*, followed by a half-illegible signature that could have been *Skye Darwen*.

"No way. You painted this?"

She nodded, then glanced at the fridge, where a colored-pencil sketch of little pink flowers was stuck with magnets. He had absentmindedly noticed it when dealing with the food, and now gave it a second glance. "You're an artist." He looked back at her and got another nod. "A barista and an artist. There, see, I'm getting to know you even if you won't talk."

She picked up her latte and wandered out of the kitchen with it.

Unsure about whether to follow, he went back to chopping.

She returned in a minute with a sketchbook, spiral-bound with black cover. She set it next to the tomatoes on the table.

"Do I get to look at that?"

She nodded.

Grady wiped his hands on the dishtowel he'd hung over his shoulder, and picked up the sketchbook. Inside it was mostly black ink or pencil, and the first several pages showed various everyday scenes: rain pouring off an umbrella as someone huddled beneath it, a dog curled up beside a cafe table, a sailboat tied to a buoy, close studies of flowers and other plants.

"These are awesome." He glanced at Skye, hoping for a smile at least, but she only watched the pages.

He turned to the next one and paused. "More surreal now?" It was like something from a fantasy film, or steampunk maybe: a tree-top village with rickety bridges overhung with strings of mismatched lightbulbs, and ramshackle houses wedged between trunks. "That is super cool."

Skye breathed faster; he heard the swift little sounds through her nose. She looked pale, her eyes bright. Her gaze latched onto the book, then onto him. He gazed back at her, trying to understand.

She reached out and turned the next page herself, then looked at him again.

He frowned at the sketch: another in fantasy style, a gremlin-like creature crouched on all fours, its limbs like twigs, its razor teeth show-ing in a grin, a ring on a tattered string around its neck. The sketch was all in graphite, except for the stone on the ring. She had colored that a brilliant red, making it stand out like an evil eye. "Wow," he said. "Creepy. You have serious talent, you know that? You can draw all these different styles."

Her lips tightened and she released a sigh through her nose, sound-ing exasperated.

"What?" he said. "You do. I'm not just saying that. I can't draw at all, so maybe I'm no judge, but I think it's amazing."

She took the notebook back, tucked it under her arm, and sipped her latte. Without looking at him, she murmured, "Thanks."

"Ah, so you *are* going to talk to me." He picked up the knife, and began dicing a jalapeño. "Okay, I'm not just going to ask you yes/no questions, then. Where'd you study art?"

She parted her lips, considered, then walked to the counter. She picked up a small note pad and a pencil, wrote something, and brought him the pad. She held it up to show him.

Univ of Puget Sound, it said. Her writing didn't suggest an unhinged mind to him. It was free-spirited and graceful.

"Cool. Did you graduate?"

She nodded.

Earning a degree at UPS wasn't usually something the unhinged did either, as far as he knew.

"Okay. Is writing easier for you than talking?"

She tilted her head, as if to say *Sort of.*

"What about with your sister? You talk to her, at least?"

She scrawled *Not much lately.*

"You're left-handed," he noted. "Okay, so you write messages for her, lately?"

Not much, she wrote.

He looked at her, bemused. "But you're willing to for me?"

She nodded again, gazing into his eyes with a hint of desperation.

"Why? You said, 'I pick you.' I'm almost sure you said that. What does that mean?"

She glanced away, looking miserable.

"You pick me to talk to? To write to, at least?"

She tilted her hand side to side. *Sort of.*

"You got to know how confused I am here," he said.

She nodded wearily.

"It's weird, but I like being with you. I may not know why you picked me, but I'm glad you did. It feels…right." His heart pounded at delivering this quasi-romantic speech, but then, none of the usual court-ship rules applied here, it would seem.

She still looked sad and haunted. But she dropped the notepad on the table, moved closer, twined her hand around his upper arm, and kissed him there. He felt the chill of her fingers and the warmth of her mouth through his flannel shirt. He trembled with each breath. What was this crazy pull she had over him? Why did he already want her so much?

He kissed the top of her head, inhaling the fragrance of her wet hair. They stood like that a moment, almost an embrace, definitely something intimate, he didn't know what to call it.

Whatever it was, it wasn't what her sister was paying him for.

He shifted away an inch, and smiled when Skye looked up. "Going to help me make lunch or what?"

CHAPTER TWELVE

IT DISTURBED SKYE HOW MUCH SHE WANTED TO TWINE HERSELF AROUND GRADY, AND DRAG HIM TO HER ROOM OR the couch or, better yet, some bed of moss deep in the woods. It was the magic at work; she felt that clearly enough.

She retained enough of her un-ensorcelled logic to recognize she would have liked him anyway. A date with him under normal circumstances might have gone smashingly well. But she'd never know, because normal circumstances were far from her reach.

She tried to meet his efforts halfway, or at least quarter-way. After their lunch of breakfast burritos, she helped him put away the leftovers. Then they sat across the small kitchen table from each other, knees almost touching, texting each other questions and answers. She could say more that way, and Grady told her with his cute grin that it made him feel less like he was babbling.

He told her he was twenty-one. She answered she was twenty-three. Their eyes met a moment over the table. A certain humility now mingled with the desire she saw there. Totally endearing. She returned her attention to the phone and thumbed in a question about his cousin.

She learned Grady often came to Bellwater for a few days in summer, to stay with Kit. He and Kit got along well, he said, though Grady didn't exactly feel like he knew Kit inside and out.

She told him she'd grown up mostly without a father, since the divorce had happened when she was so little, and he had moved so far away. He lived in New York now, and they were hardly in touch; just occasional awkward emails a few times a year.

Grady told her he came from a big and affectionate family; he was the third of five siblings. His dad was a contractor, his mom a substitute teacher. Though she didn't cook professionally, she was awesome at it, and Grady had originally learned to cook from her.

Skye told him how she had been trying to get graphic design work last fall. *Then*, she texted, and her thumbs froze. It was all she could do to press *send*, and throw him that unfinished thought.

Their gazes lifted from their phones, and met over the table again. "Then?" he asked.

She made the same despairing gesture she had made to Livy on the front porch yesterday: the sweep up her whole body, ending with a toss of her hand in the direction of the woods. Frustration tightened her face.

"Then you started feeling like this," he said softly.

She made one of her side-tilted half-nods. True but not the whole story. He'd learn the whole story before long.

His blue eyes held hers, intent. "Was there something that happened to you?"

Livy had asked, of course. Her therapist Morgan had asked. Everyone had asked. Every time, she was unable to nod or to shake her head. Maddening for all involved.

She held his gaze, begging him to read her mind, if by chance the magic went that far.

"Can you show me, if you can't tell me?" His words were quiet, treading delicately.

She stood and reached for his hand.

They put on coats and shoes. She led him into the woods.

But you couldn't summon goblins unless you came alone, and couldn't do it in the daytime. Nor did she exactly want to. Still, she brought him to the spot on the trail where the magical path had opened up to her—which in turn wasn't far from where she had met Grady a few days back.

She stopped there, let go of his hand and crossed her arms, and looked off into the trees in frustration.

Grady glanced around too, his breath clouding in the chilly air. "Something happened here?"

Again, she couldn't nod or shake her head.

"If someone attacked you, if there was anything illegal—look, you've got to tell someone. You've got to find a way."

Now she shook her head, irritated. Illegal? The law didn't even address what had happened to her. Or rather, it had happened under a different set of laws, and it *was* legal under those. Her own stupid fault for calling out to them, and for accepting their invitation.

"I'm sorry." He sounded crestfallen. "I don't understand. I want to help, but—"

She stepped forward and grasped his fleece coat, leaning up to his face.

His eyes locked onto her. He fell silent. Their breath mingled in misty white clouds. The mate-magic was stronger out here; he must have felt it too, though probably not as strongly as she did.

He gave in with a whimper, took hold of her shoulders, and kissed her.

She clung to him, drinking in the kiss. His lips were so soft, balanced by the scratchy little points of stubble surrounding them, which scraped pleasurably at her face as she nipped his lower lip and trailed kisses up his cheek. He was breathing fast, his eyes heavy-lidded, dark lashes veiling the blue as he watched her. She curled a hand up around his ear, and would have smiled in fondness at the way those ears stuck out a bit, if she could smile.

Grady ducked his head and began kissing her neck. "What *is* it about you?" he murmured. "Why am I so obsessed?"

Skye clung tighter to him, closing her eyes in pain. *Because I'm de-*

stroying you with magic. But the pain was mingled with sweetness. She felt terrible for it, but she did still prefer to be linked with mate-magic to him than to any of the goblins.

They kissed on the path for several minutes, draped in wet, cold, fir-scented air, arms wrapped around one another. It took all her restraint not to pull him deeper into the woods and become his proper "mate" on top of one of these fallen logs. Just as well that an elderly couple appeared, out on a walk along the path.

Skye and Grady disentangled, and Grady smiled at the couple. "Afternoon."

They said hello, beaming as if they knew perfectly well what they'd interrupted.

After they passed, Grady sent a sheepish glance down at Skye, then squinted up into the trees. "It's weird. I almost do understand why you brought me out here. How it's…something to do with the forest." His words became thoughtfully indistinct. "Or at least I will understand. Same way it feels right with you." Then he gave her a brighter, clearer smile. "Now I'm the one not making sense. What time is it?" He checked his phone. "Crap. Almost two. Didn't you say you had to work at two?"

She nodded and laced her fingers into his, turning back toward town.

CHAPTER THIRTEEN

WALKING TOWARD THE GARAGE AFTER DROP-
PING OFF A REPAIRED CAR AT ITS OWNER'S HOUSE, KIT SPOTTED LIVY'S
Forester parked in the small lot at the marina. The low afternoon sun
turned the clouds pink, and sparkled on the water between docks. He
gave in to impulse and veered down there.

She wasn't in her car, so he strolled down the aluminum gangway,
steep now since it was low tide. He stepped onto the wooden boards of
the marina, which bobbed a bit with each step. He didn't have to search
long. In less than a minute, Livy came out from the marina's small tack-
le-and-gift shop, carrying a paper cup with a black plastic lid.

She chuckled upon seeing him. "Got to stop running into each other."

They stopped beside one of the thick posts, upon which barnacles
and mussels and sea stars clung up to the height of his head. At high tide,
he knew, the whole marina would rise and cover the critters completely,
and the gangway would be almost horizontal. "I was on my way by," he
said. "Saw your car. Thought I'd let you know Grady and Skye seem to
have survived the day together."

She smiled. The cold wind whipped the ends of her long curls; the
sunlight turned them reddish-blonde. "I know. I texted her to make sure.
She's working this afternoon, and I guess she got there all right."

Kit lifted his eyebrow. "He walked her there."

"Oh really?" She sounded intrigued.

"Yep, told me so. Came to the garage afterward. He's holding down the fort while I run errands."

"She didn't tell me that part. Just said 'Fine' when I asked how it went." Livy's smile became wistful, and she looked down at her cup. "Even in texts she hardly talks lately."

"Sounded like Grady got a few words out of her, at least. Maybe they'll be good for each other."

"I hope so." Livy looked up again. "What brings you down here?"

"Taking Edna Burke's car back to her." He nodded southward. "She had a flat, plus the brakes needed adjusting."

"You make house calls? Good service."

"Eh, I wouldn't for everyone, but she's getting on in age, and it's not far for me to walk."

"Considerate of you."

Yeah, least he could do for his neighbors, since occasionally he stole from them. Usually not from the people in Bellwater maybe, but from *someone's* neighbors, in other towns. He looked away, at the bare sailboat masts lined up in the marina docks, a forest of white poles swaying as the water moved. "Gives me an excuse to go wander around the marina instead of doing actual work." He smiled at her. "What about you? Shouldn't you be doing actual work?"

"I was, kind of. I went to a meeting, then I had a conference call, which I decided to take out here instead of cooped up inside." She lifted the paper cup. "Then I was freezing by the time it was done, so I got some tea."

"The marina. Snack place of champions since—I don't know, but before I was born."

She squinted at him, eyes green in the sun. "I remember seeing you down here when we were teenagers."

"'Course you did. This was the place to be." He remembered seeing her too—some of her swimsuits and cutoff shorts in particular—but he knew better than to mention those out loud.

"There was this one time," she said. "I don't even know for sure if it was you, but I feel like it was. I was about eighteen, and it was summer, and I had walked down here and bought a bottle of juice. When I came out, you and some friends were sitting against that wall in the shade." She glanced back at the outer wall of the store, a few feet from the boat gasoline pumps. "You saw me drinking the juice and said, 'That looks good. Can I have some?'"

Kit had been grinning ever since she mentioned the juice. "And you handed it to me and let me have a sip." He remembered it too, in a flash, though he hadn't thought of it in years—Livy, fully developed and showing it in that bikini top, pausing to look at him in disdain while he hung out with some out-of-towner kids on vacation. Then her expression had shifted to a curious almost-smile, she'd handed him the bottle, and he'd sipped a mouthful of sweet strawberry-kiwi juice, looking her in the eyes. When he'd handed it back, she'd sipped it again without wiping it off, which had struck him as weirdly sexy. Then she'd strolled away.

Livy laughed. "So it *was* you."

"God, I was such a little punk. You should've poured it on my head."

"Nah, you were cute. I had the impression your girlfriend didn't appreciate it, though."

"Huh. Right." He remembered that too, now that she mentioned it: Jenna sitting next to him, smacking his arm after Livy walked off, then pouting and bitching at him all day. "That relationship wasn't destined to last anyhow."

Livy folded her fingers around the tea cup. "Still living the bachelor life these days?"

"Yeah. It's the compassionate thing to do. No one deserves to have me inflicted on them for life. What about you?"

She sipped the tea. "Same. Bachelor life. Except when I come down to the marina to pick up guys, of course."

"With your seductive offers of juice."

"Works every time."

Kit grinned. Here he should have said, *Anyhow, I'll let you get back to it,* and walked her to her car.

He didn't say that.

He liked her looks and the way she treated him. He wanted to do something nice for her. Even if, technically, getting involved with him wasn't much of a favor.

"You want to play hooky a little longer and walk down the beach with me?" he asked.

She lifted her eyebrows and considered for a few suspenseful seconds. "Sure."

My move, Livy thought. He had invited her on another almost-date, and as with the first one, she was enjoying it. Kind of a lot actually.

Since it was low tide, they had plenty of beach to walk upon. They followed the shore southward, clambering over small docks belonging to houses, skirting oyster beds exposed by the tide. This was no flat sandy beach like the ocean; Puget Sound's beaches were nearly all rocks, varying in size from grit to boulder, many of them covered with barnacles. The wind tore down the strait, and would have set her shivering if it weren't for the exertion of tromping through the bumpy terrain.

"You've lived here your whole life, right?" she asked.

"Not quite. I was born here, but after my folks died I moved away for a couple years. Rented out the house, and tried living in Idaho, then Wyoming." He squinted against the wind, hands stuffed into his jeans pockets. "Turned out my troubles just moved along with me."

"As they have a way of doing."

"So, I figured I might as well come back here. I missed this." He nodded at the Sound. "The water, the tides." He grinned at her. "The marina, the girls."

"Other towns have girls too, so I'm told."

"Still." He returned his gaze to the shore that rippled off into the distance. "This feels like home. And the cabin still technically belonged to me, so."

"Waterfront. I'm jealous."

"That's about the only awesome thing about it. Everything needs repairing, always."

"I guess I was similar to you," she said. "I tried to get away. Went to college, planned to travel…but then, I don't know. What I really wanted was to take care of this area." She lifted her mostly-empty cup toward the landscape. "The beaches, the forests. We're spoiled with how pretty it is around here."

"Has its dangers. But it is pretty."

"Dangers? Well, okay, earthquakes. Volcanoes. Really cold water."

"Bigfoot."

"Indeed," she said. "Mysterious creatures in the woods."

He shot her a keen glance.

"Skye and I used to make up stories," she explained. "Teeny-tinies, we called them. Forest gnomes or something." She glanced at the tips of the conifers, darkening to black as the sun set. "Sometimes when I was younger, I even could have sworn I heard them. Music, or laughter, or…" She caught his intent look, and subsided into a chuckle. "It was my imagination. Just, the forest can inspire those kinds of ideas. In someone weird like me, anyway."

Kit's glance slid away from her. "No, me too. You can tell by the crazy stuff I carve out of driftwood." He slowed, glanced at the orange sky in the west, and turned around. "We better head back before it gets any darker. Hey, and this way the wind's at our backs. Score."

Livy turned with him. The wind pushed her hair over her shoulders, tickling her chin. She chose her next words carefully. "I remember hearing about your folks. I'm sorry."

"Yeah. They died within a year of each other. It was…" He balanced on top of a buoy anchor before stepping down and continuing forward. "Not the easiest time ever."

"Wow. I bet." She bit her lip as they trudged along, debating how personal a question to ask next, but he spoke up himself.

"They had me kind of late in life, so they were both around sixty when they died. Still, that's kind of young, you know; they both drank too much, and had for a long time, which I'm sure figured into my dad's heart disease. And my mom's cirrhosis."

"God, you were so young, dealing with that. With no siblings to share the load."

"Yeah." He kept his hands in his pockets, and gazed ahead at the marina. "Worst part was she got Korsakoff's during the last couple years. I don't know if you know what that is."

Livy shook her head.

"It's kind of like dementia, or Alzheimer's. Happens with alcoholism sometimes. She lost a lot of short-term memory. In fact, a lot of memory in general. By the end, she practically didn't remember anything from the last five years. I'd go see her in the hospital, and she'd be confused and say, 'But, Kit, you look all grown up. You're only twelve.' Every time." He made an almost-laugh, a little puff of breath out his nose. "So—Skye not acting like herself, believe me, I do get how that might feel for you."

"Jeez." Livy exhaled, resisting the impulse to stop and hug him right there in the middle of the muddy oysters. "Compared to all that, Skye's problems are a walk in the park."

"Oh, I doubt it. From everything I hear about depression, it feels about as terrible as life gets." Kit glanced at her. "And it's just you dealing with it?"

"Mostly. I'm sure Mom would come up if we asked, but…she worked so damn hard for us after the divorce. I was twelve, Skye was nine. Dad moved out, we saw less and less of him, and Mom was just *always* working, always tired. It's why Skye and I got good at taking care of each other. Anyway, recently, Mom's finally been seeing a great guy, and she's moved in with him down in Portland, and her job's taking off—she's a realtor. And…" Livy shrugged. "How can I mess that up for her, you know? How can I tell her to drop everything and come look after us again?"

"She's your mom. She probably would."

"I know she would. Which is why I can't. I'd have guilt issues." She threw Kit a self-conscious smile.

"And your dad?"

"He's in New York. We haven't been in touch a lot. He didn't try to take care of us as kids, so now it'd feel weird if he did."

"I see."

"But…" She sighed. "If it gets to the point where I need to ask them for help, I suppose I will."

"In the meantime, I'm glad Skye's got you around."

"Today I'm glad she's got Grady around. I really think he'll improve things for her."

"His cooking does work wonders," Kit said. "It's made me not totally hate having him in my house all these weeks."

When they reached her car it was almost dark; the western sky was pale lavender, fading to blue, and the lights had been switched on at the marina. Their sterile reflections rippled in the water between moored boats.

"Give you a ride to the garage?" she asked.

"That'd be great, thanks." He hopped in beside her.

Amid apologies, she pulled maps and empty coffee cups off the passenger-side floor and threw them into the backseat. "I work from my car a little too much."

"Reliable car, though." He tapped the dashboard and cast a professional eye over the interior as she backed out of the parking space. "Had any issues? Head gasket? That's sometimes a problem with Subarus."

"Been okay so far. Should I have you look at that?" She paused before the turn onto Shore Avenue, and glanced at him.

He was already gazing at her, his light brown eyes and wind-tousled hair unfairly sexy in the glow of the dash lights. "Maybe. But now I'm just finding excuses to make you come see me."

Warmth rushed through her, and she smiled. "I'd come see you anyway. Got to see how that mermaid turns out."

He smiled too. She looked ahead and drove on through town.

Definitely her move.

The drive to the garage was all too short. She pulled into the parking lot within two minutes. Inside the quiet auto shop office, she caught a glimpse of Grady with his head bent over his phone or maybe a book. She rolled to a stop near the garage doors, out of Grady's sight line.

Livy pulled the parking brake but left the engine running. She looked at Kit. "Did that count as a date?" she asked.

"Our second, I would say. First was at Carol's."

"Well, then. Come here."

He leaned toward her, his gaze slipping to her lips. She met him over the parking brake and kissed his cheek, right at the corner of his mouth. The texture of rough whiskers and the scent of sea wind and masculine skin enticed her to linger a second. His hand cupped her face and held her steady, then he turned and enfolded her in a proper kiss, full on the mouth, but with an exquisitely light touch that brushed tingles throughout her.

"There." His voice rumbled low, close to her. "That's what sixteen-year-old me wanted to do to you instead of just borrow your juice bottle."

Livy grinned. "Is *that* all he wanted to do."

"It may not be entirely all."

She let her nose touch his, then drew back, trying to find her bearings even as the moisture from his kiss still cooled her lips. "You said you're content with your bachelor life," she began.

He conceded with a nod. "But I do like some company from time to time."

"So that's what's on offer. Some company." She hadn't exactly meant to sound so blunt, but hey, might as well lay this out from the get-go.

He lifted his eyebrows and glanced toward the office. "I'm...willing to have my mind changed. Never know what might happen." He returned his glance to her, and there was a gentle frankness in it she liked. "Just figured it's fair to tell you how it usually goes."

She pulled in her breath, and chewed the side of her lip, considering. "Okay. Well. I can't promise anything serious right now either, given everything I've got going on. But some company..." Their gazes met. "I like the sound of that."

A spark kindled in his eyes. "Then come here."

She leaned across and kissed him again, longer and with less restraint.

"Let's get together soon," she said, "and you can show me what else your teenage self wanted to do."

"Yes, please."

As he kissed her, his hand drifted down to coast across one of her breasts, sending a shiver of pleasure through her. Then he pulled back with a sigh. "Grady's going to come out here to see what we're doing any second. I'll go in. You free tomorrow?"

"I can probably be in town for a long lunch."

"Perfect. Could show you my place on the island, if you want."

"Sounds good." She smiled, though her heart beat hard enough that she felt it in her eardrums. "Oh wait, here—" She hauled her pack out of the backseat, found her wallet in it, and extracted a handful of twenties.

"Give this to Grady. His wages."

Kit took it, and settled his fingers on the car door handle. "All right, although I'm betting he'd gladly do the job for free. Hanging out with a Darwen girl—I know where he's coming from." He exchanged a long smile with her, then said, "Talk soon," and slid out of the car.

Kit scrubbed the stockpot under the kitchen faucet; dishes were his job when Grady did all the cooking, which was nearly every meal lately. Meanwhile his mind told him, *Here's what you really shouldn't do*: *a local woman.*

Moreover, a local woman he respected and didn't want to hurt. Far better to stick to the vacationers who were very clear about the lack of strings attached in their hookups with him. But this was winter and there weren't any vacationers around. And he had been as honest with Livy as he could, and she'd even said she wasn't looking for anything serious herself, so his hormones *really* intended to go through with this. Their noise was drowning out the worried rational portion of his brain that asked him to consider how badly this might end.

Maybe it wouldn't be so bad. It could end just as tidily as any of those vacationers.

What about the possibility of telling her the truth? Holy shit, when she'd said she'd heard strange music and voices in the woods, had envisioned "Teeny-tinies" living out there—damn, that was precisely the kind of person he might be able to tell.

Except. Enjoying fireside faery tales was one thing. Honest-to-God belief in a tribe of goblins was another. He had tried to tell exactly one person in his life, not long after he inherited the job. It was the girl he was dating; he was freaking out and needed to talk to someone.

She'd looked at him with the iciest loathing he ever saw, and said, "You know, if you want me gone, you could be man enough to say so, instead of making up some completely idiotic story. I get the message." End of relationship.

What could he do? Prove it by telling her to go out in the woods alone at night and trying to summon them? First of all, dangerous idea. Second of all, no one in their right mind would say yes to that. Yep, the goblins had their liaisons seriously screwed over. No doubt they laughed their asses off over it every night.

So the bachelor life it was. Congenial sex with no lasting relationships. Apologies about how he had a lot of "issues" and wasn't ready for anything serious. It sucked.

Although admittedly it would suck more if he didn't even get the congenial sex.

Grady was being unusually quiet over in the living room. Kit glanced at him, and found his cousin gazing out the window into the night with a vague frown.

"So you're going back tomorrow?" Kit asked. "To cook for Skye and Livy?"

Grady seemed to awaken. He glanced back at Kit. "Yeah. Same time. If that's okay."

"No problem. I talked to Justin today, the guy who used to do the mechanic work while I lived out of town. He's got a job at the hardware store now, but he can use extra hours, so he'll come in sometimes if I need him."

"Good, yeah. I'm sure he's more use than me."

"And I'm sure you'd rather hang with Skye."

Grady acknowledged that with a cautious smile, then returned to gazing out at the dark trees.

While Grady hung with Skye tomorrow, and Justin covered the garage, Kit might be procuring some congenial sex from Livy Darwen. To judge from the way his body revved up at the thought, that wouldn't suck much at all. At least, he had high hopes it might rock before it started to suck.

CHAPTER FOURTEEN

IT WAS WET THE NEXT MORNING, A JANUARY DRIZZLE A FEW DEGREES ABOVE FREEZING. THE RAIN WAS SO THIN AS TO be almost a mist, a gray gauze shrouding the water. As Grady drove across the bridge to the mainland, he could barely see anything on either side. Even the marina, just down the beach a mile, was now invisible. Two lonely round buoys in the middle of the inlet, one red and one white, were the limit of his vision, and looked like they were hovering on the edge of the world.

His insides cartwheeled in excitement as he carried his latest load of groceries to the Darwens' door. Livy greeted him, let him in, then dashed off to get ready for work.

Grady entered the kitchen.

Skye was already showered and dressed this time. She sat at the table, sketching. Her pencil flew back and forth in her notebook.

"Hey." Grady set the groceries on the counter.

She looked up, gave him a nod, and went back to sketching. She had a plaid flannel shirt on today, teal and black, not a baggy skater type but one of those cute tight stretchy ones, with the top two buttons undone. Her damp hair waved loose down her back. In a flash he imagined unfastening the rest of the buttons and sealing his mouth to her warm skin underneath.

He managed not to whimper. He resolutely put the groceries in their places, said goodbye to Livy when she left for work, and found the pots and pans he would need today.

He at least had to cook lunch as he was hired to do before making out with Skye on top of the kitchen table.

Skye could draw a goblin, but she couldn't draw the goblins seizing her and stuffing fruit pastries into her mouth. She had tried, lots of times, and it ended up like her attempts to write the words: her pencil turned the shapes into something different. What was meant to be Skye on the page became a butterfly or a frog; the pastries became burgers, candy canes, coffee cups.

But Grady was starting to get her. Kind of. So maybe if she used symbolism, he'd understand. Warning him was the absolute least she could do for the poor guy. (The poor, adorable, sexy-smelling guy, her mind amended.)

"So today it's soup," Grady told her. "Scotch broth. Sounded good for weather like this."

She nodded without looking up, finished shading in the cloak on the figure she had drawn, then examined the sketch in full. Not her most polished work, but it would do. She spun it around and pushed it toward Grady.

He scooted aside the measuring cups, and leaned on his knuckles to study the drawing. "Huh. Snow White kind of thing? Looks like an evil queen in the woods, holding a poisoned apple. A very creepy evil queen. Are those fangs?" He looked up at her, and his curious expression altered to concern.

Skye kept staring at him with as much intensity as she could sustain. *This is important, Grady. Get it. Understand.*

"When you look at me like that," he said, "I feel like I'm close to the truth."

She kept looking at him like that. *Come on. Please.*

"This means something?" He ran his eyes over the sketch again, and furrowed his brows. "You…got hurt? Cursed?"

Breathing fast, she reached across and gripped his wrist.

He snapped his gaze up to hers again. They stared at each other. "In the woods," he said softly, as if to himself.

Their eye contact stretched out several seconds. She saw he was no closer to understanding, and why would he be? No one in their right mind would look at her situation, her sketches, and say, *Ah, I get it, it's a magic spell, thrown on you by goblins in the forest!*

She let her grip on his wrist go limp, and dropped her gaze. It didn't really matter if he understood right now anyway. He'd find out eventually. Even if he knew the truth, he wouldn't have any idea how to save them, any more than she did. She just wished she could warn him. She'd feel less guilty.

Grady wrapped his warm fingers around hers. "Then I kissed you. That broke the spell for Snow White, right? I see some similarities here."

Yes, but for Grady and Skye the kiss did the opposite. Dragged him down into the spell along with her. She blinked back tears.

"It's all right. You keep sketching. I'll puzzle you out one of these days."

He spoke with such gentleness. How could she have done this to him?

In defeat, she pulled her notebook back over.

The urge to speak through art had passed for now. She closed the book and helped him prepare the soup. She echoed words when he talked, enough to make sense as conversation. Then, while the soup simmered, they plopped onto the sofa side by side, and opened the photos on their phones to show each other pieces of their lives. Grady displayed shots of his siblings, his parents, a couple of friends, and his home and hangouts in Moses Lake. Skye showed him last year's photos, herself and Livy and their mom and some of the cafe employees on Halloween and Thanksgiving.

Grady took the phone from her to look at a shot of Livy and Skye lifting their wine glasses on Thanksgiving, grinning. "I don't think I've ever seen you smile. You're...really beautiful." He looked at her. "I wish I could make you smile."

"I wish." God, she did wish it.

The corner of his mouth curled up. His eyebrow rose too. "Are you ticklish?"

She mirrored the eyebrow lift, a clear invitation.

Within two seconds, he had planted a knee on either side of her, the phones were bouncing onto the sofa cushions, and his deft fingers were dancing up and down her ribs, armpits, and hips.

Stupid fucking curse. Normally she was the most ticklish person alive. Today, though she squirmed and twitched like someone electrocuted, she still didn't laugh nor even smile.

"Wow." Grady stopped, letting his weight settle halfway onto her. "Not even with tickling, huh?"

She shook her head. This was comfortable, this position. The heat where he touched her felt like a luxury. He smelled intoxicating, like male skin with fresh whiffs of the celery and parsley he'd been chopping.

Maybe she couldn't smile. But she could make him happy another way.

She slid her leg outward so that he dropped further between her thighs. He caught his breath and tucked his lower lip under his teeth, his gaze drifting to her mouth. His hands rested on the sofa on either side of her ribs, caging her in. Skye lifted her shirt, exposing her navel and a few inches of skin above it.

He blinked, a flutter of dark lashes, then watched his own hands as they settled onto her bare waist, as if it were the most important event happening in the world. She pulled the shirt one rib higher.

He sank onto her with a long exhalation, and kissed her throat as his hands slid upward. She craved him, felt heat flooding her for him. When he discovered she wasn't wearing a bra, he groaned against her neck, and pressed hard against her thigh. She caught his leg between hers and squeezed it tight.

"Jesus," he breathed.

Skye wasn't lushly curvy like Livy. She'd always been skinnier, and was approaching gaunt these days, what with the stress and vanished appetite during the last month. She could go without a bra because you could do that with A-cups, and she occasionally felt like apologizing when it came time for a lover to place his hands on her unimpressive little breasts. To the boys' credit, they usually seemed to enjoy it regardless, and Grady's appreciation of her was blatantly evident.

He caressed her as he rocked slowly against her, his kisses dampened her neck, ears, mouth. Though his breath rose and fell faster than ever, he kept his movements unhurried, as if demonstrating he wasn't going to push her. The restraint was so luscious that she was provoked into unbuttoning her shirt until it fell open.

That capsized some of his restraint. He leaned his face against her chest, and groaned again. "God, you're sexy." Then he lifted his face to squint at her, looking tortured. "Why are we doing this? I'm not supposed to be doing this. This isn't what your sister's paying me for."

"Why?" Skye echoed, using all the skepticism she could muster.

"All right, I mean, I know why. Because we want to, apparently." At the word *want*, he glided one of his hands up to cover her breast. "But I feel like I…I shouldn't." With great reluctance, he withdrew his hand and pulled the sides of her shirt back over her chest.

Skye understood, sullenly. She was mentally unstable. He'd be taking advantage of a disturbed woman.

He shifted his weight off her, and she tugged herself up and hauled her knees to her chest, scowling.

"I'm not…" she managed to force out, then her tongue refused to work any further. Not mentally ill? Not having psychological problems right now? Not under the spell of aphrodisiac magic? Well, those would all be lies.

Grady, bless him, once again understood her, or at least more than most people did lately. "I know. Believe me, I want you. Jeez, obviously. But I..." He shifted to sit beside her, and ran his hand through his disarrayed hair. "There's been a time or two where I hooked up with a girl too early on in the friendship, and even though it was hot at the time, it was weird afterward, and it kind of ruined things. But I don't want to ruin anything. I want to be something good for you, not something that makes your life worse."

Well. She couldn't have chosen a nobler man to haul into an eternal curse with her. Skye buttoned her shirt, then leaned over and kissed him on the shoulder, more or less chastely. When he cast her a glance, she nodded in acceptance.

His kiss-reddened lips curved again in a smile. "Argh, you're so pretty. We'll see how long we can keep our hands off each other, anyway." He leaned down and treated her to a light nibble of a kiss.

Yeah, better him than a goblin. Or rather, better to become a goblin with him than with just about anyone else she could think of. That counted for something, in a sad way.

Grady drew back. "Let's go check on that soup."

CHAPTER FIFTEEN

KIT LEFT JUSTIN IN CHARGE OF THE AUTO SHOP, SAYING HE HAD SOME THINGS TO DO FOR A COUPLE OF HOURS AND would be back after lunch. Though Grady was scheduled to be with Skye till two o'clock, Kit texted him anyway.

Just in case you were thinking of going back to the house between now and 1, don't.

Uh why? Grady answered. *Everything ok?*

Yeah, lunch date

lol, ok, sorry I asked. Say hi to Livy for me ;)

Kit changed out of his work clothes, and scrubbed every smudge of motor oil from his fingernails. He met Livy at 11:30 as arranged, at the beachside state park just north of town. She had parked her car there, and stood waiting, balanced on a driftwood log, her long black coat wrapped around her, hood up against the misty rain. When he pulled up and turned off the engine, she strode to the passenger side of the truck and climbed in, not waiting for him to get out and open her door, though he had intended to.

"Hi." He watched her fit a cloth shopping bag onto the floor by her feet.

"Hi." She flipped back her hood. "I brought fruit and cookies, though I'm sure whatever Grady made is better."

"Pretty cheap of me, right? Serving you leftovers I didn't even make myself." As if the date was really about food. As if she didn't know that.

"Nah, I'm looking forward to it." Her cheeks were pinked up by the chill, and she smoothed back the strands of hair that had escaped her barrette. She looked luscious, and smelled like some sort of perfume that made him picture her naked in a soapy bath.

She surprised him by leaning across and kissing him on the mouth. Then she smiled, bringing out a dimple he hadn't noticed before. "There. Don't you hate when you're wondering if you're supposed to kiss or not? Now we don't have to wonder."

"I like how you think." He gazed mesmerized at her another few seconds before remembering to turn the truck back on.

Small talk about jobs and neighbors and weather carried them for the short drive out to the island. Soon the truck was rattling down the gravel driveway between the stands of trees, and his brown cabin with its slanted roof came into view.

"Here's home." He turned off the truck and pulled the parking brake.

Livy peered out through the windshield. "Even more sculptures! I didn't know these were back here. You can't see them from the road."

Nearly everyone in Bellwater had walked across the bridge and around the loop road of the island at some point. It was a scenic way to get exercise, if you didn't want to bother hauling out a boat to row.

"Yep. I work on them here sometimes." He hopped out and came around the cab to her door. She had opened it by the time he got there, but he took her hand as she jumped down.

She shouldered the grocery bag and walked through the gap in the split-rail fence. Heedless of the drizzle, she strolled between his projects, studying them. "Wow, check you out," Livy said, touching a gear on one of his metal-junk creations. "Is this the Statue of Liberty?"

"You recognize it. I'm glad."

She laughed, admiring the goofy thing: a bunch of pipes and gears and washers and other bits, all welded together into an approximate Lady Liberty shape, six feet tall. Livy tipped back her head to look at the orange taillight the statue held aloft. "Does the torch light up?"

"Of course." With the toe of his boot, Kit knocked a switch at the base. The light came on.

"Awesome. Why don't you take this into town? You could sell it."

"Eh, she's heavy. I don't know, I've gotten kind of attached to her. Some of these I'm used to now, and I don't want to sell them, even though I should. So instead I've got junk cluttering up the yard. The neighbors really love me."

"It's not junk." Livy wandered a few steps and set a wind-spinner rotating with a touch of her finger. "It started out that way, but you turned it into art. What inspires you to do it? A way to escape the monotony of work?"

"A way to escape a lot of things. Well, and it pays, too. When I actually bring myself to sell them."

She lowered her chin at him in respect. "True, but this isn't the work of someone doing it just for money. You dig it, and you have talent. Anyone can see that."

"Thanks." Kit smiled, more touched than he expected to be. "Well, come on inside. No point standing around in the rain."

Having kicked off with that kiss in the car, Livy had thought she could carry on the bold seduction act through the whole date, like she had in her sporadic other instances of casual sex: acting sassy, being alluringly direct in her physical desires, keeping the doors to her inner life firmly shut.

But it was too late for that last part already, wasn't it? Tormented by worry about Skye, she'd told Kit her problems during their first two dates, effectively erasing any possibility that he hadn't glimpsed her vulnerable, messy, true self. He'd even reciprocated, sharing tragic details about his parents. This *was* a physical attraction and they had laid those ground rules about not promising more, but nonetheless, it was also a friendship. Stranger still, he was a neighbor, or close enough, which was a first for her as dating went. All taken into account, this wasn't quite like any other hook-up of Livy's.

Maybe this was how Kit operated every time, though. Could someone just be that open a person?

Inside the cabin, he took her coat and hung it on a hook by the door, along with his leather jacket. His main floor was all one room, except for the bathroom tucked away against the south wall. The kitchen transitioned into the living room, and in front of the fireplace the sofa bed lay open, with folded clothes stuffed under it and hastily-smoothed blankets spread on the mattress. "Grady's lair?" she asked, nodding at it.

"Yep." Kit waved toward the interior balcony that spanned half the room. "Loft's mine."

"Cool. I love it." She set the bag of fruit and cookies on the island counter in the kitchen, and ran her fingers over one of the barstools. Their polished wood surfaces gleamed in a wild swirl of grain colors: reds, pinks, and browns. "Madrone?"

"Indeed." He came up beside her, close enough that their arms touched. "Nice ID skills."

"Guess all those forestry courses paid off. So did you make these?"

"Yeah, topped a set of old stools with them when I had some wood left over from a statue."

"They look great." Livy hopped onto one and let her feet dangle.

Kit hung out beside the counter, appraising her with patient brown eyes and a smile. "So, you want to see the array of wonders Grady left us for lunch?"

"Maybe not just yet." With one of her dangling feet, she hooked his leg and gave it a tug. Seriously, playing footsie? She was acting like a teenaged virgin.

Lucky thing her date was a smooth enough operator to make up for her clumsiness. He rested his hands on the counter, one on each side of her. His thighs leaned against her knees. "Yeah, I could wait on food." He sounded a little bashful, like he wasn't sure how she'd respond.

With him this near, she could smell him, fresh air and leather jacket and the indescribable scent of *guy*, the same scent that had surrounded her in those kisses in the car last night, and her diffidence began melting away. She met his beautiful eyes, finding not only desire in them but what looked to be a sea of loneliness; and she thought of how he didn't really have anyone except maybe his cousin, just like she didn't really have anyone except Skye. Everyone else, her friends and ex-lovers and family, had all drifted away from Livy's life.

Now she didn't even have Skye like she used to. Maybe Kit Sylvain, of all people, got how she felt.

Then he kissed her, and she closed her eyes and let go of those dark thoughts to make way for warmer ones.

Half her lunch break later, Livy stretched across his bed, sated and pleasantly limp. Every scrap of her clothes now lay in a heap on the floor of his loft bedroom. Kit, returning from disposing of the condom, climbed onto the bed on his knees and ran his gaze down her legs.

He caught one of her heels to examine the tattoos on her ankles. "Ooh. What are these?"

"Earth. Air." She pointed to the two on her right ankle. Then, on her left: "Fire. Water."

"Ah. The four elements."

"I have a soft spot for them, even though I'm a scientist." She wiggled her toes, watching the tendons flex the little symbols in green, purple, red, and blue. "They were for my twenty-first birthday. Skye designed them. She even came along to the tattoo parlor to make sure the guy wielding the needle did it right."

"Ha. Well, they turned out awesome. So, show you mine?" He twisted around to display his back: halfway up on the left side curved a whale, the size of her hand, decorated in swirls of black, red, and white.

She touched its fins. "Oh, beautiful! I love whales."

"Who doesn't? That was the first chainsaw carving I did that sold, so this was a way to commemorate it. Plus whales are...I don't know, free. They get to swim the world, thousands of miles a year. They're cool and mysterious. They seem deep."

She grinned, letting her fingers drop. "Deep. That they are. So is that what you want to do? Travel?"

"I'd love to. That and restore cars—the dream of most mechanics. But both of those take a lot of time and money, and..." He shrugged, his gaze dropping away. "No one's ever got enough of those, do they."

They ate a lunch of Grady's leftovers, sitting at the counter, chatting and laughing. They were both barefoot and not totally dressed, Kit with his shirt half-buttoned and Livy wearing her sweater but leaving her bra off till the last possible minute.

"It was...fun," she told Skye that evening, and heard the note of wonder in her own voice.

Skye lifted her eyebrows, gaze fixed on Livy across the kitchen table.

"I mean, I know." Livy spooned up some Scotch broth and blew on it. "He's had plenty of practice, if the gossip is true. He *ought* to be able to make it fun. It's not like it means anything. But still."

"Fun," Skye said, as if agreeing fun was worthwhile in itself.

"Yeah." Livy sipped the spoonful of soup. "This is yummy. Grady's doing a good job." She noticed Skye's gaze slip down to the table. "Is it okay, having him around? You can be honest."

Skye nodded resolutely. Instead of looking Livy in the eye, she gazed out the dark, fogged kitchen window, toward the forest.

CHAPTER SIXTEEN

MAYBE NYMPHOMANIA WAS PART OF SKYE'S CONDITION, GRADY THOUGHT THE NEXT DAY, AS HE TRIED TO CONCEN-trate on ripping up romaine over a colander in the sink while Skye held him in a languid hug from behind. Her hands trailed up and down his chest, slid over his hips, and inched dangerously close to his crotch. He could feel her warmth and breathing, could smell her shampoo, could remember so clearly the softness of her breasts and the slickness of her mouth when they'd kissed yesterday…

Her hand slid between his legs and rested there. His lettuce-tearing motions faltered, and he closed his eyes, tortured with want.

"You're being a very disruptive kitchen helper." But he made no move to escape her touch.

Skye responded with a firmer caress, and kissed his shoulder blade through his shirt.

Wouldn't Livy have warned him if she knew Skye was a nymphomaniac? That was the kind of thing you would warn someone about if you were going to leave them alone with the person.

To be fair, though, he was reacting almost like a nymphomaniac himself.

"Didn't we say yesterday we should slow down?" he tried.

"Yesterday," she pointed out.

"What, like that was yesterday, this is today?" He was still pulling apart lettuce, but only slowly.

Her hand still petted him. "Mm." She slanted the sound with a tone that suggested *Sort of.*

He glanced partway back, only enough to catch her shoulder in his view. "Or you mean, like, we waited a whole day, so that counts for something?"

"Mm." Closer to agreement this time. Her fingertips circled his groin.

He swallowed and tried to focus on the romaine. "I should at least finish the salad."

Skye withdrew her hands and stepped away, the motion exuding sulkiness even though he couldn't see her with his back turned.

He glanced over his shoulder, and examined the frustration burning in her eyes. His gaze traveled down the black hoodie she wore over a tank top. Her nipples made visible peaks through both layers, and he set his back teeth together to keep from groaning. "But maybe, just for a second…"

She stepped forward. He dropped the head of lettuce into the colander and snatched her up with his wet hands. A second later he had her propped against the fridge, their lips and tongues entangled, all four of her limbs wrapped around him. She had on black leggings, so thin you could almost feel skin through them, and she gasped in pleasure.

His mind filled with strange, bizarre wants: not just stripping her down and plunging into her, the way he'd usually fantasize about at this stage of things, but also the woods. Sex with her in that mossy, semi-spooky forest, down in the undergrowth where he'd landed after he kissed her and got tripped by blackberry vines, or high up in the trees, in some kind of treehouse—the ones she drew, maybe—the two of them powerful and reckless like animals…

What the hell?

"God," he said. "Okay…okay, just…" He slid her down till her feet landed on the floor, and wrenched himself back a step, though it almost physically hurt to break contact with her. He stretched out his fingers in front of him as a barrier. "Remember? How I didn't want to do anything you'd regret?"

"Regret?" Her face beautifully flushed, she looked down and shook her head. She seemed mournful almost, as if there might be many things she regretted, but not this specifically.

Grady raked one of his damp hands through his hair. "I'm so confused. I'm sorry. But this whole thing, it's making me want things, think things, that I don't understand. And too much of the time, I don't even care that I don't understand. That scares me. It makes me think I'm going to do something I definitely will regret."

Skye tightened her lips and nodded, her gaze still cast down. Turning her from sexy nymphomaniac back into sad depressed waif made him feel like a complete asshole.

He stepped forward and took her hands. "Listen. You have no idea how much I want you. Or—well, you probably do. I'm sure you can tell. But let me get the salad done like I'm supposed to, and then maybe we can try to be responsible grown-ups who do this right. Okay?"

"Right." She tipped her head forward to lean it on his chest. Then she chose another few words of his to echo, in a whisper: "I want you." But erotic though the sentiment was, she sounded just as conflicted and disturbed as he felt.

Skye backed off and let Grady finish assembling the salad. She understood his reasons for resisting, and could add a reason of her own: namely, that it was surely wise to fight the magic as long as they could. Maybe they'd even find a way to reverse their spell. How, though? She couldn't even Google the question; the words wouldn't transfer from brain to fingertips. She had tried.

On the other hand, she didn't see a lot of point in resisting, because at least kissing and fondling him felt good. Not nearly enough of life felt good for her lately. She had to admit, with a guilty sort of thrill, that it was a turn-on to know they'd be unable to fight their mutual magnetism much longer. Given this was the one single aspect of the curse that actually involved pleasure, why wouldn't she pursue it?

While Grady assembled ingredients and whipped up salad dressing, she sketched various parts of him, divided into random-sized boxes around the page. In one, she drew his big feet in their black socks against the kitchen tiles (he'd taken off his shoes at the door). In another, the back pocket of his jeans, with the shape of his phone making a rectangle of faded denim within it, and his T-shirt's rumpled hem draped just above. The back of his neck, near-black hair inching halfway to his shoulders, vertebrae showing in subtle bumps. His hands selecting a knife. His profile, eyelashes swept downward, full lips set.

As she finished shading in the stubble on his skin, he glanced at her and smiled. "I'm being lazy for this lunch. No actual cooking required. I brought some chicken that I cooked last night." He pulled down two plates from the cupboard. "I figured, less time cooking, more time…doing other stuff."

She nodded, and slid the sketchbook out into the center of the table.

He didn't notice it yet. He loaded both plates with salad, already tossed with its dressing, sprinkled crumbled goat cheese on it, added chopped chicken and walnuts, and pulled over a plastic bag of something dark red. His hand was inside it, closing around a fistful of the stuff, when Skye recognized it as dried fruit.

Her voice surged to the surface. "No!"

He jolted and looked at her, then back at the bag. "Oh. That's right. You're off fruit."

She nodded, lips pressed together, stomach clenching. Would the goblins make her eat that disgusting magical fruit again when she did finally join them? Would she actually like it at that point?

"Then no dried cherries. No problem." He twisted up the plastic bag to close it. Turning to face her, he rested his back against the counter. "There was an apple in one of those pictures you drew. Evil queen with an apple. I feel like fruit is another clue."

Skye looked sadly at him.

"It sometimes seems like I'm starting to get it." His gaze wandered to the table, and halted at the sketchbook. The haunted look dissolved from his eyes, and his sunnier everyday expression slipped back in. "Hey. You drawing me?"

She drew in a deep breath to settle her queasiness, and nodded.

He came forward and planted his knuckles on the table to study it. "Dang. You're good." He flicked a nail against the drawing of his sock. "Even got the holes in my clothes." He kissed her forehead. "I love it. Can I take a picture of it?" When she nodded, he got out his phone. "Then we can have lunch."

After their salad, they settled on the couch, Skye nestled against Grady's arm, to chat via text. This time the topic was past relationships. Both of them had gone through a share of drama, now worn down to amusing by the passing of time.

It was probably inevitable that they'd detour through the woods again before he walked her to work. Probably just as inevitable that she'd end up leading him down a side trail into the quietest depths of the forest. She hopped up onto a fallen log, which had landed at a slant, propped against an upright tree. She pulled him in for a kiss.

After what she'd started this morning, it was also inevitable that he'd slide his hands under her wool coat and grip her. Or that her hand, before long, would roam across the front of his jeans.

He groaned against her mouth. Awash in spell-magic and normal lust, unable to tell anymore how much she owed to each, she clung to him and urged him on with rhythmic writhes. Moss squished and crumbled under her, his tongue tangled with hers, their hands teased and pressed.

"We should stop," he begged, not stopping.

"Should," she said, also not stopping.

He gasped against her neck. "Or not."

"Or not," she agreed.

She took a foil-wrapped condom from her pocket and slipped it into his hand, a minor victory for human responsibility in the face of reckless magic, she felt.

Grady turned it over in his fingers. "Brought some myself," he admitted. "Just in case."

He lifted his blue eyes to her. Here was where he should have smiled, where the old Grady would have smiled. Instead his gaze searched her face, drenched with desire, drugged with magic.

This was terrible of her. She knew full well *they* were watching. She couldn't see or hear them; no one would in the daytime; but they were most certainly there, ogling the two of them as free entertainment, laughing, commenting to each other in the crudest and most offensive ways. She knew it, and Grady didn't know it yet, and she did this with him anyway. Because that was how much she wanted him, and because in the house Grady might be able to resist her, but out here he couldn't.

Afterward, they caught their breath, her forehead against his temple. He shivered, tucked his coat back around his body, and hugged her. He looked with wonder at the evergreens swaying above. "Well," he said, his voice a bit unsteady. "This is my new favorite place in the whole world."

Skye could only cling to him and hide her face on his neck, in sorrow.

CHAPTER SEVENTEEN

KIT HAD LIVY OVER AT THE CABIN AGAIN THE NEXT DAY AFTER WORK. HE ARRANGED TO HAVE GRADY BE ELSEWHERE, and Grady cleared out willingly, almost cheerfully. Probably "elsewhere" was wherever Skye was, like down at Green Fox for her shift.

It wasn't unusual for Kit to see a woman more than once. If it got to more than four or five dates, then that would be shading into unusual. His vacationer hookups usually only stuck around town a week, if that. But being treated again to Livy's soft curves, slick heat, enthusiasm, and laughing wit was enough to make him start formulating plans he didn't often entertain.

To his surprise, she voiced one of them, lying comfortably beside him afterward. "So are we friends with benefits?"

"I would not object to that." He touched the cute plump tip of her nose. "Though at the moment I may have a teeny crush on my 'friend.' Hope that doesn't complicate things."

"You need a teeny crush for these things to work." She lifted herself up on her elbow, wheat-colored curls tumbling around her bare shoulders. "Does this mean I can booty-call you if I want?"

"Yeah. Why would I ever say no to that?"

She laughed. "Thank goodness. This winter was looking bleak otherwise."

After she went home, Kit gathered up all the ugly gold-plated forks from the box under his bed. He drove across the bridge, parked at the edge of the vast forest, and tromped in.

He summoned the goblins with a whistled trio of notes. They sang a few other notes in response, and a path opened between trees. Luminous ferns this time, sparkling like they were coated with glow-in-the-dark frost.

"It's not even the full moon," Redring greeted, after morphing into her human-ish shape. "To what do we owe the pleasure, Kit darling?"

He held out the handful of forks. "I want to add another person to the list of the protected. Her name's Livy Darwen."

Behind Redring, among moving silhouettes and floating lights, laughter erupted. As usual.

Redring seized the forks, sniffed them, and rubbed the tines between her fingers. "You just invoked protection for your cousin last month. You cannot add anyone else until a year has passed."

"I get one per year. I usually don't even use it. I added Grady in December, and it's January now, so it's a new year and I get a new person."

"As if we care about your calendar dates. I just told you. The agreement is, one year *between* the times you add each person. You added him, then a year must go by, then you add your little toy."

"A year?" Shit, think what they could do in the space of a year. And Redring probably wasn't lying in this particular instance, since when it came to their nonsense rules and contracts, the goblins did stick to what was agreed. He reached for the forks to take them back, but Redring scrabbled six feet up a tree, eerily fast. The move looked especially bizarre in her human form, dressed in pajamas and robe.

"We still get these!" she said, while the rest of the tribe hooted behind her like a bunch of damn monkeys.

"Well, fuck you too. Seriously?"

"*Maybe* they'll convince us to be kind to this woman, whom we smell so strong upon you. Perhaps."

Her minions kept giggling.

The razzing, the stealing, the smelling people on him, the way they'd wrecked his life and his ancestors' lives for generations now…fury swept over Kit. He grabbed a fallen branch, thick as his arm and heavy with soaked-up rain, and swung it like a baseball bat at Redring's legs.

He felt the crack and heard her feral screech, but he barely even got a glimpse of the damage, because goblins leaped onto him from all directions. Knobby hands covered his eyes; claws and teeth ripped at his scalp, his cheek, his hands, his legs. The creatures smacked him down on the ground, and he pummeled blindly at them. It felt like fighting a pile of stinky, moving tree branches.

Then, as if answering some call Kit couldn't hear, they all whisked themselves off him. He sat up, looked at his scratched hands, touched his throbbing cheek and came away with blood on his fingers. He glared at Redring.

She still perched halfway up the tree, in human-like guise, looking totally uninjured. She waved the forks at him. "That hurt, you ungrateful pup. Lucky for me, we heal fast. If I were you, I'd remember that you do not."

One of the goblins flung down the branch Kit had used against her. It whacked his shinbones, hard enough to make him grit his teeth.

Kit rubbed his shins and looked away into the darkness, refusing to answer. He felt a warm drop of blood trickle down his forehead from his scalp.

"Then we'll see you at the full moon, Sylvain." Redring darted upward to disappear into the treetops.

The others followed her, cackling.

"Kit. Kit." It was a whisper; submissive, for a goblin.

He glanced toward it. The creature they called Flowerwatch crawled toward him on the ground, bending the ferns. She was a small female, and around her neck hung an ancient, tarnished pocket watch with a flower carved on its cover. She'd always been one of the meekest in the tribe, as far as Kit had seen, and sometimes she looked at him with pity, which was more than any of the others ever did. If his ancestors' records were correct, she'd been an abducted human long ago. Then again, maybe all of them were, and they didn't all behave like Flowerwatch did. He had no idea why she acted different, and right now he didn't care to figure it out.

"What," he said.

"You do not have to worry about Livy Darwen." Flowerwatch glanced back fearfully toward the rest of the tribe before looking at Kit again. "The locals, they like her. She respects the forest and the water."

"Yeah. She does. But what…"

"Flowerwatch!" Redring's snarl from above sent Flowerwatch yipping and scurrying back from Kit. "Your mealy-mouthed weakness for humans is foul and disrespectful to all of us. To me!"

"Yes. Yes. I'm sorry." Flowerwatch cowered so low her nose squashed against the mossy ground.

"You undermine me!" Redring cracked a branch against Flowerwatch's back, making the smaller goblin yelp. Kit winced too. "I have warned you, do you hear? I will only hurt *them* more if I see you behave this way—and I will hurt you too!"

"Of course. Apologies. Of course." Flowerwatch scrambled away with only one quick glance back in Kit's direction.

Redring pranced after her, swinging the branch like a nightstick. That was how she'd held onto her dictatorial position all these centuries, he figured: tyranny and punishment, interspersed with favors and rewards. It seemed even immortal beings shied away from pain or the denial of pleasures, and they had lots of creative ways of punishing each other.

Kit watched them disappear. The rustles and whispers of the goblins faded until only the wind in the trees remained. The glowing ferns and little lights winked out. Kit heaved himself to his feet, switched on the flashlight on his phone, and limped back to his truck, not encouraged despite Flowerwatch's enigmatic words.

Grady sat in the steamy warmth of Green Fox Espresso at a small table close to the counter. A book lay open on the table, whose pages he ignored in favor of gazing at Skye as she made drinks. It was dark out, after dinner now, and the little coffee shop was half-filled, mostly with teenagers. Not much else for the high school set to do in Bellwater on a wet winter night, he supposed. He barely gave any of them a thought except to be grateful they provided a crowd he could blend into, so he could sit here and bask in the sight of Skye without anyone thinking him strange.

If they did notice and think him strange, he didn't even care.

She wore a black apron over her tank top; she had taken off her sweatshirt to leave her arms bare among the heat of the espresso machines. Her hair was wrapped up and held with black-and-white painted chopsticks. It looked like her boss had moved her off the order-taking duties at the cash register (probably because she barely spoke), and had her mostly putting drinks together. She did everything he'd seen baristas do a thousand times—measuring ground coffee, packing it into the machine, punching buttons, swirling foam in—but now every move plucked a chord deep inside him.

He'd ordered a latte, and left it untouched for the first fifteen minutes because Skye had made a heart on top with the foam. It struck him as a declaration, a Valentine of sorts, and he didn't want to destroy it.

He couldn't love her yet. It wasn't possible. But, God, it was starting to feel that way. He started drinking the latte, his lips dragging the heart all out of shape, just to prove he wasn't being over-sentimental, and because anyway it would be a waste to let it get cold.

A while ago a woman in her twenties had come in and talked to Skye for ten minutes. (Skye only nodded or echoed a word here and there; the woman did most of the talking.) Someone else behind the counter called, "Hi, Jamie!", and Grady recognized her as Skye's friend from some of the photos on her phone. Jamie wore a puffy red winter coat and a green hat, and had rosy plump cheeks. Skye hadn't mentioned her much lately. From the regretful twist to Jamie's lips when she gave Skye a goodbye hug, Grady got the impression Jamie didn't see her often anymore and didn't know what to do with Skye when she did see her, and was sad about it.

He ought to ask Skye about Jamie, and about other people in her life who cared about her. It was completely the kind of thing he would ask her about, if he were behaving normally himself. But that was just the thing. He wasn't. Though he recognized it as unhealthy and felt unnerved by it, he knew he'd choose the path of keeping Skye all to himself.

She seemed to glow in his vision like a spotlight had picked her out. The rest of the cafe, the rest of the world, fell into shadow. She kept looking at him too, between orders, when she had a moment, and he would have sworn she was promising *Soon*. Soon they'd steal another hour alone like this afternoon in the woods. Soon they'd do more than that. Soon he'd understand what had silenced her and erased her smiles, and how to fix it.

Soon they'd never have to be apart, could be together in the woods forever, dropping society's rules and adopting new ones.

That thought was crazy. It was unlike him. It was frightening.

But it all came wrapped up with Skye, and somehow he knew he had signed onto it the minute he started kissing her in the forest without so much as a "What's your name?"

A text buzzed in from Kit. *Livy's heading home. Come back whenever you like.*

Cool, see you in a bit, Grady answered.

He finished the latte and brought the foam-stained mug back to the counter. Skye wandered up on the other side.

"Livy's on her way home," Grady said.

Skye nodded. She'd probably gotten a text from her sister saying as much, and it was likely Livy would stop here first to see her.

"I should go. Just wanted to say goodnight properly."

Skye hadn't told Livy about this relationship yet. Grady didn't like the whiff of secrecy, but he agreed telling Livy or Kit would raise more questions than he currently felt like answering.

Skye glanced behind her, ascertaining her two coworkers had their backs turned. Then she leaned across the counter to meet Grady in a kiss. It lingered a few seconds, coffee-flavored and steamy, enough to amp up his already-sky-high hormones. "Goodnight," she whispered.

CHAPTER EIGHTEEN

"JESUS, WHAT HAPPENED TO YOU?" LIVY TOUCHED THE BRUISES AND SCRATCHES ON KIT'S FACE.

He stepped back to let her into the cabin. "Oh, yeah. I was fixing someone's flat alongside the road, and slipped into the ditch. Which of course was full of blackberries."

It wasn't even the first time he had gotten into a fight with the goblins and had to lie to people about the bruises. It had happened two or three times before, in the earliest years of his liaison position. He'd behaved since then, up until snapping last night. He didn't entirely regret lashing out at them. They needed to know when they'd crossed a line. Nonetheless, he hated lying every bit as much as he hated stealing.

Livy seemed to buy his excuse. She winced in sympathy. "Ouch. I know the evil ways of blackberry vines. Or holly—God, that stuff's sharp. And don't get me started on nettles and poison oak."

He sank onto a barstool and drew her close, hands around her hips. "That's what you got yourself into, choosing the Forest Service."

"Yeah, yeah." She spread her hands along his shoulders. The soapy smell of her perfume calmed and aroused him, simultaneously. "At least I got to save a frog today."

"Just today? Just one frog? Shoot, I was under the impression you were out there saving frogs by the hundreds every day."

She laughed. "I am, of course, but usually I don't see them. Today I was working with the volunteers, clearing roads and trails after the windstorms we've been having. And we moved a log, and this college girl looked down and said, all sad, 'Oh, a dead frog.' So I came and checked it out, and told her, no, he's probably alive, just hibernating. Gave her the whole spiel: how they can look dead during winter; in fact, they can even freeze. Like, ice can form in their blood, but then in spring they thaw right out and come back to life."

"They can freeze? Really? I never knew that."

"Yep. They're pretty amazing, frogs. So we made him a new bed of dead leaves in the log, and tucked him in. With any luck he'll be hopping around and eating bugs again in spring."

He curled his fingers under the warm hem of her sweatshirt. "Olivia Darwen, preserver of life and happiness." In the past week they'd shared their full names. She'd seemed intrigued when he told her his first name was merely "Kit" on the birth certificate, and wasn't short for anything.

Her smile faded, and she threaded her fingers through the ends of his hair. "Well. Some varieties of life and happiness, anyway."

Kit spread his hands, holding her steadier. "How's Skye?"

She shrugged, keeping her gaze on his collar. "I still think it's good for her to have Grady around. They seem to be friends now."

"I kind of get the impression he's smitten. Don't worry, though; I'm sure he'll be honorable about it."

"Oh, she can handle herself there. And he doesn't seem the aggressive type. I'm not worried. Just…"

"What?"

She finally stopped fiddling with his hair, and met his eyes again, for a second. "She still isn't herself. I don't know how they're getting along, since she's talking even less than ever."

He slid his arms further around her back, holding her in a loose hug. "These things take time. You're doing what you can. Grady's helping too, maybe, or at least he's probably not doing any actual damage."

She touched her nose to his. "Let's hope not."

"If he does, let me know, and I'll do something appropriately evil to him."

"Like what? Hide the oregano?"

"Worse. Make him cook with margarine instead of butter."

She laughed, and wrapped her arms around him.

How have you been, hon? Skye's mom asked in email, after a paragraph of news about exploring Portland with her boyfriend. *I miss seeing your art. How are you feeling?*

Skye rested her elbows on the counter at Green Fox as she read the message. Sadness overtook her as she dwelled on childhood memories of the rare times her mom was relaxing at home instead of working, and Skye would clamber into her lap with a handful of crayons and insist on drawing with her. Gone, all of that, gone. She might never see her mother again, or her father. Her parents and Livy and Jamie and the rest of the world would never know why she'd vanished or what had happened...

CHAPTER NINETEEN

"THE MERMAIDS DIDN'T KEEP THE RAIN OFF YOU DURING YOUR PADDLE?" KIT TUCKED THE BLANKET OVER LIVY'S shoulder.

Her hair was still damp from the rain, sticking itself into ringlets. "Not their department. I think they try to get people extra wet."

"Oh, just like me, then." He captured her laugh in his mouth, rolling her onto her back. He lay kissing her another minute or two, still turned on even though they'd just had sex.

It was Saturday afternoon and she had pulled in to his beach on her kayak, as pre-arranged by text. Grady and Justin were manning the garage from lunch till closing today. Owner's privilege, getting to take the afternoon off, he'd loftily told them. Of course, they knew what he'd be doing instead of working.

"This is fun," he murmured. He'd found himself saying it during most of their dates over the past couple of weeks. It was the most fun he'd had in a while, actually. Livy surprised him. When he got her alone, she blossomed from formidable, chilly Forest Service scientist into naughty, up-for-anything friend with benefits. Even setting the sex aside, they hit it off great. They made each other laugh, and kept finding interests in common.

His "little crush" was developing into something that made him think about her at all hours. And worry about her safety at the hands of the goblins, even though Flowerwatch had said they wouldn't touch her. He didn't trust any goblin.

"Ever gone swimming at night in summer, when the bioluminescent plankton's sparkling in the water?" Livy asked.

"Mmm. I love it when you say things like 'bioluminescent plankton.' Yeah, 'course I have. It's awesome. Like swimming through stars."

"It's times like that I see why people used to believe in nature spirits. It totally looks like magic. So I don't know about mermaids, but some kind of sparkly water faeries—maybe I could believe in those. Almost."

She still grinned, but Kit's heartbeat began doing funny things, the way it did when he was about to try something especially stupid. "Huh." He slid off her, leaving one arm draped across her. "What about the forest? You spend a lot of time there. Any…run-ins with the fae, like you and Skye used to make up stories about?"

"The fae?" Livy lifted her eyebrows, teasing but impressed. "Scholarly word there."

"It's what people call them sometimes." He wasn't even smiling now. He just watched her, and waited for her answer.

She smoothed her hair back and folded an arm behind her head, gazing at the log beams of his ceiling. "Well…I could almost believe it some days. Once in a while."

His heart beat against his ribs. "Yeah? Why's that?"

"Skye's said this too. Like, there's been a couple of times we swear we saw a path that wasn't there before. Then we couldn't find it again later. Just goes to show how easy it is to get turned around in the woods."

"Was this at dusk? At night?"

"Hmm. I guess right as it was getting dark, yeah. Things get harder to see then, is probably why."

"Listen. You ever see a path like that, don't follow it."

Her eyes turned to him, bemused. "What?"

He lifted up onto his elbow. "I'm serious. Promise me you won't follow paths like that."

"Why not?" Doubt sharpened her voice.

"There's…" He dropped his gaze to his hand, which he ran along her warm skin, between breasts and navel. "My family, we've all seen things, things people wouldn't believe, things *I* wouldn't have believed until I saw them myself. First and foremost, between dusk and dawn, do not follow paths that weren't there before."

She hitched up onto her elbow too, dislodging his hand. "You're kind of freaking me out. What is it you think would happen?"

He was almost shaking. He couldn't just go telling people, especially someone he liked as much as her. But now he'd said this much, and he needed to finish, or he'd sound like a serial killer. Or at least someone aiding and abetting a serial killer.

"Well…you know how there've been people found dead in the woods, like that fisherman a while back?"

"He died of exposure, if I recall. It was cold. I mean, yeah, people get lost and die in the woods once in a while, all over the world. It's not usually foul play."

"I'm not talking foul play, exactly. Not by other humans." Kit already wished he hadn't started down this road, but now he was stuck on it. "It's more like…enchantment."

Her eyes narrowed. She waited.

"Fae," he said, his voice weak. "Goblins, technically. A type of fae. They…followed my family here, generations ago. It was…"

"Wait. What?" Her voice had gone flat, her demeanor buttoning itself all the way back up to hard-line scientist, even while she lay there naked. "*Goblins?*"

"Yeah."

"You're messing with me. Right?"

He shook his head. "I wish."

She studied him a few more seconds. "You really believe this."

"It's a long story and I know it sounds crazy. But I can prove it."

"How?"

"In order to hear them yourself…it's dangerous and I don't recommend it, but you could summon them in the forest. They might answer. They'd open a path to you, then if you *don't* take the path you're all right; that's the important thing. But you'd at least see the path, and hear them, so you'd know it's true…"

Livy scooted off the bed and grabbed up her underwear, bra, jeans. She started putting them back on. "Okay, that? Freaks me out even more. You realize you sound like a murderer? You do know that?" Her voice quivered.

His heart dropped as he realized how badly he'd frightened her, how horrible he'd made himself look. "I'm not. I swear. Wait—Livy, come on. Listen to me, please. I've never hurt anyone. What I'm trying to do is to keep them from hurting anyone."

She rushed into her socks, her sweatshirt. "In that case I'm thinking we have very different belief systems. I should…go back and check on Skye…I just have a lot to deal with." She wouldn't look at him.

"God, don't—all right, wait, there's another way." He scrambled out of bed and pulled his boxers back on. "I have the letter from my great-grandmother that explains it all. It's here in the house. I'll get it and show you."

"No, I really ought to go. Maybe we can talk about it later." Dressed in all but her boots, which she'd left by the front door, she padded quickly to the spiral staircase and descended.

Kit chased after her. "Livy, I am not insane. You know I'm not. Give me a chance. Stay and listen."

At the door, she held up her hand to silence him. Her eyes closed a moment, then opened to regard him with something between compassion and hurt. "I really don't have time. Right now. For this." She said the last two words softly, but they fell upon him like hammers.

As she stuffed her feet into her boots, he stood watching, shirtless, barefoot, trembling. "You think I'm crazy. I don't blame you. But I am begging you…"

Livy slid into her coat and rounded on him. "Goblins? You're begging me to listen to how there are goblins in the forest? I'm a scientist, Kit. What do you think I'm going to say?"

"I think you should look for proof. Not run off."

She zipped up her coat, lips set tight. "Yeah, well, maybe there's more wrong here than just the goblin story. I'll see you later." She slipped out and trudged down the beach to her kayak.

Kit stood with the door open, letting the cold wind slice against his skin, watching her shrink in his line of sight without a single glance back at him.

He slammed the door shut, kicked it with his bare toes, then closed his eyes and leaned his forehead on it. If the curse was going to kill him young the way it had for his ancestors, he fervently wished it would get on with it.

Livy slashed at the water with her paddle. The cold air stabbed her lungs, and her shoulders burned with exertion, but she kept at it. She paddled farther than necessary, past the tip of the island and out into the middle of the inlet. The afternoon wind picked up, rocking her kayak and frothing the little waves into whitecaps. Belatedly, she recognized the danger of being out here alone in hypothermia-inducing waters.

Though probably it was no more dangerous than having sex with a delusional freak.

She bowed her head and let her paddle rest across the top of the kayak. Damn it. He had seemed so fabulous. Of course he'd have to turn out to be deranged.

She plunged the paddle blade into the water to swing back toward shore.

A gray wave slapped back. Stiffened with cold, her hands fumbled. The paddle escaped her grip and knifed into the water. She grabbed at it, but it washed out of reach, floating away from her with the next wave.

She looked around in despair for something else to use as a paddle—her water bottle? Driftwood? Where the hell were the stray flip-flops sailing through the water when you actually needed them? All the while she kept an eye on her paddle, which hadn't gotten *too* far away yet. But if it did, maybe someone on shore was watching, and would figure out she needed help, or at least she could phone someone to bring out another boat and tow her in before it got dark…

A madrone log bobbed up alongside her kayak, five feet long with an end full of twigs. She seized it. Drenched in chilly salt water, it numbed her hands at once, but she plunged it in and managed to use it to turn the kayak toward her drifting paddle. She stretched the branch toward it, aiming to catch the blade in the twigs. Her first three swipes fell short by several inches.

Tears stung her eyes. "Come on," she wailed. "Please."

Something poked up from the water and batted her paddle back toward her. Something like…a hand. Except green, and webbed. It dunked back under before she got a good look. Her paddle, meanwhile, skated a foot closer. Livy smacked the branch down on top of it, raked it in, and pulled it back aboard.

"Oh my God," she mumbled in relief.

She tossed the branch back in the water, then sat motionless, watching the choppy surface where the hand-thing had disappeared. *What* had she just seen?

Seal flipper, maybe. Fish happening to jump at a lucky moment. Sodden log or trash getting pushed to the surface for a second.

Definitely not a mermaid or a water-goblin or anything of that sort.

God damn Kit Sylvain. He was making her see things now.

The sun was setting by the time she hauled the kayak onto the public dock in Bellwater. Her arms shook with exhaustion and her hands stung with cold.

She sat in her car a while after loading up the boat, staring alternately at her phone and out the window. Kit hadn't tried to contact her in the hour since she'd left. She wasn't sure whether to be relieved or hurt.

When the streetlights came on at the dock, she switched on the car and drove home.

Skye had just returned from her shift when Livy walked in. The smell of espresso wafted off her even from five feet away. She was hunched over the kitchen counter, texting someone. Not Livy, it would seem. Probably Grady. Skye and Grady seemed thick as thieves lately. Ugh, Sylvain men. Fucking womanizers.

Livy threw her keys onto the counter and kicked out of her boots. Skye gave her a double-take, concern entering her otherwise impassive face.

Livy shook her head, and shuffled forward to get a glass of water. "I know how to pick 'em, Skye."

Skye lifted her eyebrows.

Livy swallowed half the glass of water. "Yeah. Kit. He's…ugh. How do I not see they're crazy until after I've slept with them? How do they hide it so well?"

Skye stood up straight, elbows leaving the counter. "Crazy?"

"I know. Judgment-laden word, not cool. Sorry. Either he honestly believes some weird shit, or he's trying to mess with me in this lame and bizarre way. Or he's actually dangerous. I mean, maybe I should be thankful I'm here and not wrapped in duct tape in his crawlspace, right?"

"Duct tape," Skye said, skeptically.

Livy finished the glass of water, set it down, and pushed her tangled hair out of her face. "Oh, I know, I should listen to him. Just—God, I'm embarrassed even to tell you what he said. It's so…I'm sorry, the only word is 'crazy.'"

"What he said?"

Livy shuffled to a chair and flopped into it. "I would never tell this to anyone but you, Skye. He says, get this, that I should be careful in the woods, because *goblins* live there." Livy covered her face in mortification. "He seemed genuinely concerned. What the hell?"

Skye's hissing intake of breath made Livy drop her hands and frown at her.

Skye had gone white. She stared wide-eyed at Livy, lips parted but without saying a word.

Alarm flashed through Livy. "What? What's wrong?"

Skye turned and ran out of the kitchen. Her footsteps thumped down the hall to her room, then thumped back, and she smacked her sketchbook down in front of Livy on the table, open to a page where she'd drawn a creepy gremlin creature.

Livy frowned at it. "Okay? You showed me this before. What? You're saying…this is a goblin?"

Skye just stared into her eyes, breathing hard. She seemed unable even to nod or shake her head. That always did happen when Livy tried to ask important questions about what had happened to her, though…

Livy examined the picture again, then looked back at her sister. "This is something you believe too? You seem as concerned as he did. Look, I don't—"

Skye grabbed Livy's wrist and pulled her out of the chair. Next thing Livy knew, Skye was shoving her boots at her, grabbing car keys and the sketchbook, and hauling Livy to the front door.

"Skye! What? What are we doing?"

Skye stalked down the front path, beckoning impatiently to Livy. Stumbling into her chilly, damp boots, Livy hurried after her.

"Where are we going?" She followed Skye to her silver Volkswagen.

"Kit," Skye bit out, in the numb-tongued way she did when she had to come up with a word instead of echoing it. She swung into the Scirocco's driver's seat and started the car.

Livy jumped in, but only to keep Skye from harm, not because she approved of this errand. "Skye, whoa. I really don't want to see him."

Skye tightened her lips and backed the car out of the driveway.

Though Livy kept up a stream of "Skye," and "Come on," and "No," Skye drove them straight through town and across the bridge onto Crabapple Island.

CHAPTER TWENTY

KIT OPENED HIS SECOND BEER. GIVEN WHAT ALCOHOL HAD DONE TO HIS PARENTS, HE RARELY DRANK HIMSELF, BUT HE figured tonight got to be an exception. He had gotten dressed again, but otherwise had been doing virtually nothing but pacing around the inside of the cabin like it was a jail cell. He circled the kitchen island, glowering at the frail old letter encased in a plastic sheet protector that he had dug out from the file box.

Not long after dark, Grady came back from the garage. "Hey. Nice afternoon?" When Kit just exhaled through his nose and kept pacing, Grady slowed in his approach. His eyes took in the empty beer bottle on the counter and the newly opened one in Kit's hand. "Oh. Um… dinner, then?"

Kit looked away. "Whatever."

"Well. Then I'll…"

Then Kit had to stop prowling the kitchen. Right. Kit grabbed the letter, and took it and his beer to the front door. After throwing on his leather jacket and boots, he stalked out into the dark.

His front deck was just a rectangle of boards a cinder-block's height off the pebbles at the top of the beach. He crossed it in two strides, descended the one stair, and crunched out onto the shore. The dark silhouette of a heron glided through the dusk, reflected in the faint purple surface of the water. Kit glared at the peaceful scene. He rolled up the letter in its plastic casing, stuffed it into the inside pocket of his jacket, then recommenced pacing and drinking.

A few minutes later, headlights splashed across the sculptures at the side of his house, and he caught a glimpse of Skye's car with two people in it. This could be a decidedly ugly visit. He walked back up the slope, bracing himself.

The car shut off, and soon not only Livy but Skye came rushing around the side of the house, Skye in the lead, her hair all loose and wild.

Kit met them in front of the deck. "Hey." He glanced behind her at Livy.

Livy flung up her hand, harassed and apologetic. "She insisted on coming here. I don't know."

Skye shoved a notebook at Kit, opened on its spiral binding to a page in the middle. He took it in his free hand and tilted it toward the light from the house.

Then he had to set down the beer bottle on the deck and use that hand to grip the boards to steady himself. He took in the drawing of Redring for a few seconds, then looked at Skye. "You saw this?"

She breathed unsteadily. She didn't answer, just stared at him with a plea in her eyes. Then she turned the page to show him the sketch of the goblin dwellings, exactly as he'd seen them by looking up from below. But she'd drawn them from a closer perspective than he'd ever gotten.

"Oh, God," Kit said. "This is what happened to you."

Skye's eyes filled with tears. She rolled her lips inward, as if biting down on sobs.

"Oh, no. I'm so sorry. I thought of it, but then…I hoped…"

"Is someone going to tell me what the fuck this is about?" Livy shouldered her way in next to Skye, glaring daggers at Kit. "What did you do to her?"

Skye placated her sister with a hand on her arm, and shook her head. She thumbed away the tears on her cheeks.

The front door opened, spilling more light out. Grady paused there, then came forward. "Skye. What—?"

Skye flew up the stair and buried herself in Grady's arms, crying.

Grady's eyebrows furrowed. He looked at Kit, and his voice went harsh. "What did you do?"

Kit exhaled a sigh. "It isn't what I did. It's what our great-grandma did." He looked at Livy again, whose eyes still sparked with anger. "Come in," he said. "I'll explain."

Skye thought she might pass out. Someone knew. Kit knew, and he was going to explain. *Please, please let there be a way out of this.* She clung to Grady as they trooped into the cabin.

Her sister still looked ready to pulverize Kit. Arms folded, Livy planted herself with her back to the cold fireplace, and refused to sit down. "Okay, Sylvain. Explain."

Kit pulled some papers wrapped in clear plastic from his jacket, and unrolled them. "It's a goblin curse. They must have caught her at night, and lured her down one of their paths. She can't talk about it because that's how the spell works. Right?" He glanced at Skye.

She couldn't nod, so she straightened her posture, keeping her eyes on him.

"Yeah." Kit smacked the papers against his palm. "Can't even nod or shake your head when anyone asks about it. Sounds like the kind of thing they do."

Grady sank to sit on his folded-out sofa-bed, drawing Skye with him. Skye leaned her head on his shoulder.

Livy gave them a second glance, as if finally registering that they were acting like a couple. Then she narrowed her eyes at Kit again. "I'm going to need a lot more explanation than that."

Kit pulled the papers out of their plastic sleeve. "Where to start. How about the beginning."

"Good idea." Livy sounded as icy as a January night.

"Well then, here." Kit held out the sheaf of papers, but she kept her arms folded. "Testimony of my great-grandmother, Élodie Roux." He nodded to Grady. "*Our* great-grandmother."

Grady nodded, still silent, frowning in confusion.

Livy didn't move to take it. When she glanced at Skye again, Skye whispered, "Please."

Livy snatched the pages from Kit.

"Go ahead." Kit folded his arms, copying Livy's former position. "Read it."

Livy smoothed the top page. The paper crackled, as if brittle with age. She began reading aloud.

CHAPTER TWENTY-ONE

7 August 1954

I, Élodie Fabre Roux, now that I am ill and do not have long to live, write this confession of the goblin curse I brought upon myself and my descendants. I hoped it would die with me, but the last time I was strong enough to go into the woods and see the goblins, they told me it would transfer to one of my children, that it was a curse that would run through our bloodline for a thousand years. I cannot bear this thought and I write all this down for my children in the hopes that they will find some way to break the curse. Even if they cannot, it is only fair they know what has happened to them and why.

As you know, I was born in France and lived there for my first twenty years, before we came to America. I was of a poor family, in Nantes, in Brittany. From childhood I loved your father, Jean-Baptiste Roux, or Jeannot as we called him. He loved me too, but he was from a prosperous family, and when we were eighteen he gave in to pressure from his parents and became engaged to a girl who met their approval. Her name was Françoise. I did not hate her nor even know her very well. She seemed meek and well-meaning. But my heart was broken and I knew there was no love between them, nothing like what Jeannot and I felt for each other.

We were Catholic, of course, but in Brittany the ancient ways were also strong, and I had always felt an affinity for the spirits of the land, the fae. I had sensed them, heard their music and voices at night in wild places, seen glimpses of them, and understood there were many kinds of them, in different *forms and with a variety of powers.*

I also knew it was dangerous to call upon them to use their powers. There were many stories about how this had gone badly for people. But I was young and heartbroken, and determined to try even if it meant danger.

I went into the woods alone at night under the full moon. I cried out to the fae to appear for me.

It was my ill fortune that it was a goblin who answered. I did not know, at that time, how devious they are.

The creature looked no larger than a goat at first, and all composed of branches and earth, or so it appeared. But as it crawled down the tree and into the moonlight, it changed before my eyes until it became a strong old woman in peasant dress. She would have looked normal enough in passing, but when she spoke I saw she had sharp teeth like a wolf. It made me shudder.

She said her name was Redring, and I told her mine.

At those words, Skye sucked in her breath, and everyone paused to glance at her.

Livy had felt the hard resistance in her own voice soften like melting wax the further she read, as confused wonder took over her anger. Skye's gaze darted to the sketchbook, which Kit had set upon the square side table.

Kit leaned down and picked it up. He held up Skye's drawing of the goblin for everyone to see: limbs like branches, teeth like a wolf's, a ring strung around her neck with its stone filled in with blood-red pencil, the only color on the page.

"Redring," Kit said. The name hung in the quiet room.

Livy felt chilled all over with fear, the way she'd felt watching scary movies as a kid. Grady looked like he felt the same, silent, his arm rigid around Skye. Skye and Kit gazed steadily at Livy, willing her to understand.

Kit set the sketchbook back down and folded his arms. "Go on."

Livy drew in a breath, found her place, and kept reading.

Redring asked what favor I wished from the fae, and I told her my predicament.

Yes, she said, they could make it so Françoise would not marry Jeannot. All they'd ask in return was my ongoing cooperation: a monthly gift of gold, for as long as I lived. "Just a tiny bit, an amount equal to the weight of this little ring," she said, holding up the silver one she wore on her necklace.

Indeed the ring was an ordinary size, but I knew gold was costly. I told her I was poor and could not get it, not every month certainly.

Redring said, "We will gift you with magic so you can always steal and not be caught, as long as you steal for us."

I thought of the rich who treated people cruelly and kept getting away with it. Certain clergymen, politicians, merchants, unkind society women. It would only be fair to steal gold from them, I reasoned. Besides, they were rich and would not miss it. I could live with this rule.

But I wanted to make sure they would not kill Françoise if I accepted. Of course not, Redring assured. They would just make her not want to marry Jeannot anymore. She would wish to leave him. Then the marriage surely would not happen.

I agreed. God help me, I agreed.

Redring shook my hand to seal the pact, and in so doing she sliced my palm with her nail, which was like a cat's claw. I cried out. She licked away the blood, which repulsed me, then she told me my tribe and hers were now linked. She let me go, telling me to come back at the next full moon with my first payment of gold. She promised that in the meantime Jeannot and Françoise's engagement would fall apart.

And so it did, but not in the way I expected. Within a few days, I heard Françoise was acting strangely, hardly talking, seeming withdrawn and ill, but no doctor could find anything wrong with her. Not in body, at least, only in her mind. She never seemed happy anymore.

Fearful, I spoke to Jeannot. He seemed troubled, but he did smile for me before we parted, and said he was grateful I was still my old self. It filled me with guilt, yet also with hope.

From gossip over the next few weeks I learned of Françoise's increasing distance from everyone. She slipped away to wander in the woods often. She didn't want to eat or speak. She had no interest in Jeannot or the upcoming wedding anymore.

Then one night she disappeared. Her family, the police, and Jeannot searched the woods and neighboring villages for days. Finally, deep in the woods they found the clothes she had been wearing, all except her gold engagement ring, which was gone along with her. They never found any other trace of her. Most people assumed she had been kidnapped or murdered. Some speculated she had run away with another lover, and we all hoped so. I hoped so most fervently, even if it meant the goblins had enchanted her with a love spell.

Jeannot was upset but not heartbroken. Meanwhile, I had to begin to steal my ration of gold.

I started by picking the pockets of rich folk right under their noses, taking rings and watches and coins. When I said the magic phrase beforehand, "For the tribe," no one paid any attention at all to what I was doing. Those thefts were enough for the first month's payment, and when I brought the gold at the next full moon, I dared to ask Redring if she knew what had happened to Françoise.

"Of course I know," she said. "She is alive and well, stronger than ever."

"And she is happy?" I asked. For truly I did not wish her to be otherwise.

Her whole tribe was laughing—they laughed at everything, it seemed. "As happy as we are," Redring said.

I had no way to know if she told the truth. I hoped she did. I returned to my life as best I could.

Jeannot eventually came back to me. We became engaged.

I kept stealing. From the church I took a candlestick. I walked right into *the mayor's house and carried off several of their gold serving plates. I never liked it. Getting away with it was not satisfying, not even when I reflected on the pomposity of the people who owned these things. But it was the deal I had struck, and I feared what Redring and her tribe might do if I failed to come at the full moon with their gold.*

Then, about a year after I married Jeannot and was pregnant with our first child, I found out what had really happened to Françoise.

Livy stopped speaking and paged ahead, needing to know what became of people under this curse, unable to take the delay involved in reading aloud.

Kit told her, after a spell of silence, just as her searching eyes found the information herself. "She became one of them. A goblin. Far as I can tell, she's still there. Their whole tribe came here, followed our great-grandma to America when she moved. My ancestors say Françoise became known as Flowerwatch, and…there's still a goblin they call that. I've heard them say it. I've seen her."

Livy stared aghast at Kit, then at Skye. Skye didn't look shocked, just miserable. Like she already knew, and had known for some time.

Livy sank into a wicker chair by the fireplace. Her legs felt weak, her insides hollowed out. "So that's…"

"That's likely the curse on you," Kit said, his gaze on Skye.

Grady, pale and grave, nuzzled Skye's head. Great, Livy thought, a new relationship to make this mess even more complicated. But that hardly mattered right now.

She leafed frantically through the pages. "Then how do we stop it? What did they learn? Where's the goddamn handbook on this?"

"Oh, I've got lots of information." Kit sounded exhausted. He still stood with arms folded. "Whole box of it. Every liaison kept records, as best they could. We've put together some clues, at least, about how the goblins do things. But how to stop it…" He rubbed his face. "That,

I don't know. No one's ever caught one of these enchantments early enough to have a chance to stop it. Seems like in every case so far, no one realized it was a goblin curse until after the person had disappeared for good. After that, I'm not sure there's any bringing them back."

"Then this time we're lucky, right?" Livy refused to give up. Not when Skye still sat right there in front of her. "We can figure out a—I don't know, a counter-curse. A way to break it. There has to be one."

"Look…I want to say yes." Kit paced back and forth. "But I also have to point out that if there was a way to break it, my family's done a shit job at figuring out what it is, because we're still stuck with this curse, four generations on now."

Everyone absorbed that for a moment.

Kit caught Grady's glance, and added, "You're protected. I mean, from getting enchanted. So even though you're in the family, at least you don't have to worry about them trying to take you. As to whether they'd make you liaison if anything happens to me…I don't know. I don't think I get to choose what they do there."

Grady and Skye exchanged a silent, charged look. "Protected?" Grady said.

"It's all in there." Kit gestured toward the pages Livy held. "Once our great-grandma realized the goblins sometimes enchanted people into leaving the human world forever, she got scared they'd do that to someone close to her. Her kids, her husband, who knows. So she asked them for some sort of guarantee, and they said she could request one person a year, and they'd never enchant that person for their whole life. In return for that clause, of course…" Kit sighed. "The monthly payments in gold would have to keep going through future generations too. That's why I'm stuck with it, and my dad, and his mom, and so on."

"Why would anyone agree to that?" Livy said.

"If you read through it, you'll see. She was tricked. That's how they operate. There's always loopholes. They said, 'We'll let you protect one person a year, but if we do that, we have to make your agreement go for a thousand years.' And she said, 'But I'm not going to live a thousand years,' and they said, 'Exactly, then go ahead and agree to it.' So she did."

"Okay, damn it." Livy rose to her feet, reanimated by anger. "I want to meet these people, these *things*. I need to see this. And if it's for real, I'm going to find out how to end this."

"I doubt it's as simple as that," Kit said.

"Just tell me how to see them! I have to start there. I can't even believe all this until I see it, or hear it, or something."

Skye made an urgent sound, a sort of whimper. Livy and Kit glanced at her. Her eyes were wide, and she managed a small head-shake at Livy.

"If she doesn't take their path, it'll be okay," Kit assured Skye. "They can't get her if she doesn't take it."

Skye looked back to Livy, and acquiesced with a nod.

"How do I do it?" Livy asked Kit. "How do I summon them?"

"I'm not sure they'll come, but…here." He sighed, and held out his hand. "Let's see your phone."

CHAPTER TWENTY-TWO

LIVY HAD LEFT ON HER OWN, UNDER KIT'S IN-STRUCTIONS. GRADY AND SKYE STAYED BEHIND WITH KIT, WHO DRAGGED out the box of goblin-related files and sat at the kitchen island with it, digging through notebooks and scowling.

Grady remained seated on his bed, with Skye huddled under his arm, and examined the ghoulish picture that had finally crystallized into focus in his mind.

Desperate words clogged his throat like a logjam. He would have spoken if he could have, lots of times. He would have told Kit and Livy how the woods had been calling to him too, how this all wasn't exactly a surprise because the eerie truth had been sneaking up on his brain ever since he met Skye. After all, for the past couple of weeks—and he wouldn't tell them this part, but—he'd been having various kinds of sex with her daily, out there in the woods, despite drizzle and chill, despite having to lie on damp moss or prop themselves against muddy trees. He could have done all this with her in her room, so why had they kept at it that way instead? The forest must have drawn them, made them unable to resist. He had worked that out already, bizarre though it was, though he didn't know why it was happening.

Mostly, he wished he could tell Kit he must be wrong about Grady being "protected," because the goblins had fucking gotten him anyway.

By now Grady couldn't speak of it either. His words had been getting locked down inside him more and more over the past few days, and now that he was dying to speak, he couldn't. About other topics, he could still talk more freely than Skye could, but not about that.

Grady glanced at her, and their eyes held for a long moment. The curse was spreading in him, and he could tell she knew it. Had known it from the first day. Her gaze overflowed with sorrow, as it always did when she looked at him, and now he fully understood why.

He ought to be furious at her for doing this to him. But he couldn't be. *Help me* had been her first words to him; she had been drowning, casting out for anyone's hand, and Grady's happened to be available. He couldn't regret going to her. She was his mate and he never wanted to be separated from her, and soon he would never have to be, and that, at least, was a comfort.

But everything else in his human life—his parents, siblings, hometown; the career he might have had; the man he might have been—for all that, about to be swept into the trash heap of history, he felt immense sadness. Because he was still human, not a gleeful, callous goblin. Yet.

Skye stirred, slipped out of his grasp, and walked across to the bathroom.

As soon as the bathroom door shut, Kit glanced over at Grady. "You're quiet."

Grady let his hands dangle over his knees. "Yeah."

"I get it. I was pretty freaked when I first found out too. Also I guess you and her are…" Kit sighed, and chucked a notebook back into the file box, then plucked out a different one. "Shit, man. If I'd honestly thought that was what was wrong with her, I'd have warned you. I'd have done *something*. What, though, I have no idea."

"Yeah," Grady whispered again.

Kit paged through the notebook. "Look, maybe Livy's right. Maybe catching it early this time, there could be some way to break it."

"Maybe." Great, now he was echoing words too.

"But it's like I said." Kit kept leafing through pages. "At least you're protected, so you don't have to worry about yourself. If that's any consolation."

Grady stared at him, furrowing his brows, willing Kit to look up and understand that he *wasn't* protected, that it *hadn't* worked, that he was cursed right along with Skye. Kit kept searching through their ancestors' records without looking up, his face grim. "If she doesn't call after half an hour, I'm going out to find her," he muttered.

Kit said you had to go to the woods alone at night, so that's what Livy was doing. He also said it was rare for the goblins to show up on Crabapple Island, so she drove back across the bridge and through Bellwater toward the national forest. He reported he'd only seen the goblins on the island a couple of times, when he was trying to avoid them and they came to bug him anyway. They didn't like it out there, probably because they had to get people alone to work their magic. That tended to be tricky on the island, where there were too many houses close together, which, Livy figured, must be why Kit continued to live out there instead of on the mainland. That way, at least at home, he could usually avoid them.

Good God, how was she even thinking about this rationally? As if goblins were a real thing? She gripped the steering wheel tighter, continued on out of town, and made for the nearest Forest Service road. First things first. She'd test this "summoning" procedure and see if anything even happened.

She bumped Skye's car along the muddy road, her headlights washing across dark tree trunks, fallen fir needles, and the waving arms of ferns growing over into the roadway. A couple of miles out of town, she decided she'd gone far enough, pulled over, and turned off the engine.

She creaked open the car door and stepped out. Cold wind whispered. The forest canopy moved high above, just visible against the night clouds. She told herself she wasn't afraid.

She tapped the voice-memo option on her phone, and listened to the playback of the six notes Kit had whistled as a recording. She let it play a couple of times into the darkness, and looked up, waiting.

The wind gusted, the trees swished. Nothing else.

Maybe it had to be her own voice, not a recording. She whistled it herself, imitating the notes. The partial tune sounded eerie to her; a minor key, if she wasn't mistaken, more suited to Halloween than to the middle of winter. She wondered what the rest of the song sounded like, and her heart pounded at the possibility that she'd know in a minute, if anyone answered.

No one did. Just the wind, rustling and moaning. Unless the moaning was something else.

She shuddered, picturing ghosts now and actually believing in them in a setting like this. She drew her back up against the car, her gaze darting around the dark forest.

Still nothing.

Her fear ebbed, and frustration surged in. Skye's sanity, maybe her existence as a human, hinged on finding out what was going on in these woods. This explanation, absurd though it was, seemed to have absolutely convinced Skye and Kit, so Livy would unearth the truth behind it, whatever it took.

"Hey!" she shouted, her own voice shocking her in the stillness. "Goblins! Show yourselves! You out there? Huh?"

She was alone. It was dark. She had whistled the tune and shouted out their name in invitation. These creatures ought to be opening up glowing pathways to her about now.

Nothing happened.

"Hey!" The rage ignited her voice. "What did you do to my sister?

How do I fix it? Show your faces and *tell me!*"

No one answered.

Livy stood there a few more minutes, shivering, stamping her feet to keep them from going numb. Even after her eyes had adjusted to the dark enough for her to watch individual branches moving in silhouette above, nothing glowed, and nothing unearthly showed up.

Screw this. Tomorrow she was going to call Morgan Tran and set up a psychotherapy appointment for herself; in fact, maybe for Kit too; she'd drag him along whether he wanted to come or not, and she'd bring Skye and Grady as well, have a nice, big group session.

She turned to the car. As she laid her fingers on the door handle, something fell from the trees, bounced off the VW's roof with a clink, and hit her in the eye.

"Ow!" She scrunched up her eye, rubbing at it, and looked down at the ground to see what had hit her. It had felt and sounded like metal rather than a fir cone or twig.

After switching on the flashlight bulb on the back of her phone, she found it, and picked it up: a ring. Gold and heavy, with rounded edges, smooth and slightly tarnished as if it had been handled by many owners for many years. It had designs engraved into it, which she examined as she turned it around in the flashlight beam: a mushroom, a feather, a sun or maybe a flower, a cockle shell.

She looked back up, as if she might be able to see where it had come from, which was unlikely given all the darkness.

Except suddenly it wasn't dark up there.

Fear and wonder splashed over her in a cold wave. She sucked in her breath and reached out to steady herself against the car—then stumbled, because the car wasn't there. Neither was the road; bushes and trees stood all around her, as if she had walked out into the middle of the forest without noticing.

That would have been alarming enough. But none of it astonished her as much as the little lights, the figures, flitting and crawling in the trees, some of them descending toward her.

"No," she said. "Oh, no. I did not take any path. This shouldn't happen unless I take your path!" She shouted it up at them, as if defiance might change reality.

Something floated down to the level of her nose. The thing was about the size of her hand, and looked like a frog with wings, its whole body glowing in a nimbus of pale gold light. "You picked up our token," it told her, in a voice like a tree-frog's chirp. "That is the same as a path."

She opened her palm to glare down at the ring. "Well, he didn't tell me about that."

The frog thing laughed, as did the others, in a ripple of chittering sounds. The creatures weren't beautiful, or at least not in a human way, like the faeries in children's books. Instead they took forms from the natural environment: a clump of lichen ambling down a tree trunk, a foot-long dragonfly with a quasi-human face, a gnome whose hat you could easily mistake for a pointy brown mushroom, a bushy flying twig of spruce needles with a green smile.

They didn't particularly look like the spooky creature Skye had drawn, but then, apparently goblins could shape-shift.

"What did you do to Skye, and how do I reverse it?" she demanded.

"The goblins enchanted her," the frog said. "Not we."

"You aren't goblins?"

They all reacted again, this time in what sounded like offended grumbles.

"Of course not." The frog continued hovering in front of her, glowing gold, its wings not even moving, as if they were just decoration rather than a means of levitation. The air wafting off the creature smelled oddly warm and pleasant, like beeswax. "The goblins are invaders. Weeds. They followed the liaison and took over much of the forest. We are the proper fae of this land."

"Oh. Sorry. I've never…well, I never knew any of you were here, exactly."

"Most humans do not. But you, Olivia Darwen, respect our forests and our waters, and therefore we wish to assist you. You called out, so we are answering."

Livy drew in a breath. "Good. Are you…well, if I can ask, I know the goblins used to be humans…"

"Yes, most of them."

"Is that what you are too? Humans who were changed?"

"Only a few of us. For the most part we are merely fae, and always have been."

She glanced around at the glow-spangled nighttime forest. "And where are we now, exactly?"

"You are in the forest as before, but you have stepped into the fae realm. It is always here, overlaid upon your world, but humans usually cannot see it or enter it."

"But they can get stuck in it, if someone like a goblin gets hold of them?"

"Yes. That is always a danger. That is why such paths are treacherous."

"How can I save my sister?" Livy asked again.

"Her enchantment was within magical law. Unfortunately she asked the fae to appear, and the goblins, common weeds that they are, answered her. They showed her a path and she took it. This makes it fair, even if some of us do not like it. They have been taking more than they should, and pushing the boundaries of the rules too far."

"So what can I do? Is there any way to stop the spell? Or is she just doomed to become one of them?" Livy's heart wrung itself tight at the thought.

"When the time comes for her to leave you and go to them, then you may act. For then *you* are the one wronged, to lose your sister, and you never accepted such a deal."

"No, I didn't. So when does that happen? When does she go to them?"

"We do not know. Only that it would surely be at night, and probably soon."

Livy swallowed, fear sweeping over her. "What do I do then?"

"Come to the woods, any woods, and summon us. Keep that ring." The frog-faery nodded at her clutched hand. "Possessing it enables you to see and hear us."

"Then what happens?"

"Then you will have to be brave, Olivia Darwen." The frog looked grave—Livy was beginning to read expressions better on its stretched, wide-lipped face. "We will help you overcome their magic, but it must be you who approaches and infiltrates them."

"Why me? You're the ones with magic. I don't have any."

"We would like to defeat the goblins. Since coming here they've been pests to us. But magic has rules that we cannot break, and the goblins are always out of our reach unless they overstep rules themselves. They do so sometimes, and we do retaliate, but it has only taken their numbers down a little. They build them back up with new victims. They are strong. Weeds always are."

"Yes." Livy thought of her battles against Himalayan blackberry, Japanese knotweed, and English ivy. "They are."

"But you, a human from the tribe who was wronged—you, with our backing, may be able not only to save your sister, but to open a way for us to eradicate the goblins. Are you ready to be so brave, young human?"

It sounded scary. Maybe the kind of thing a person never returned from, like all those people who disappeared into the woods or the water and were never seen again. But she thought of Skye—the Skye who used to laugh, tease, gesture enthusiastically, spend a whole weekend perfecting the colors of a painting while listening to loud hip-hop. The

Skye who was already almost lost to her and would never come back unless Livy stepped up.

"Yes," she said. "I'll be ready."

CHAPTER TWENTY-THREE

KIT SUCCUMBED TO HIS EDGINESS A LITTLE
BIT SHY OF THIRTY MINUTES IN, AND TEXTED LIVY. *DOING OK?*

While he waited he drummed his fingers on the cover of a fifty-year-old notebook, absently watching Skye and Grady as they stood by the front window, leaning against one another. The water was an expanse of black outside, with a streak of light rippling across it from one passing boat. Wonderful, Kit thought. On top of everything else, his goblin problem was breaking his favorite cousin's heart. He should never have let Grady stay in this town.

His phone buzzed.

Yeah, Livy texted back, and Kit breathed freely again. *Met them, or at least some like them. Will come explain.*

That was mystifying, but it sounded like he'd get the story soon. He responded, *ok then, see you*, and set the phone down. "She's all right," he told Skye and Grady. "She's on her way back."

Skye nodded to him, relief relaxing her features for a moment. But no smile. God damn it, why hadn't he realized she never smiled? Livy had even said so.

Not like he could have done anything if he had added up the clues, though. Except beat himself up for being useless, and for being the unwilling reason the goblins were here at all.

In a few minutes, the sound of Skye's car rumbled up to the cabin.

Kit met Livy at the back door and let her in. She looked shaken, her lips set, cheeks flushed from the cold air. Grady and Skye came into the kitchen as well.

"Okay, so," Livy said, "I didn't see or hear the goblins, but I met the *other* fae. The ones who aren't weeds." She set her keys on the island counter.

"Weeds?" Kit said.

"You know. Invaders. That's—the others kept calling the goblins weeds. I don't know, it stuck with me." She took a thick gold ring from her jeans pocket and rolled it between her finger and thumb. "This, too. I need to keep this."

The other three exchanged glances. "What's with the ring, there, Frodo?" Kit joked, examining her carefully.

Livy gave him an annoyed glance. That reassured him; she looked decidedly un-enchanted. "This was weird, all right? I'm still processing it." She set down the ring in the middle of the counter, where they all stared at it. "They gave me this. It makes it so I can see and hear them, if I summon them and if they answer."

"So the locals do exist. Damn." Kit scowled at the ring. "I've never seen them."

"Kind of surprising, for someone who meets with goblins every month," she said.

"Not really. It's because I'm meeting with the goblins. Makes the good ones stay away from me. Anyway. What did they say?"

"Well. They said there's hope." Livy looked across at Skye, who listened, silent but attentive. "I…apparently can't act until the goblins make their move, though. That is, when they actually take you. When you…go to them."

Skye's chest lifted and fell in a tremulous breath, and she looked toward the window at the back of the house that faced the woods. Rather than seeming scared or angry, she wore a look of what Kit would have called longing, like she was already distant from the human world. Then she snapped out of it, pulled her gaze back to Livy, and nodded. But that look had worried Kit, and surely Livy too.

"I'll go after you when that happens," Livy went on, her voice unsteady. "They'll help me, they said. I guess I find out the details at that point. They did say that, whatever it is I have to do, it might even take down the goblins for good."

"Then I want to help," Kit said. "I don't know how much the liaison spell will let me. The rules are weird. Whatever I can do, I will. You know I want to be free of this."

Livy nodded. "I know. But they only mentioned me. They said it had to be me."

"Still, there ought to be something we can do. Me and Grady. Right?" Kit looked over at his cousin, who stood with his arm entwined in Skye's. The bottom dropped out of Kit's stomach. Grady was gazing out toward the woods with the exact same expression that Skye had worn a minute ago. "Right, Grady?" Kit said, louder.

Grady drew his attention back to Kit. He didn't nod. He didn't say anything. He just breathed in and out, shallowly, nostrils flaring with each breath. Kit and Livy stared at him in silent dread, but Skye only watched him sorrowfully. Finally Grady stepped away, picked up Skye's sketchbook from the side table, and brought it to them. He set it on the counter, opened to the drawing of Redring. He looked straight at Kit.

"No," Kit said hoarsely. "Not you too."

Grady swallowed. A shimmer of reflected light in his eyes suggested tears.

Kit curled up his fists, wheeled away, sought something to punch, and, finding nothing suitable, settled for shoving the box of notebooks off the counter. It crashed and spilled on the kitchen floor. "How?" he shouted. "You were protected! I set it up, goddammit!"

Skye and Grady looked at each other in sadness, then looked silently at Livy and Kit again.

"I…" Livy blinked rapidly, distressed. "I could try summoning the other fae again. I could ask them. Maybe they know."

"Oh, I am going to ask the goblins myself." Kit stormed back and forth, kicking a notebook out of the way. "This is—no. How did they…" He pushed his hair off his face with both hands, and blew out a long breath. "God, man. I'm sorry."

Grady gave a nod. "I'm sorry," he whispered.

"No, don't *you* be sorry—argh." Kit went back to pacing. "I see. You're echoing. Fucking great."

No one said anything. Misery settled on the room, thick as snow.

"Well," Livy said at last, her voice hushed, "tonight there may not be a lot we can do. It's kind of late. We haven't even had dinner. Have you guys eaten?"

Kit shook his head, still prowling the room, and Grady murmured, "No. We have leftovers."

"Yeah." Kit did an about-face and headed for the nail by the door where his keys hung. "Start heating those up. My turn to go out." He grabbed the keys and slammed out of the cabin.

It was almost nine p.m. now, though it felt to Livy like she'd already been up all night. It had been around five when she came home and told Skye the crazy thing Kit had said. Just four hours ago, and her world had been completely changed.

Livy and Grady pulled food out of the fridge, creating a buffet on the counters. Lining it up, she realized what she should have noticed at home: over the past two weeks, his cooking had gotten less and less ambitious. Plain cooked pasta, pre-packaged shredded parmesan, unadorned green salad, bottled dressing, carrot sticks, rotisserie chicken cooked by the store, hard-boiled eggs—none of that, now that she thought about it, compared in the slightest to coconut curry soup or tandoori steak wraps with mint or any of the other wonders Grady used to make. God, how had she neglected to pick up on that? Or on the fact that she hadn't seen him smile recently?

They were eating in near-silence when Kit returned. Livy gasped when she saw him, and leaped off her barstool.

"Jesus," Grady said, staring at his cousin.

Kit pulled the bloodstained towel from his nose, leaving red smears all over the lower half of his face. "Looks worse than it is. It's not broken." He limped to the sink and started cupping water in his hands to rinse his face.

Livy darted to his side. "What did they do?"

"My fault. I have a habit of trying to attack them when they piss me off." Kit squeezed the towel under the tap, sending rivulets of blood-stained water down the drain.

"Oh my God. Why are you limping?"

"One of them smacked me against a log. Nothing broken there either. Just a bad bruise."

Skye and Grady came around the kitchen island to him.

Kit pulled a fresh paper towel off the roll, wiped his nose and mouth, and turned to face them, leaning against the counter. "So," he told Grady, "what they claim is, *they* didn't enchant you. *She* did." He nodded toward Skye. "I gather it was because she kissed you. Chose you as her 'mate' somehow."

Skye dropped her gaze as if she couldn't bear to meet anyone's eyes. She looked so ashamed Livy couldn't take it. Grady didn't seem surprised at all; he only glanced down solemnly at her, and brushed her hand with his fingers as if to forgive her.

"But it was *their* spell she was under," Livy protested. "Their magic that—that spread to him, or whatever."

"Uh-huh. That's what I told them, that they were full of cheating shit." Kit examined the now faint streaks of blood on the paper towel. A bruise was forming on the bridge of his nose. "They laughed. I grabbed Redring and tried to strangle her."

Livy was trembling with anger. "Okay. No. This is—they can't do this!"

"So you would think. Yet they have been, for years and years. Probably centuries; it's just my records only go back as far as our great-grandma, when our bloodline got involved." Kit stuffed the paper towel into the trash, and limped over to pick up a plate.

Livy watched him spoon out pasta and salad, then looked in dismay at Grady and Skye. They leaned against the island counter, Skye's arms around his waist, her head on his collarbone. Grady rested his cheek on her hair, while his tired blue eyes followed his cousin. So Skye had kissed Grady at some point in the past month, and infected him with the spell? Livy still didn't get it, couldn't make sense of these weird magical procedures, then decided it didn't really matter how it had happened.

"I just have to get you both out of it, then," she said.

Skye and Grady glanced at her, but didn't speak. It was unnerving how they both clammed up when this topic arose. She wanted to shake them, shout at them to say something. But she could see in their eyes that they longed to speak, probably had a hundred things to say; it was just that their voices were shackled. The silence wasn't their choice.

Kit turned with his plate, and forked up a pasta shell. "These local fae better have meaner moves than I do. Otherwise I am not liking the idea of you taking them on, Liv."

"I don't like it either!" She shouted it at Kit, since shouting at Grady and Skye wasn't going to accomplish anything. "I don't like any of this! I don't like finding out that there *are* Teeny-tinies in the woods only to learn that they're fucking stealing people. But, fine. The locals tell me this is how we get out of it and there is no other way. You're the goblin liaison and therefore the locals can't come to you. These two are...magically compromised." She flung a hand toward Skye and Grady. "So it's down to me. Do I want it like this? No. But that's how it is."

They all stared at her. She expected Kit to tell her she was crazy, argue with her, maybe tell her she was being a bitch. But in Grady's face she found gratitude; in Kit's, admiration; and in Skye's, a fierce, loving approval.

"In that case," Kit said soberly, "I'm glad we've got a knight in shining armor, because it looks like there's three of us in this tower to rescue."

Livy and Kit stood by the VW in the sodden, cold night, trying not to watch while Grady and Skye kissed goodnight for two or three minutes among the sculptures outside Kit's cabin.

"I can't believe I didn't know they were together," Kit said. "Or that I didn't realize he was under a spell. Or that I tried to attack the goblins, again. God, how am I so clueless?"

"I didn't know any of that stuff till tonight either." She glanced at her sister, who was still drinking in Grady's kiss like they couldn't breathe unless they were connected at the mouth. "Guess that explains how they've been spending the past couple weeks."

"Yeah, I wondered, but..." Kit shook his head. "This is awful. I mean, we have to wait? Till they give in, and walk into the woods alone some night? We just stand by and watch, *then* act?" He sounded anguished.

"I hate it. But that's what the locals said."

"They better give you one hell of a magic sword to take with you, that's all."

"I'm hoping it's more like a magic shovel. I don't know how to use a sword."

Kit snorted.

She met his gaze. "I'm sorry," she said after a moment. "For not believing you. For all the things I said."

"Hey, it's a sign of your intelligence that you didn't believe me."

"Living with this, all these years..." She exhaled, puffing out her cheeks. "I can't even imagine what it's been like for you."

He scraped a mud fleck off her side mirror with his fingernail. "I hate that it's involved all of you. But at the same time, I've got to admit, it feels really good to tell someone."

"I bet. I'm going to have more questions for you tomorrow." She nodded toward her sister, who was finally disentangling from Grady. "But we should call it a night."

"Yeah." Kit turned to Skye as she approached the car. "I'm sorry," he told her gravely.

She nodded, and squeezed his upper arm through his jacket, a gesture of solidarity, or forgiveness. Probably both.

Kit opened the car door for Skye, and she slid in.

Grady shambled up too, hands stuffed in his hoodie pockets, and when Livy looked at him, he said, "I'll still come tomorrow, but don't pay me anymore. Please. You shouldn't."

"I should. I insist."

"I'm barely even cooking lately." He sounded wretched.

"You're still better at it than me," Livy said. "Besides, you're bringing us groceries. I at least owe you for that."

Unconvinced, he bowed his head and looked away, his sigh becoming a cloud of fog.

Kit shut Skye's door, and he and Livy locked eyes again. "Well. Goodnight," she said.

"We'll talk soon."

"Yeah." She hovered, tempted to kiss him, thinking it was the least she could do. In the end she turned away instead, and slogged around to the other side of the car, alone.

CHAPTER
TWENTY-FOUR

WHEN SKYE AND LIVY HAD DRIVEN AWAY,
GRADY STAYED IN THE YARD BEHIND THE CABIN, HUGGING HIMSELF, GAZing up at the treetops.

Kit's step crunched the gravel off to his left. "They live up there," he said. "Up in the trees. Not here on the island really, but in the national forest on the mainland. I guess you know that, though."

Grady had begun to guess as much, but he couldn't nod or otherwise answer. He looked at Kit a second to show he was listening, then let his glance get pulled back up into the woods.

"They have these weird houses up there, like a treehouse village, like Skye drew. You can't see it unless they invite you in and you take their path. Which you've never done, I guess. That's what I made them promise they wouldn't do to you. Lot of good it did."

Right. Instead Skye had invited him—*Help me*—and he'd taken her path, stepping off the main trail and through the underbrush to reach her, to taste the enchanted fruit of her mouth. Grady forced his gaze down instead, to the solidity of the ground.

"They're getting too damn bold." Kit sounded bitter. "There's no precedent for this, for them taking someone close to the liaison. Not that I've found in the records, anyhow. They usually just pick on random people." Kit sighed. "Not that that's any better. And I guess liaisons before me were better at protecting the people they ought to protect."

Grady shook his head at Kit, with a slow blink to signal *Not your fault, no hard feelings.* Really, not Kit's fault. Just rotten luck.

"Sucks for you too," Grady said. The curse let him say that, at least.

"Oh yeah. That it does."

Though it was cold out and starting to drizzle again, Grady wanted to linger out here a while, absorbing the air alone. But Kit hovered a few feet behind him, and finally said, "Will you come in? You're making me nervous. I don't want you to wander off into the woods this very night if it's all the same to you."

Grady could tell he was trying to sound ironic, throw a pinch of humor into the situation.

Grady nodded, and resisted the forest's pull, following Kit back inside.

He tucked himself into a chair by the dark front window, his computer open on his lap. "How to write a will" was a Google search he'd never run before, never thought about nor wanted to think about; but now he ran it, and with cold fingertips copied and pasted a legal-looking template into a document file. He filled in the blank spaces with his name and the date, and read over the boilerplate.

I, Grady Michael Sylvain, being of sound mind…

Was he of sound mind? Probably couldn't claim that anymore. But a lawyer wasn't going to take a goblin hex into consideration, so he kept on filling in blanks. Pushing down the whirlwind of grief and terror, he typed his intention to divide his modest goods and bank account among his parents and siblings if he died—or at least, if he went permanently missing and was presumed dead. Probably it would be better for his family if they thought he was dead, so they wouldn't have to wait and hope endlessly for him to return.

Then, if they found this document, they'd likely think he had killed himself, even if Kit—who would probably be the last to see him "alive"—swore up and down that Grady wouldn't do such a thing. For what other reason than suicide would a healthy twenty-one-year-old in a seemingly safe lifestyle write a will?

He shut his eyes a moment, feeling so sad and nauseated he couldn't even look at the screen. The thought of his family regarding him as a suicide hurt just as much as the thought of them waiting forever for him to come home. Screw Kit's reservations on the issue. Grady opened his eyes, made room for a new paragraph after the preliminary boilerplate, and typed:

I am not dead. But I cannot come home. It is my wish that my cousin, Kit Sylvain, tell the truth about what happened to me, just as he told it to me shortly before my disappearance. He isn't to blame in any way, but he has the explanation.

He was tempted to add Livy's name, call her in as a witness as well. But he supposed it best to let the Darwen clan write their own letters and explanations in the ways they saw fit. After all, if they couldn't break this spell, Skye would be leaving her family in the same bereft condition.

Grady rested his head back against the wall, looking at the ceiling's log beams. He wondered if he should text Skye, ask her if she'd written a will. Maybe she didn't need to. Her family was smaller than his. Everything she owned would surely go to Livy, who would know what to do with it. Livy seemed to know what to do about most stuff in life.

He grimaced at his makeshift will, which struck him as useless, and he closed it without saving it.

God, how he hoped Livy would know what to do here, and soon, before he and Skye gave up their human skins and crawled into the treetops.

"So I know you'll have to go out into the woods alone eventually, one of these nights," Livy said when they got home.

Skye shivered, feeling the tug of the tribe, tasting the increasingly appealing syrupy fruits, hearing the frolicking songs...

"But," Livy went on, "if you could please stay inside tonight? Just—can it not be today? Please give me one more day with you…" She held her hands clasped before her chest, her eyes pleading.

Skye nodded. She was so tired anyway, she probably could just fall asleep in her bed and not be too tormented by the thought of the fresh air and starlight and glee she was missing.

Those thoughts had plagued her every night since the goblins captured her. She felt like a teenager grounded by her parents, exiled to solitary confinement while all the people she wanted to see were partying without her. Also, Grady wasn't with her at night, and she pined even harder for him than she did for the forest. It should have been enough to know she'd see him the next day, in a matter of hours. Like anyone addicted to something, she had trouble seeing past her cravings, her current lack of the desired thing.

Even tonight, though she obeyed Livy's request and stayed indoors, she stood by her bedroom window a long while after turning off the lights, and stared out into the forest. It had become a habit for her, a behavior she indulged anytime she couldn't sleep, and one she performed every night before she went to bed. Livy didn't know; Skye always shut her door, and moved quietly around her room.

Tonight drizzle spattered the windowpane, hitting harder in erratic gusts of wind, and all she could see of the forest was a vaguely shifting wall of black. Would it be cold and wet, living up in the treetops on a night like this? Would the gusting wind make the houses sway? Did the weather bother the goblins, or did they swing through the bending branches like squirrels, and splash into the rain like frogs, always in gleeful communion with nature?

She guessed it was the latter. That didn't sound so bad. It had to be better than feeling torn in half like this.

Skye was well aware of what the others hadn't realized until tonight: that Grady had become increasingly quiet and unsmiling ever since being enchanted by her. He'd grown less interested in cooking, in his job hunt, in any life outside of Skye and the forest. Even when alone together lately, they didn't talk much anymore, not the way they had those first few days. They replaced most of their conversation with touch, and with gazes in which they seemed to be trying to read each other's minds (unsuccessfully, but she still felt comforted by the attempt). It was almost enough. It felt intimate, and was intimate in most definitions of the word.

Being able to speak freely had become one of her strongest cravings, and he undoubtedly felt the same. Who wouldn't? Turning into a goblin would restore that to them, though presumably they wouldn't speak the way they used to, exactly. None of the goblins seemed to think like humans did, even if that's who they used to be.

Still, what could she do? She was supposed to join them before Livy had any hope of shattering this spell. Much as they all dreaded it, that was the only instruction they'd gotten from the other fae.

Strange that she was so safe from her fate during daylight hours. Livy could leave her and go to work as usual, in the knowledge that Skye couldn't be taken. Skye considered going out in the woods during the day and holing up there, waiting for night, letting it happen already. But that last sliver of humanity left to her was strong. It wouldn't let her. When she did go out, she returned home before sunset, every time.

Grady came over today as usual. She felt an extra flutter of nervousness before his arrival. He'd been quiet in text—ordinarily they kept in touch every few hours—and she dreaded seeing the sadness or accusation in his face, now that he knew everything with clarity and had had all night to mull it over. Indeed, now she herself knew much more than she had before.

When he arrived, an hour after Livy had left for work, he set down the grocery bag and just held her, in the front entry, their chests rising and falling against one another. The scent of him, through the soft flannel of his shirt, made her tear up. Surely he wouldn't smell quite like this anymore after their transformation. *But I won't care; I'll be happy then,* she reminded herself.

A glance downward into the grocery bag, gaping open by her feet, proved how far his interests had tumbled: pre-wrapped deli sandwiches. Canned soup. Boxed crackers. The real Grady would have thrown this Grady out of the house in outrage.

The human world would lose two artists when the tribe took them. Would she and Grady still use their skills in the goblin village? Would she be designing their next treetop houses? Clumping together glowing mushrooms to make light fixtures? Or—a shudder shook her at the thought—would Grady be mixing up next month's batch of jinxed fruit pastries?

She lifted her face to him, hardly able to breathe in her panic. He read her expression, and leaned down to soothe her with a kiss. She closed her eyes, felt his heat melt her sharp edges away, and sank into it. This magic brought all sorts of cruelty, but being with him eased the pain. Almost.

CHAPTER TWENTY-FIVE

"SO WHEN DID YOU FIND OUT?" LIVY ASKED. "DID YOU GROW UP KNOWING ABOUT THIS?"

They were sitting in Carol's Diner again, this time with Grady and Skye. Each of them had a cup of coffee. A shared plate of hash browns sat in the middle of the table—mostly untouched, Kit noticed. Not a lot of appetite among the four of them today.

He glanced at Livy, beside him. "Nah. My dad told me during his final illness, seven years ago. I thought he was off his head with pain meds, of course. He told me where to find the ancestral records, and I read them, but I still thought it was just a hoax, my ancestors keeping up some weird story for fun, or maybe they were all honestly crazy. I put the box away. I didn't know what to think. Then one night after he died, these voices started calling to me from the trees. I followed them and…met them. And realized all those obligations Dad told me about were true."

"Did your mom know?" Grady asked.

Kit nodded. "He says she did. But she'd forgotten by then, what with her own illness." He dragged his fingertip around in some spilled salt on the table. "Explains why they seemed so stressed a lot of the time when I was growing up."

"So when you said you moved to Idaho and Wyoming, but your problems moved along with you," Livy said, "does that mean they followed you?"

"Yeah. They showed up wherever I tried to go. I'd think I had escaped them, then within a month they'd be chirping at me again. Calling down from trees to tell me they were going to start stealing people
if I didn't fall in line." Kit formed the salt into a square, boxing it in on
each side with the edge of his finger. "Same thing happened to our great-
grandma. When she and her family emigrated to America, she hoped
the gob—" He cut off the word, glanced around, and continued, "She
hoped they would get left behind in France. But no. They followed her
across the ocean, then across the continent. Then all the way out here."

"How?" Livy asked. "In a boat, or…"

"They can shape-shift. They probably became fish or dolphins or
something. Then birds, on the continent. Who knows. But it's definitely
the same group. Riding us to keep getting their gold."

"That's why the locals called them weeds." Livy sounded glum.
"They actually are an invasive species."

"Yet another way Europeans have fucked up America."

"Gold," Grady echoed. "Why?"

Kit's gaze moved to Skye, at Grady's side. She watched Kit, dark
brown eyes pinned to him like a student who knew the answer and
wanted to be called on, but who couldn't talk if he did call on her. "It's
their magic material of choice," Kit said. "They can make just about
anything out of it. Anything inanimate, at least. Maybe living stuff too,
I don't know."

"What do they make?" Livy asked.

"Everything. Their houses, their furniture, whatever they want. The
other month they wanted an espresso machine and a milk steamer."

Grady's eyebrows lifted in disbelief.

"They did not," Livy said.

"They did. They're into food. Not only because they like it, but because it's one of the ways they tempt people. If they can get you to eat or

drink something of theirs, you're under their spell right away."

"I thought you just had to follow their path," Livy said.

"That's how you see them. You might be okay if you follow the path and don't eat anything. But…" He looked at Skye again, feeling guilty for bringing it up. She lowered her face. "It doesn't mean anyone's gullible or anything, if they get enchanted. The tribe probably does whatever they can to cast that spell. They basically assault people, so I wouldn't doubt if they…forced food on someone." He said the last few words softly, since, to judge from Skye's traumatized face, that was exactly what they'd done.

"Did they?" Livy demanded of her sister. "Did they force you to eat?"

Everyone watched Skye, who only closed her eyes a moment, cringing. No nod, no head-shake.

"What else did they force you to do?" Livy's voice shook. "Did they—they didn't—was there anything sexual?"

Grady slipped his arm around Skye, gaze fixed on her, hardly seeming to breathe.

Skye straightened up and shook her head, just a little. She met Livy's gaze.

Grady breathed again, and touched his lips to her shoulder.

"They better not have." Livy clenched her hands in fury, on either side of her mug. "This is just…oh my God."

Kit felt sick. He wished he could assure them the goblins never molested anyone sexually. But the past liaisons had heard of them doing exactly that. As with most of their crimes, it was nothing anyone could prove; more like hearsay and bragging from long after the deed was done. They mugged, ensorcelled, and assaulted people, and sometimes left them to die, so why would they draw the line at groping or raping someone?

From the little that Redring had said about Skye's spell and the "mate" status she had conferred upon Grady by choosing him, they probably had played a slightly different game than usual with Skye. He got the impression they wanted to keep her rather than abandon her like they did with the fisherman a few years back, so they had cast some sort of mating magic on her with the idea of making her choose one of them as a mate. Instead she'd chosen Grady, which was a clever loophole find on her part. Then the goblins had outfoxed her by claiming Grady for their side too.

Grady cleared his throat. "The gold. The stealing. How do you do it?"

Kit glanced around uneasily. No one in the diner seemed to be eavesdropping; only a few other groups of people sat in the place, all talking to their companions, several booths away. "I hate it. It sounds like this awesome opportunity, like you get to be Robin Hood, right? But it isn't. It sucks."

"There must be people who deserve to be stolen from," Livy said. "Or who have so much they wouldn't miss it."

"Yeah, and sometimes I do go to rich people's houses, or ostentatious boats at marinas. But still, say you find gold, what's it likely to be? Jewelry, right? These days it's hardly ever coins or anything. And jewelry's got sentimental value, and I don't know the story behind it. Maybe this rich guy is a dick, but what if this necklace was his mother's and he's saving it for his daughter, who's a perfectly nice person? How can I know?"

"Hmm." Livy tapped her fingers on the table. "Fair point."

"So for the most part I don't even try to get gold, not during the thefts. I just look for cash. Cash is impersonal. Then I use that to go buy gold, somewhere or other."

"Pawn shops?" Grady suggested.

"I go to those too. With them, I don't mind lifting gold quite so much, at least in the ones where the owner seems shady. Still, the stuff might've been stolen in order to end up in the pawn shop, and someone out there might miss it."

"What about big chain stores?" Livy said. "They can afford it. Or those overpriced jewelry stores in downtown Seattle. Or banks! Can you rob banks?"

"Would you keep your voice down? And yeah, I can. Sometimes I hit all those. Even then, it sucks for someone. If a couple thousand dollars goes missing from the till, a bank or a store can absorb the loss, but what's going to happen? They're probably going to fire whoever was on duty. So then I'm responsible for some innocent teller or cashier losing their job."

"Oh. Huh." She frowned at her coffee mug.

Skye and Grady abstractly gazed at the table too, maybe trying to imagine how they'd go about stealing if they had to.

Livy squinted at him. "How does it work, though? You just walk into some store or house, with some magic word…?"

He smiled bitterly. "I say, 'For the tribe,' before I walk in. That makes the magic kick in, and then, yep, they just don't even notice me. Made me sick to my stomach the first few times I tried it. Thought for sure I was going to get arrested."

She lifted the coffee mug to her lips, but didn't drink. "Every month for the last seven years," she mused, speaking against the mug's rim.

"Yeah. I spread it around, a lot of different stores, houses, towns." Kit tensed his shoulders. "But it's a pain in the ass, and I still end up feeling like a thug. Which I am. I'm completely a criminal, there's no way around it."

"No." Livy set down her mug. "You've got no choice. We'd all do it, if it were that or have people get assaulted. Not that it seems to stop them assaulting people."

He shut his eyes a moment. "Well, that's the rest of it. Sometimes…I come up short for the month. I can't stand to go out and steal, or I don't have time, or whatever. And then…well, there's no way I can be sure, but those seem to be the times they act out against people. Like it gives them the right, if I don't hold up my end. My ancestors' records suggest that's how the magic works."

"So before they got Skye…" Livy was clearly putting the clues together.

"I came up short that month." He stared at the salt crystals. "They
were pissed. The timing matches up. I brought them more stuff a week
later, but in that time…" He trailed off, and looked at Skye.

She met his glance for a second, then looked forlornly out the window.

Everyone was silent for a stretch.

"Where did Redring even come from, anyway?" Livy said in despair.
"Why is she like this?"

Kit pulled Élodie's letter from inside his jacket, and leafed through
to find the right part. "That's in here. Or at least, as much as we'll ever
find out." He handed the relevant page to Livy.

She frowned at it and read aloud Élodie's words:

*"I asked her once, 'Who are you? Were you once human as well?' And she
got angry and sneered, 'What does it matter? What could you want to know?
Once upon a time there was a girl whose whole family was slaughtered by Vikings, and she swore revenge and called upon the fae, and one answered her.
He made her a goblin like himself, and she became his mate, and though he
was but one lone creature when she met him, together they became powerful
and amassed a mighty tribe, who drove out any humans who tried to live in
their forest. When he overstepped his magical bounds, the nasty neighboring
fae stole him and transformed him into a river-nix who cared nothing for her
anymore, only for the water and its creatures, but the tough goblin girl kept
on. She has survived and her tribe is one of the mightiest in the world, and
everyone knows you cross her at your peril.' "*

Livy let the page sink.

"Vikings?" Grady echoed.

"Yeah," Kit said. "We're talking a long, long time she's been doing this."

"We've got to end it," Livy said. "Whatever it takes. This is absolutely unfair, to everyone involved. Including her."

They paid for their food and went back outside. Kit needed to return to the garage, and Livy had an afternoon of work to do.

Grady and Skye wandered into the sculpture garden, arms around each other's waists.

Livy watched them. "If this doesn't work, I guess I have to stay on good terms with you," she said to Kit. "How else will I find out how she's doing?" Her voice cracked on the last words. Tears pooled in her green eyes.

Kit's heart squeezed. "Listen." He grasped her wrist, at his side. "This *will* work. We will do this."

She tried to smile, a twitch of an expression that soon slipped away.

What he didn't tell her, because he didn't want her talking him out of it, was that he'd had enough. He planned to offer the goblins whatever the hell it took to let Skye and Grady go. Twice the monthly gold, ten times, he'd do it. Even his life, if they wanted it.

It would be worth it. He was done.

CHAPTER TWENTY-SIX

KIT SUMMONED THE GOBLINS THAT NIGHT.

They were cackling extra hard, as if they'd never finished laughing about his beating last night. He did his stoic best to ignore the laughter, and focused on Redring. "I want to talk about adjusting our deal."

"We do not adjust deals. Deals are sacred. If you wish to make a new deal, we could talk about that."

"Fine, a new deal. What do you want in exchange for letting Skye and Grady go?"

"Oh, but we have invested so much time in them, and grown so fond of them. We could not let them go."

Kit clenched his fists, reminded himself not to attack. "We're fond of them too. We're their *tribe*. What do you want for them? More gold? I'll do it."

"Really?" Redring skittered closer. She didn't quite move like a person; more like a two-legged lizard. Kit tried to hide a shudder. "How much more would you give us? Twenty times the weight of my ring?" She picked up the ring from against her chest and swung it by its chain.

"Twenty? Are you seri—okay, look." Get the rules straight. Look for the loopholes. There was sure as shit going to be loopholes. "Say I did. Say I got you that much every month from now on."

"For the next thousand years."

"Oh, no no. I'm not falling for that." That made the rest of the goblin tribe scream with laughter, like tricking Élodie had been one of their best jokes ever. "Just for *my* lifetime."

Redring sighed in disappointment. "Fine. Twenty times as much, every month, for your lifetime."

"Then you'd release them from the spell?" Even with this onerous new obligation about to fall on him, his heart sped up with hope.

"I would, much as it would hurt me."

He scanned the deal, and found the loophole. "Immediately? You'd let them go right away, effective today, and never bother them again?"

The tribe cracked up anew, and Redring said, "Oh, I cannot promise *that*. After all, we are entitled to *some* time enjoying them."

"Wait. I thought after they became one of you, they couldn't go back."

"Well." She shrugged, as if it didn't really matter. "We can return them, but we almost never do."

"And do they come back…" He thought of Stephen King stories and other creepy tales. "…the same as they were?"

"Who does time and experience ever leave unchanged?"

He expelled a breath through his nose. "Nice. And just how long were you thinking you were 'owed' with them?"

"What do you think is fair?" she asked over her shoulder to her minions, who shouted all sorts of nonsense numbers from "five thousand" to "three-eighths." She turned to Kit again. "Seven years."

"No. The fuck? All right, what if…" His tongue felt dry; he swallowed to moisten it. "What if I offered my life? Myself. What if you could have me instead? Then would you let them go?"

"Why would we want you? We've already chosen such a delicious one, and she hooked us another. Two lovely, juicy, young ones."

"But couldn't I exchange myself for them?"

The goblins catcalled him; he heard at least one, "I'll take him!", but most of the remarks were along the lines of "Ewww" and "Never." Like

Kit was the repulsive one in this assembly.

"Oh, Sylvain." Redring sounded pitying. "You are worth far more as our liaison than you'd ever be as our tribemate."

His body sagged in defeat. "And you'd just latch onto a new liaison if you did take me. Grady or some other poor relative of mine."

"But of course. That is the deal."

"What about taking my life? Just killing me. Is that worth anything, any magic, anything that would erase all these deals?"

She snorted. "No. No use."

"Are you kidding me?" He spread his arms. "I'm offering complete self-sacrifice here. That ought to be worth loads of magic."

"Not to us. We prefer the deals the way they are. But this idea of extra gold, I am liking that."

"Forget it." He turned away.

"Are you sure?" She was cackling now too. He was apparently pretty damn hilarious. "But it is such fun to make new deals."

"No new deal. Forget I stopped by."

There was no way he'd come out the winner in any arrangement with them. A banker's box full of written records back in his cabin had already told him as much. He was a slave, a procurer of gold; even his life or death counted for nothing. Evidently all he could do was wander around Earth trailing destruction after him.

The clouds blew away and a clear freeze crystallized western Washington. The sky became bright again, a blue Grady hadn't seen since autumn, arching over a frigid, dry land. As he walked through the woods with Skye, the ground resisted, hard and brittle under their boots, without the usual sliding give of mud and moss. The fallen leaves had been transformed from a carpet of mundane brown into a mosaic of individual shapes, every leaf standing out individually, veins and serrated edges highlighted in frost. The twenty-degree air iced his lungs with every inhalation, and Skye's hands were cold in her fingerless gloves. He wrapped his hand around one and pulled it into his coat pocket.

They investigated a row of icicles hanging off a branch like clear jagged teeth. Below the icicles, a puddle in the path had frozen over. Skye crunched her boot heel against it to crack it. She picked up a shard, looked at the sun through its milky clarity, then shivered, let it drop to shatter on the ground, and stuffed her hand back into Grady's pocket.

With his free hand, Grady grasped the needles of a Douglas fir, drawing them through his fingers. They were still green and supple. "Why don't these freeze?" he murmured aloud.

He looked at Skye, and she shrugged. Her gaze traveled up the trunks to the evergreen canopy, and his followed.

She shrank closer to him. He slipped both arms around her, although through their coats and scarves and other layers, the amount of heat from the embrace was minimal. He knew they were both thinking the same thing: how somber, how dismal, to live outside on a day like this.

Or, perhaps, how glorious, for probably they'd become as impervious as the evergreens, as tough and eternal as the stones.

It merely came at the cost of your life as a human.

CHAPTER TWENTY-SEVEN

IT BECAME A PATTERN OVER THE NEXT COU-
PLE OF DAYS: LIVY FINISHED WORK EARLY, BEFORE DARK, AND WENT
home. Then she and Skye went to the Sylvain cabin on the island, where
they collectively put together dinner (they didn't make Grady do it all
anymore) and researched goblin magic. They read the journals and notes
from previous liaisons, and Kit and Livy searched the internet for new
ideas. Skye and Grady put on hopeless expressions when Livy suggested
they run searches too. Apparently the spell wouldn't even let them type
queries related to goblin curses. Of course not. Why would it?

Not that it would have helped. What Livy found was that the internet supplied a million theories, anecdotes, and legends, but nothing that
seemed to change the actual existing spells.

She insisted Grady and Skye turn their clothes inside out. No luck.
She found beach stones with holes in them, and made them wear the
stones on strings around their necks, along with packets of sea salt.
Didn't change a thing. She lit a black candle and wrote down the details
of the spell on a slip of paper, and burned the slip in the candle flame.
Spell remained unbroken.

Kit watched with his chin in his hand. "My ancestors have tried all
that, you know. I've tried all that. We're dealing with a stronger kind of
magic here."

"Damn it." Livy chucked the pack of matches across his kitchen island. "Who do we know that has magic? Other than the locals? Aren't there human witches or sorcerers or…"

"Tried them too." Kit didn't move from his perch on one of the madrone stools. "People have sage-smoked the place, hung bundles of sticks over the doors, incanted all kinds of interesting words while ladling spring water over my head. Didn't make a difference."

"Spring water," Grady said dubiously, from where he lolled on the sofa-bed with Skye.

"Yup."

"Over your head."

"Uh-huh." Kit scratched at a drop of black wax on the countertop. "Closest I got to success was one dude who claimed he could see faeries. Like, everywhere he went, not just here. I found him on the internet and convinced him to come meet me. He looked at me, looked around the woods, and said, 'Oh yeah, they've got hold of you, all right.' Then when he learned it was goblins in particular, he got terrified, and scrambled back into his car, telling me he wished me all the best, but goblin curses were the kind of thing no sane person ever got involved with. Then he was out of here at top speed."

"Great," Livy said. "So we're back to what the locals told me. They're our only shot. I'm our only shot, with their help."

"The only shot we know about."

"Which is insane."

"Yup." Kit caught her glare, and added, "I believe in you."

"Good, because I don't." Livy scooped up the ashes from the burned slip of paper and dumped them into the trash. When she glanced across the room again, she got an eyeful of Grady and Skye tangling tongues, still sitting upright on the sofa-bed but looking likely to slide into a prone position any second now.

Kit had glanced at them as well, and when he met her gaze, his mouth twitched up into a dry smile.

She cleared her throat. "Hey, um, it's still light," she said to him. "Want to go outside for some fresh air?"

"Sure." He hopped off the stool. "Nice day to hit the beach."

It was nowhere near a nice day to hit the beach. Bundled in scarves, hats, and coats, they picked their way down the pebbles to the ebbing water. The temperature hadn't risen above freezing all day, and a frigid wind blew from the north.

"Did they not have enough sex this morning when I left them alone together?" Livy said.

Kit chuckled. "I am not going to ask. You can if you want."

"Should we even let that happen? If the spell is making them do this, or at least altering their minds so they'd do things they wouldn't normally...well, shouldn't we discourage it?"

"I'm concerned too, but again, I don't think I'm going to get into that subject with them."

Puget Sound almost never iced over, with its constant seawater flow in and out, but the high-water line from an earlier tide had frozen into a solid rope of seaweed and sticks. Also juice-box straw wrappers and snack-size chip bags. Livy paused to wrench the plastic and foil loose from the frosty seaweed, stuffed it into her coat pocket, then kept walking down to a square wooden dock belonging to Kit's neighbors. The low tide had stranded the dock on shore.

Livy looked at the sky. "Clouding up. Snow's on its way."

Kit stepped onto the dock and walked a couple of paces on its creaking planks. "Yeah? They still saying that?"

"Two to four inches overnight."

"Damn. Not nearly enough people came in to buy tire chains, then."

Livy put a snow-booted foot on the dock's stone anchor, half buried in the mud. "I've been going out every night lately with that ring, trying to summon the locals. Get some answers."

"Still no luck?"

She shook her head. "They haven't shown. It's like they're refusing to deal with me until…it happens."

"Don't take it personally. The fae—well, I've only met the goblin type, but I gather they're all pretty weird by human standards. They don't think like us or act like us."

Livy regarded his profile as he gazed down the island, the wind whipping his hair. "So, being the liaison. I imagine that's put a crimp in your relationships."

He nodded, still looking off down the beach. "Can't really tell anyone, and if you can't tell anyone it's not much of a relationship. Last person I tried to tell, other than you, was right after I inherited the job. My girlfriend at the time. She, uh…" He hunched his shoulders, burying his hands deeper in his jacket pockets. "Didn't buy the story. Thought I was a jerk, maybe crazy. That was the end of that."

Wincing, Livy scraped her boot against the barnacles on the anchor. Exactly the way she'd reacted, and the way it would have ended, if Skye hadn't dragged her back to Kit's doorstep. "God, that must be lonely."

"I've learned to deal. The art, and doing what I can for people, it's enough. But at first…well, when I said on our date at Carol's that I understood about depression, that's why. When I realized I was screwed and honestly couldn't do anything about it or even tell people, that made life pretty dark. Still does, some days." He shot her a brief smile. "At least I can talk about it with you guys now. Believe me, that's huge."

She stepped up onto the dock next to him. "I'm so sorry. I should've listened, not stomped off."

"You already said. It's okay."

"I know things haven't been the same the last few days…" Unlike Skye and Grady apparently, Livy and Kit hadn't indulged in any sex since she'd rocketed out of the cabin a few days ago on the heels of his revelation. "But it's not because I want it to be over," she added. "It's just everything's been so scary. And tiring."

"Plus we're not under some aphrodisiac spell. Which is a real shame. They couldn't have given me that instead?"

She grinned. "Careful. Those deals may sound good, but there are always loopholes."

He flicked his hair out of his face. "I know it. Anyhow, don't apologize. This isn't...I mean, I hope it's not over too, but the way it's gone for me with women during the last seven years, thanks to all this—hey, even if it's just casual, even if all you want to do is hang out, then I'd still count myself grateful."

She nodded, but something unflattering stabbed at her from within those statements. "Thus the 'no strings attached,' I guess."

"Right. Wouldn't be my first choice, but it's what I'm stuck with. I haven't wanted to saddle anyone with my issues." He kept his hands deep in his pockets. His gaze followed the ripples of wind across the water.

"But if someone actually knew, and was willing to help..."

He smiled, glancing at her for a moment. "Yeah. This is new. I hardly know what to think."

She smiled too, though anxiety still swirled around her like the incoming storm. "I know this was supposed to be casual, and I can do casual, but...well, let's just say I'm open to more." His clear brown eyes met hers, keen with interest. She shoved a loose curl back under her hat. "I mean, assuming we live through this, and all."

"I've been hoping you'd say that," he said, with gentle surprise. "I've been hating to think I'd have to let go of you too. You're the first I've..." He seemed to get shy, and huffed a laugh, looking away. "The first for a lot of things. I'm definitely open to more too, assuming you can still stand the sight of me after whatever it is we have to go through."

"Which I wish we knew."

"Maybe it's better not to know."

Livy was about to argue with that when something white flicked across her vision. She lifted her face. A tiny, cold spark hit her cheek, then another on her eyebrow, and her lips. She held out her arm. Even in the deepening twilight, she easily spotted the white specks of snowflakes on the dark green of her coat sleeve.

"Hey," she said. "Snowing."

Kit tipped his head back. "Huh. So it is."

The wind gusted and the flakes thickened, cascading down past trees and cabins. Livy breathed in the smell of snow, as pure and cold as if the wind had traveled straight here from the peaks of the Olympic Mountains. "Skye and I should go soon. The bridge will be getting slippery."

"You guys could stay the night." Kit kept gazing up into the storm. "If you want."

Livy considered it. Snowflakes pattered down around her nose and ears. "True. We're not right up against the national forest over here. Got some water between us and them. Might even be safer."

"Could buy us a night."

"I'm betting Skye and Grady won't mind sharing a bed."

Kit smirked.

"Hey." Livy stepped up to him, tilted her head, and kissed him.

He caught the front of her coat to pull her closer. After a long kiss, he slid both arms around her and lowered his head to sigh against her neck. She settled her chin on his shoulder and stood holding him, watching snow collect on the beach.

CHAPTER TWENTY-EIGHT

SKYE AWOKE. THE ROOM LOOKED LIGHTER
THAN IT SHOULD HAVE FOR THE MIDDLE OF A WINTER NIGHT. SHE PEELED
away from Grady's sleeping warmth, and tiptoed to the front window of
the cabin, shivering in her bare feet and T-shirt and a pair of soccer
shorts borrowed from Grady. She caught her breath at the beauty outside. Everything glowed a magical subdued white. Three or four inches
of snow muffled every surface except the dark expanse of water and the
undersides of tree branches. The clouds lay thick overhead, reflecting the
town's lights.

The soft breaths of her three companions rustled through the cabin, from Kit and Livy up in the loft and Grady on the sofa-bed. She
registered their company, but couldn't pull her eyes from the transformed landscape outside. She longed to be out in it, the way she always would feel when waking up to a beautiful snowfall, but stronger
now. More feral.

Something gave way inside her. The scrap of humanity she'd been
clinging to now seemed about as inconsequential as a dead leaf. She relaxed her grip and let it fall.

Though not dressed for winter, she eased back Kit's deadbolt and
turned the doorknob. It squeaked as the door scraped against its frame,
and she paused, her heart beating fast. The slumbering breaths of the
other three didn't alter.

Skye stepped out and shut the door gently. She gasped at the shock of the snow against her bare soles. Shuddering, arms around herself, she walked forward. Tiny snowflakes brushed her cheeks and lashes, like kisses. From the deck she stepped down onto the snow-topped gravel, and padded across it until she stood in the shadows under one of the largest trees, an alder between Kit's property and the neighbor's.

"I'm ready," she whispered upward.

She said it so quietly. They must have been waiting, for they responded at once.

"Skyyyye. Daaaarling."

As if the snow was made of white clay, it curled up into spiral shapes on either side of a path leading between the trees. Teeth chattering, she walked down it. When she looked over her shoulder a few seconds later, Kit's cabin and all the others on the island were gone.

Redring and a dozen more goblins crawled headfirst down the tree trunks. They didn't bother morphing into human form this time. Instead Redring reached out her twiggy fingers, a tiny round berry held between finger and thumb. "Warm up, my dear."

Skye opened her mouth and accepted the berry. It tasted like a black huckleberry, on the moldy side, but nowhere near as revolting as the fruit tarts from that first night. As soon as she swallowed it, warmth spread through her body, reviving the blood flow in her bare toes and fingers. In relief, she looked down at her feet, flush with warmth and wiggling unconcernedly in the snow. She felt like she was submerged in a pool of perfect temperature.

"Welcome," Redring said. "We are so glad. Shall we, new friend?"

Skye looked around at the goblins. Their faces now seemed more diverse from one another, livelier, friendlier. Her tribe.

She tried to remember her old tribe: her sister, mother, friends… sadness tugged at the back of her mind. Those memories were fuzzy, and she shoved away the sadness. She'd had enough of it.

She smiled at Redring. *Smiled*. God, how good it felt. "Yes. How do we get off the island?"

They cackled.

"Oh, that is easy." Redring stretched out her arms, which lengthened and became wide, dark wings. A heron's beak grew on her face, and her legs became skinnier, her toes elongating into bird talons. Five of the other goblins changed too, until a group of extra-large blue herons hopped about in the snow. "When we are done with you two tonight," Redring added, her voice now croaking like a heron's, "you will be able to do this, as well."

You two. "My mate will come?" Already his human name seemed insignificant, nothing worth remembering. He'd have a new one soon. They both would.

"How could he resist, sweet one?"

Skye lifted her chin and repeated the vow: "I'm ready."

The six herons wrapped their talons around her arms, three on each side. They beat their wide wings and lifted her into the air. Snowflakes ghosted past. Twigs and heron feathers swiped her nose and legs. They broke through the canopy and Skye gasped in wonder. How gorgeous the wild island and the inlet looked from up here, all frosted with snow. Across the water sprawled the vast forest: home.

As they soared across the inlet toward the woods, Skye began to laugh. In fact, she cackled.

Grady awoke with the impression he had heard something. The bed lay empty beside him, and he looked around the shadowy room for Skye. It had been so sweet to fall asleep next to her, and too easy to sleep deeply. He threw back the covers and crept across the room until he could see that the bathroom door stood open and no one was inside. He turned to the front window, caught sight of the snow-blanketed deck and beach, and drifted across to look. He settled his hand on the doorknob, feeling a strong pull to go out. That might have been what he heard—Skye slipping out ahead of him, following the same urge.

Grady hesitated, unmoving, hand on the cold metal, listening to the barely-discernible sounds of Kit and Livy breathing upstairs. *Goodbye*, he thought, with only the slightest twinge of regret, nothing at all like the torture he'd gone through when trying to compose a will the other evening.

Everything was all right now. Or would be soon. He felt light as a snowflake.

He slipped outside and silently shut the door behind him. Shivering in his socks, pajama pants, and T-shirt, he followed Skye's footprints until they stopped under a tree. He looked up into the branches. Falling snow scattered across his face, making him blink. "I want to follow her," he whispered. "Let me come too."

A handful of voices giggled above, and a glow caught his eye from below. A path appeared in front of him, lined on both sides by curled snow sculptures that reminded him of seashells. Skye's footprints led down it, filling up with falling snow. He followed the prints until they stopped again.

"Thank you, clever boy," a voice said.

Grady saw a tarnished brass key, dangling low, followed by the goblin who wore it as a necklace. Somehow he knew it was a she. She crawled headfirst down a tree trunk, barely a foot from his face.

"Hi," he said, unconcerned.

"We could not summon you. Rules are rules. But if you summon us, then all is well!" She and the rest of the goblins laughed.

Grady nodded, still shivering, arms wrapped around himself. The snow was soaking through his socks.

"Here." The goblin thrust a huckleberry toward him.

Some faint part of his mind screamed, *Don't eat anything!*, but he'd left that portion of himself too far behind now to heed it. He had come to be with his mate. His tribe.

He ate the berry. The chef in him cringed at the dismal quality of the fruit, the moldiness of the flavor, but he dismissed that thought too. And soon forgot it in the delightful rush of warmth that flooded him. Even his sodden feet burst back to full comfort levels.

"Better?" the goblin asked.

"Oh yes."

"Ready?" She changed into a giant bird—as did all the others.

He watched, pleased, and felt himself smiling. "I am." He unfolded his arms and reached up to his new tribemates.

CHAPTER
TWENTY-NINE

LIVY KNEW SOMETHING WAS WRONG EVEN BE-FORE SHE OPENED HER EYES. SHE LAY LISTENING, BUT HEARD NOTHING except Kit's steady breathing. No wind from outside. No sound from Grady and Skye downstairs.

She loathed to climb out of the luxurious warmth of the bed. It was her first night staying over with Kit, and she'd found it cozy even though they hadn't tried to have sex, not with Skye and Grady within earshot. She longed to cuddle up close to his heat and go back to sleep, but...not if something was wrong.

She slipped out of bed, shuddered at the drafty air, and padded across to the loft's half-wall to look down into the living room. The house was dark, but the snow coating the ground outside sent a filtered light through the windows, enough to see by. Enough to tell the sofa-bed's blankets were thrown back, and the pillows unoccupied.

Livy darted to the spiral stairs and flew down them, mostly trying to stay quiet, but increasingly letting go of that concern in the face of panic.

They weren't in the bed. They weren't in the kitchen, or the bathroom, or anywhere in the house.

"Kit!" Her voice shattered the silence. She ran to the front window, then to each of the side windows, looking out in vain. No one moving. Nothing to see but snow. People had died of hypothermia in conditions like this...

Kit's feet thumped on the floor upstairs. "Liv? What is it?"

"They're gone! They're not here."

"Shit." He thundered down the stairs to the front door, which he flung open.

They stuck their heads out into the icy air.

"Footprints." She pointed.

They looked at one another.

"I'm suiting up," she said.

Within two minutes they were both dressed for outdoors, in snow boots, coats, and gloves. They ran out into the cold. Livy wore the gold ring on a length of yarn around her neck to keep from dropping it, and clutched her gloved hand around it.

They followed the footprints, seemingly Skye's and Grady's both, until they stopped under the large alder at the edge of the property.

"They just disappear," Livy said in wonder.

"They took a path." Kit's face had tensed, hardened. "Into the fae world."

"I thought that wasn't supposed to happen from the island!"

"Well, it can. Just doesn't usually."

"Okay." She turned to him. "You have to go somewhere else. Out of sight, off where you can't hear me. I have to summon the locals and I have to be alone."

He nodded, and took her by the shoulders. "Listen. I don't know what they're going to have you do. There'll probably be weird rules, things that don't make sense. So…if there's some kind of magic where they need a sacrifice, someone's life, someone taken into their world forever—I'll do it. Give them my name. I mean it. Mine, not yours."

Tears stung her eyes. "You kidding me? I'm saving all four of us. We're not handing over lives tonight."

"Livy." His voice was almost just a breath. His grip tightened on her shoulders. "It may be you don't have a choice. If that's how it is, pick me."

"What fun would I have around here without you?" Her voice cracked a little.

"I love you. Shit, I haven't loved anyone for—I don't know, ever. I want you to know that. But I also want you to pick me if you have to pick anyone. The rest of you have more to live for."

The tears in her eyes blurred his face. "I'm not sure I can promise that. Because I love you too."

"Nah, you don't. Maybe you could someday, and that alone makes me happy. So go save those two, okay?"

"I do love you," she insisted.

"But you love Skye more." When she hesitated, he added, "As you should. So go." He let go of her. "Bring them back."

She stepped forward and locked him into a long kiss, storing up all the details in case she never saw him again: the soft warmth of his lips, the bristle of his beard, the cozy lingering scent of pillows and sleep. Then she pulled back, bracing her shoulders. "Okay."

"Good luck with that magic shovel." They both smiled as bravely as they could manage, then he turned and walked away.

She waited until he was around the cabin and out of sight. Then she wiped her eyes, drew a deep breath of the snowy air, and wrapped her hand around the ring on its chain. "I need your help," she told the silent trees. "Please come."

This time they came. The wind gusted, and dark shapes popped up out of the snow: mushrooms, growing fast. They formed a dotted line leading between bushes and trees. Somewhere down the path, a frog-like voice said, "Come, Olivia Darwen."

Livy held onto the ring and did what she was told to never do: she took the path. It wasn't a long path, just five yards or so, but when she looked back at the end of it, Kit's cabin and all other signs of civilization were gone. Fear and wonder shivered through her. It was the wild version of Crabapple Island.

Some of the mushrooms were moving. Walking, coming up to form a circle around her, where they were joined by a few of the locals she'd glimpsed before. The flying clump of spruce needles zoomed in along with the grotesque-faced dragonfly, and the golden, luminous frog floated down to face level again.

"The goblins have taken your tribemates," the frog said. "It is time for you to be brave. Are you willing to walk a path to reach them?"

Livy nodded. "How do I do it?"

"The goblins have protected their lair with many enchantments. To guide you through them, we can open a fourfold path, one for each element."

Livy understood almost at once. She wore them on her ankles, after all. "Earth, air, fire, water." The ring's four symbols, too, now that she thought about it.

"Yes. If you take this path all the way into their dwellings, we can follow you and change the goblins into new shapes, different fae, so that they will do less harm and more good. We have long wished to be able to, but we could not break through. We needed someone from your tribe, with a rightful claim to retribution, to walk this path for us."

"Then I will. And Skye and Grady will be saved?"

"Only if you complete the task before dawn. They are beginning to be transformed into goblins now. We can change them back if we reach them before the night ends. Otherwise…" The frog pursed its wide lips. "I cannot guarantee they will ever be the same again."

Livy shivered, not wishing to ponder what that meant. "Then show me the path." She took out her phone and checked the hour. "It's just after midnight. I suppose that means I have seven or so hours."

"Time moves differently in our realm," the frog warned. "Often faster. You must not delay."

"We're on the island, right? How do we get across the water? Is there a bridge?"

"Yes, the goblins have taken your tribemates to the mainland. Our path will guide you there. As long as you stay upon it and keep hold of the ring, you will remain safe and end up where you need to be."

"So when I get to their dwellings, what do I do?"

"You must capture their central source of magic and give it to us. The token of their leader: the ring with the red stone."

"I have to steal Redring's ring?" Livy almost shouted it, remembering too clearly the blood and bruises that resulted from Kit's attempts to fight the goblins. "They're strong, they're immortal! How can I?"

The frog looked grim, twitching its sparkly wings. "You must be clever. And quick, and brave."

"Oh, holy crap." She looked down in near-panic at her phone.

"There must be no contact with your world," the frog added. "It will break the spell and strand you, and your opportunity will be lost."

Livy turned off her phone, and zipped it into her coat pocket. Mentally she said a farewell to the human domain, which she half suspected she'd never see again. But Skye was worth the risk. "Then let's get started."

"The first element of your path." The frog drifted aside. "Earth."

The ground tore itself open before Livy's feet. The coating of snow gave way to the black soil of the forest, in a yawning hole that reminded her of the ragged craters left behind when trees fell over and ripped their roots out of the earth. But this hole went deeper, and as she watched, green glowing worms and centipedes squirmed out of the dirt and formed themselves into two parallel lines, with a foot of space between them: a path, pointing straight into the underground darkness.

"I...follow that?" she said.

"You must not leave the path," the frog cautioned again. "The fae of each element will guide you. I will see you again only when you have completed the four parts. You may walk, crawl, or climb as need be, but the path is the only place you are sure to be safe."

"Safe." She pulled in a deep breath. She could think of plenty of safer approaches than crawling through a pitch-black tunnel of dirt under the forest floor. Then again, the fae's rules weren't going to make sense. Kit had warned her of that. She stepped closer, examining the opening.

"If you complete the path through the earth element," the frog said, "the next will open for you."

"*If*? Wait, what happens if I can't finish it for some reason?"

"It is hard to say. The enchantment will break, and at best you will find yourself back on the surface in the human world. At worst, the element may trap you forever."

"The element." She stared at the black tunnel into the ground, full of wriggling bugs and dangling roots. "Earth." Buried alive, in other words.

She hesitated, trying to calculate how deep this tunnel might go and whether she'd be able to dig herself out with her hands, through earth frozen solid.

The frog drifted closer. "Time is wasting. Set out now, or your tribemates may be lost."

Skye would tunnel under the earth with her bare hands to save Livy, if their positions had been the other way around. Livy knew that without question.

She walked forward between the lines of glowing creatures, and dropped to her hands and knees. The frozen earth felt hard and sharp under her gloves. The path loomed black inside the hole; the illuminated lines faded a few yards down—for down was the direction the path slanted. Livy took one look back at the hovering frog, the other fae, and the snow-covered landscape. She drew in a last breath of the open air, then crawled forward into the earth.

CHAPTER THIRTY

IT WASN'T TOO BAD AT FIRST. IT WAS PITCH BLACK AND THE AIR FELT BOTH COLD AND STIFLING, AND SMELLED strongly of dirt, of course, but Livy had enough room to crawl at a reasonable pace. The frozen ground hurt her knees through her jeans, and roots sticking out the top and sides of the tunnel scraped slimily against her on her way. She'd be a muddy mess by the end of this. But she wasn't claustrophobic, at least, so she could manage this element.

Then the tunnel started narrowing as it slanted deeper. She bumped her head against roots more frequently, and her shoulders met the side walls. Her breath came faster. This was a little too much like those dreams where you were trying to squeeze yourself through a small opening for some unknown reason. She couldn't see a thing at first except the path's lines, which glowed with a faint green light, but her eyes began to adjust after a few minutes, showing her a little more of the tunnel.

Things whisked past in the corner of her vision from time to time—earth-element fae, she supposed. One moved slower than the rest, and she sucked in a frightened breath when she glimpsed it: a tiny skeleton, like a warped four-inch-tall human, who turned a blank skull-faced stare upon her, then dug swiftly into the tunnel wall and vanished.

Onward she crawled. Clods of dirt dropped onto her head sometimes as she brushed through the dangling roots. Or perhaps not exactly dirt: something was moving in her hair. Livy hissed a breath inward and swatted at the back of her head. A clump of soil dropped down to the base of the tunnel, rose up on root-thread legs, and walked away across the back of her hand, leaving a phosphorescent slug-slime trail on her glove. She shuddered, but she was already so mucked up, she didn't even bother trying to wipe it off.

She kept forward. Where else could she go? Backtracking at this point wouldn't be any more pleasant than going onward. The lit-up path of bugs stayed with her, at least. It felt a little bit like company. Not that she cared for it at all when a small centipede—or some fae version of it—dropped onto her shoulder, crawled under her collar, and took up residence against her bare skin. She gritted her teeth and slapped at it— gently, not wishing to offend the creature—but it was cagey. Its crawly sensation vanished in the spot she'd last felt it, only to reemerge in a new spot under her clothes a minute later. None of her attempts to find it and get it off her were successful. Another test of her endurance, she sup- posed. Whimpering, she crawled onward.

Glimpses of white bony fingers and black spiders flickered alongside her as she passed. She tried not to think about them. But they made themselves harder to ignore as she progressed. The finger-bones took to stroking her legs, vanishing when she looked back, giving her only a glimpse before withdrawing into the dirt walls. And on three separate occasions, a spider—not a charming glowing green one, but black and apple-sized and long-legged—dropped down on a silk thread to hang an inch from her nose, forcing her to stop with a yelp. Each one drew upward again, letting her pass, but the centipede hiding in her clothes tickled her each time as if to tease her.

"How goddamn wide could this island even be?" she said aloud after a while. She now squirmed forward on her belly, roots clawing at her on both sides.

Don't panic. Don't panic.

Crabapple Island was narrow. So, assuming the geography hadn't changed too much in the fae world, she had to be getting close to the end of the tunnel, even if she had to crawl the entire width of the island to get from Kit's shore to the mainland-facing shore on the other side.

A glimmer of purplish-blue at eye level caught her attention. It radiated from what looked like a gemstone in the tunnel's wall. Though it lay outside her designated line, Livy gave in to curiosity and poked at it with her fingertip.

It dropped away inward, as if there were open space on the other side of the wall. The purplish-blue light streamed from the little hole. Livy put her eye to the spot where the gem had been, and took in her breath in wonder.

This couldn't be. There weren't any subterranean cave systems on Crabapple Island; there just weren't. Anyway, if there were, they'd be full of seawater. But there it lay, fifty feet below her: a cavern from a tale of treasure-hoarding gnomes, all stalactites and rock-hewn stairs and piles of precious stones in a rainbow of colors, glittering softly. In fact, the gems seemed to be the source of the light.

A roar echoed through the cavern, and a green eye as large as her head appeared right up against her hole. Livy shrieked and reared back, hitting the opposite wall of the tunnel. A rock slammed into the hole, blocking the view and quenching the light. Dirt rained down from the impact of the blow, then the earth fell silent again.

Right. Don't go outside the path. Remember that.

Livy skittered onward.

And upward. The path began to rise up again. She slogged through the frosty grime, grabbing roots to haul herself ahead, her centipede hitchhiker tickling her in the armpit, the hip, the nape of the neck. One arm-length down. Another. Another. Definitely an up-slope to the path now. Oh, please…

A breath of snowy, fresh air swept in, and the tunnel's height expanded enough for her to rise back up to hands and knees. She moved faster. Another few yards, and after ducking under a tangle of roots, she spotted the exit, a mouth of gloomy night, almost bright after the underground passage.

Livy crawled out of it and rose, feeling as triumphant as a goddess being born from the earth itself, despite the pain in her knees and back. The centipede crawled out the bottom of her shirt and dropped onto the snow. "Thank you," she muttered in relief, looking down at it. It was only an inch long, and looked about like the ordinary centipedes she'd seen hundreds of times in rotting logs. This one drilled through the snow to vanish beneath, and where it had descended, a tiny mushroom sprouted up within seconds, shining the pale green of glow-in-the-dark toys.

Livy stood still a moment, straightening her spine and looking around at the snowy wilderness. Forest lay behind her, beach in front of her; still no cabins or bridge or other signs of humankind. But from the narrow shape of the waterway she faced, she guessed she had reached the other side of the island and was looking across at the mainland, toward the huge forest where they'd taken Skye.

"Okay." She closed her hand around the ring, just in case that was necessary. "Now what?"

The path sparkled into view.

The next element was apparently water. Sand dollars and sea stars, glowing blue, blossomed up through the snow to form twin lines. They led into the Sound and vanished a few feet out from shore, under the weight of dark, cold seawater.

This piece of Puget Sound was half a mile across, and over a hundred feet deep through most of it. She didn't see a boat, a bridge, or scuba gear. Just a path to follow. Underwater.

Livy stared at it in despair.

CHAPTER
THIRTY-ONE

KIT WAITED MAYBE THREE MINUTES BEFORE PROWLING BACK TO WHERE HE'D LEFT LIVY. HER FOOTPRINTS IN THE snow vanished into nowhere, just as Grady's and Skye's did. The fae had brought her into their world.

Empty and rattled, he walked back to his cabin, but stopped at the door. What was he going to do while the three of them were in the goblins' hands? Build a cozy fire and heat up a pot of coffee in case they came back? Hang out warming his feet till then? Screw that.

He wheeled around, went to his truck, and dug out the tire chains from the metal box in the bed. He hooked them onto the tires, then climbed into the cab. If Livy did succeed, and broke all of them out of the goblin hideout, then they'd probably wind up in the national forest where those dwellings were.

Also, if they—goblins and his loved ones alike—thought he was going to sit here pointlessly while they did all the important stuff, they were sorely mistaken. He was summoning them and going in, whether anyone else liked it or not.

He drove down the bumpy, icy lane to the loop road, then out to the even icier bridge, and eased the truck across it. Bellwater slumbered on the other side, everything covered with pristine snowfall, lit up by streetlights. It was 12:30, though the timing might be different in the fae world.

He drove past the closed-up shops, up Shore Avenue, and on into the woods. His truck's weight and the tire chains kept him from skidding too much, and he arrived at his traditional stopping point without sliding into any ditches. He got out. The snow lightened the world; he saw more than he usually could when he came out here at night. But everything was quieter too. The trees still creaked in the breeze, but they sounded muffled by the blanket of snow. The winter wind rose with a moan for a moment, like a tundra soundtrack, then died away again.

Kit whistled a few notes.

It took a minute, but someone whistled them back, and a voice taunted in falsetto, "Who is it?"

"It's me." He used a neutral, conciliatory tone. After all, going in swinging hadn't turned out so well lately. "I want to come visit the dwellings. Just want to be there, for the big night. Just to see, okay?"

This was so dumb. Even if they brought him up there, what chance would he have to accomplish anything brave and useful? They'd throw him out of the treehouse the second he made a move against them. But if it bought Livy even a few seconds to do whatever she had to do, or if it inspired Grady and Skye to resist and not become goblins, then he was going in.

They opened the path for him: snow sculptures tonight, knee-high mushroom shapes leading him into the woods. They didn't glow; the snow made things light enough to see without it.

Once he reached the end of the path, three goblins crawled down the snow-dusted trunks to meet him. He glanced up at their dwellings, a hundred feet up in the trees. Things looked livelier than usual up there, like a party was going on. Lanterns and lightbulbs blazed. Bouncy music, eerie voices, and laughter floated down.

"He wants to come up," one of the goblins said.

"Yeah." Kit glanced at the three. Redring wasn't among them. "Where's your leader? She usually comes to talk to me."

"Tonight is a big night, as you say," another said. "She is quite busy. She sent us to get you."

"Super. How do I get up there?"

"Like this." One of them jumped onto his head, faster than he could anticipate, and knocked him sideways into a bank of ferns and snow.

"Hey! Get off—" But while he tried to pry loose the one on his head, the other two wrapped a gag around his mouth—a grimy cloth whose dirty-laundry taste made him shudder. They seized his hands and bound them with a chain, and whipped more chains all around his body, pinning his arms down. God damn, the goblins were strong for such puny creatures, and fast too. It always surprised him.

"Rrmmf!" He made the growl of protest as menacing as he could, glaring at them as they stood to beam at their handiwork.

"Redring's orders," one said. "You are far too troublesome to be unbound in our dwellings. But you may come and watch, she says."

"Your blood contract does not allow us to use magic to immobilize you," another said, sounding regretful about that. "So we must use clumsy human ways."

"Up we go!" the third said. She picked up Kit like he weighed about twenty pounds, and threw him over her shoulder.

They scaled a huge tree trunk. Dangling over the creature's shoulder, tied up and with his mouth stuffed with disgusting cloth, Kit watched the snowy ground sink away from him.

At this rate, Livy and Grady and Skye were definitely not going to thank him for showing up.

✢✣✢

Livy stood between the lines of glowing sea creatures, her boots a few inches from the lapping edge of the water. Was she supposed to swim? In Puget Sound, the hypothermia could kill a person even on a summer day. This was a frozen winter night.

Trust the path.

"But the path's underwater," Livy said, to no one in particular. She stared at the illuminated blue lines rippling under the clear, dark water, until they faded a few yards out. As far as she could see, the path stayed on the bottom for the whole span.

Everything here was magic. This was her path, so there must be a way.

She gripped the ring and walked forward until she waded into the shallows. She paused, ankle deep. These weren't waterproof boots; none of her current clothes were designed for being submerged. As she hesitated and took stock, she realized the water wasn't getting through her boots. She bent over to look; the water was pulling back from her feet, surrounding her ankles as if a bubble of air held it there. "Huh," she said. She waded another step deeper, and another. The water was up to her knees now, and still it didn't actually touch her. It surrounded her on all sides, but hovered behind an invisible wall that moved along with her.

"Right, so." She continued forward until the water was around her chest, then paused, looked back at the beach longingly, and faced forward again. A black expanse of saltwater gleamed at eye level, stretching far out to the mainland. "Brave." She took a deep breath and walked forward.

She closed her eyes when the water level rose above her face, holding her breath with the next step. But air continued to surround her head. Tonight it was warmer under here than in the snowy weather on land. Her squelching footsteps bounced and echoed within her bubble, like the sounds of water slapping beneath marina boards. Everything smelled of saltwater and seaweed. But she could breathe. She was dry, if clammy, and she could breathe.

She opened her eyes. Green-black water curved around her in a giant wall, like an aquarium. It had closed over her head, smearing a transparent ripple between Livy and the free air. She drew in a breath to make sure she still could, and looked at her path. The blue glowing bottom-feeders rested in their two lines, some of them temporarily exposed to the air by her bubble. One of the sea stars lazily moved an arm, curling it out with extreme slowness as if searching for a clam to snack on while it was lying here.

She kept forward—or rather, downward, for the path sloped steeply. These fjords were carved deep, as she knew well from her studies of the local environment. Now she saw what no one except divers ever saw in person: the sea floor of Puget Sound, the deep sections never exposed by low tide. It was one mucky, slippery place.

The beach pebbles and rocks at the high end soon gave way to sticky mud that she sank into up to her ankles with each step. She learned to step on rocks or shells wherever possible to avoid getting mired down. But after descending for a couple of minutes, the path became a mess of seaweed, or sea grass, or algae, or kelp, or some mix of all of those. It came in various colors—hard to tell with only bioluminescent animals to light the way, but it seemed to be brown, red, purple, and off-white in addition to green. Slipping in the knee-deep layer of slime, Livy struggled to keep her balance with every step. The lightweight glowing sea stars and sand dollars rested easily on top of it, but her full-sized human weight kept sinking until she resigned herself to crawling this path too. Even on hands and knees, she slid as she progressed, and plunged to her chin often.

The steep pitch of the path wasn't helping. She was still going down, so she couldn't have even hit the halfway mark yet. The air in her bubble was dank and chilly, her breath making humid clouds. She worried she would use up all the oxygen before getting to the other side. The fae wouldn't let that happen, would they?

Above and around her, through the magical aquarium wall, everything was black. She rarely spared a glance at her surroundings, finding it too scary to dwell on how she was crawling along the bottom of Puget

Sound in the middle of the night. But a glimmer of something light-colored caught her eye, and she paused a moment to look aside at a bank of white sea anemones, hundreds of them covering a patch of the slope, their wispy tentacles waving in the current.

She could see them more clearly than she expected, and as she continued downward, she realized other glowing things dwelled here beyond just the creatures forming her path. Whether it was because she was in the fae domain or whether bioluminescence was common down here in the ordinary world too, she wasn't sure, but she began to catch glimpses of more things emitting light. A squid darted past, no longer than her forearm, its whole body outlined in blue-white sparkles. A sea slug with long wide spikes like water-lily petals rested on the sea-floor and glowed softly in pink. A school of skinny fish zoomed around her bubble, separating into two groups as they passed and then reuniting, each fish wearing a glowing green-blue stripe down its belly. Something reddish-orange undulated next to her, which turned out to be a large octopus, lit up by the ping-pong-ball-sized glowing jellies drifting around it. Livy shuddered and hurried past. She remembered anecdotes about the wiliness of octopuses, and could too easily imagine it reaching a tentacle in to wrap around her ankle and tug her off the path into a quick drowning.

When something black and white and gigantic soared over her bubble with a rumbling swoosh, she yelped. The animal turned, a gleam of white in the murk, and glided past again, one eye upon her bubble.

Ordinarily she'd have been delighted to spot an orca. Orcas didn't tend to attack humans, she knew, but they ate nearly everything else that swam, and she probably didn't look like a typical human at the moment. Plus she had forgotten how utterly huge orcas were. This one looked to be the size of a bus, and surely weighed a few tons. If it decided to ram her bubble just for sport, could she count on magic to keep all her air from shattering into a million mini-bubbles and leaving her to drown, or die of the bends when trying to ascend?

With her attention on the orca, she didn't heed the path closely enough. Her knee hit an especially slippery patch, and she went sprawling. The steep slope became a slide—she picked up speed, skidding on her front, and grabbed frantically at strands of kelp for something to hang onto. They tore free, or slurped through her gloves like escaping eels. She pulled up a knee to slow herself, making her body pivot. Her foot swung outward—and crossed the line of blue glowing sea stars.

Instantly water poured down upon her leg, icy cold, its weight slamming her foot into the seaweed floor. With a sob of terror, she yanked her foot back within the confines of the path. The flood stopped; the bubble calmly resealed its wall.

"Oh my God," she said aloud with a whimper. She shook from head to soaked foot, and had to spend a moment cowering with her head on her knees until she regained the composure to continue.

Skye needed her. Grady needed her. Kit was counting on her, and he loved her. And the bottom of the Sound was no place to dawdle.

She unfolded herself and kept crawling.

Above, the orca circled and came back for another pass. "Hey, water fae," Livy said to whoever might be listening. "You're not going to let this guy hurt me, right?"

Something gurgled, low-pitched, from out in the depths—a laugh, or an answer. It didn't sound like a whale, somehow. A moment later, something seal-sized swirled past, then circled back and bobbed upright next to her bubble. A harbor seal, she thought at first: silver with black speckles, and long whiskers on its dog-like face. As she sent it another glance, it gestured with one flipper in a greeting, exactly the way a person might wave.

Then it spoke. "She is only looking. She wants to tell her pod about you. You are safe on your path."

The voice had the contours of a seal's bark, and the message echoed and sounded muffled, like someone talking to you while your ears were underwater in the bath. Livy glanced in amazement at the creature, who followed alongside as she slid and slogged. "Thank you," she said.

The orca kept gliding around overhead, showing up as an occasional flash of white.

"We don't mind helping you," the seal added. "You aren't like some of the others, who fling their nastiness in our water. You take it out. You think of us."

"I try." Livy decided against telling it that until lately she'd had no idea the fae even existed. She supposed her consideration for regular seals, orcas, fish, and other sea life probably still counted for something. She remembered another strange moment, and glanced at the creature. "My kayak paddle. Did one of you send it back to me when I dropped it? I thought I saw your...hand. Or flipper. Um."

The seal spread its flipper again to display it, and this time Livy noticed it was more like a human hand—albeit a long-fingered, shiny hand webbed between the digits. "My tribemate did. We were near you."

"I appreciated it," she said, still sliding downward in the seaweed, though the slope was becoming less steep. It seemed the path was leveling out at last. "I'm sorry about the other humans. The ones who mess up the water. We're working on them."

"We smash holes in their boats or overturn them with waves when we must." The seal said it matter-of-factly, which sent a chill through Livy. She recalled that fae-world values were not the same as human ones.

"So," she said. "Am I in the middle of the inlet now? The path seems flatter."

"Yes, you are at the depths for our small pool."

"Good to know."

She supposed for a sea creature, a half-mile-wide, hundred-foot-deep stretch of water was a small pool compared to the open ocean.

"We would like you to destroy the goblins," the seal added. "They steal our fish sometimes, and fling things in our waters, just as humans do. We drag them under and turn them into water fae when we can catch them, but they are often too fast."

She would have opted not to get in the middle of an otherwordly war, but apparently such was her lot tonight. She sank up to her shoulders in muck again, and pulled herself free. "I'll do my best."

CHAPTER THIRTY-TWO

SKYE SAT ON MOSSY DECK BOARDS IN THE TREETOP VILLAGE, HER ARMS SPREAD TO THE SIDES AND HELD BY TWO goblins. She didn't mind. She felt pleasantly dazed. Around her, the tribe played music and raced about gathering food for the party, their scampering feet shaking the boards and making the lightbulbs and lanterns and jars of glowing beetles swing in the branches overhead.

Grady had followed her, as Redring predicted. He sat next to her, similarly immobilized, almost close enough to touch, but she didn't have the energy to reach out. No need. Soon they'd be transformed, and free to scamper about like all the others.

A commotion drew her attention, loud screeching and yipping from the ladders leading up to the decks.

"Look who came to see us!" A goblin flung a man onto the boards, chained-up and gagged.

Skye recognized him, though it took her foggy brain a moment. Kit, the liaison. He brought gold to the tribe, though he didn't want to. An ally, but a troublesome one. Also former kin to Grady, and close to Livy, and he had tried to help Skye somehow…but it hurt to think of all that, a hurt that was thankfully dying away. She welcomed its demise.

"Such good timing." Redring crawled into view on three limbs, holding aloft a large wooden bowl with the other hand. "He can witness their transformation."

"And if he misbehaves?" The goblin called Slide, with a battered dead iPhone chained around his neck, hulked over Kit with twitching fingers.

"Then he falls tragically off the treehouse and we claim a new liaison. Our liaisons do die young. It's as if they don't like serving us."

The tribe screeched with laughter.

"Wonder who it'll be," someone called.

Redring poked Grady's leg. "Not this one. We get him instead, thanks to our new lady."

Most of the tribe cheered, but Slide grunted and curled his lip into a sneer as he raked his gaze across Skye and Grady. "He might still come to harm. He doesn't deserve to be her mate."

Disgust shivered through that fading human kernel of Skye's mind, and Grady twitched in his bonds, likely feeling it too. Flattery was what Skye felt now more strongly. She might not desire Slide and might have to claw at him to keep him away, but to be desired and fought over meant status.

"Shut up, Slide," Redring said. "Be patient. It is not as though we keep to one mate for long. You'll have your turn, as will we all." She ran her twiggy hand down Grady's leg, which made him twitch again, but his gaze followed Redring attentively.

"Rrggh!" Kit writhed on the boards, fury contorting his face as he watched, but he didn't manage to work his arms or mouth free. Slide kicked him in the midsection, and he started gasping as if the wind had been knocked out of him.

A tiny chord of protest struck within Skye, and Grady tensed up for a second. Then Redring stepped close to them, her body blocking Skye's view of Kit. She held up the bowl. Her presence soothed Skye, and the contents of the bowl fascinated her: round red fruits, possibly cherries or grapes or even small apples, glistening and sticky as if stewed a long time in spices and sugar. Exactly the kind of food Skye had detested for the last several weeks, but now she couldn't imagine why. The warm, syrupy smell curling off the fruits made her salivate.

Redring raised her voice. "My tribemates!" The music cut off, except for one low ongoing note that changed gradually as it rumbled along, like a bullfrog's voice perpetuated. The goblins crowded near to watch. "We have waited so long for our lovely new sister. She is feisty. She resisted us a good while." Redring ran a scratchy finger down Skye's cheek. "She even defied us in her choice of mate—but in doing so, brought us a new member!" She transferred her caress to Grady's jaw. He stared glassily at her. "How we have enjoyed watching your matings in our woods, young ones."

All the goblins whistled, whooped with laughter, and made mocking grunts. That sliver of humanity within Skye coiled tight in humiliation and outrage, but it had been sequestered away where it barely affected her anymore.

"Finally you've come to us." Redring wrapped both hands around the wooden bowl. "We don't need tedious ceremonies. Let us merely give you our most sacred fruits, and bring you into our tribe. Then the celebrating can truly begin."

The goblins cheered. Somewhere beneath it, Skye heard another muffled roar from Kit.

Her eyes stayed riveted on the stewed fruits. With two long fingers, Redring lifted a red globe from the bowl. A sticky drop plunked off it, and a curl of steam escaped from where it had rested. Redring held it out. Skye opened her mouth and took it.

As her teeth closed on it, that bit of human righteousness lashed around in horror. Not only was the fruit over-sweetened and mushy, but that bitter metallic tang in the spiced sauce had to be blood. Yet this was how she became one of them, she understood. Maybe it was even Redring's own blood. This was a great honor. She chewed and swallowed the cherry or crabapple or grape or whatever it was, and beside her, Grady accepted a fruit from Redring's hand and consumed it too.

The numbing warmth within Skye's body brightened to a glow of sparkling life. She stirred, flexing her limbs. Strange pains shot down them, quickly soothed by an iron strength. Her bare feet and arms darkened to the grayish brown of fir bark, and her fingers and toes elongated to digits that could grip, climb, rip, strangle. Her body shrank, but it delighted rather than alarmed her: she was becoming distilled, concentrated to an essence of wild strength. After this, she could change into so many other shapes.

Her tribemates released her arms. She leaped up, landing in a crouch on her new wiry legs and fingertips, admiring the mobile, tough creature she had become. The T-shirt and shorts hung absurdly loose on her now, and she plucked at the fabric and laughed—a cackle that twirled into the notes of a song. The tribe screeched in celebration. The music bounced into life again, matching her song and lurching the notes around in improvisation.

Her mate cackled in answer, and she turned to beam at him. He was changed too now, wiry and strong and desirable, his teeth sharp as he grinned at her. He leaped upon her, tackling her against the boards, and she fought back, the two of them tangling and rolling and tearing the ridiculous human clothes off each other.

Slide growled in frustration. Redring shoved him away. "They may have each other tonight, Slide. You can try for her tomorrow."

"And I will scratch out your eyes," Skye said to Slide, as she clutched her mate close to her. Her voice squeaked and rasped now, a beautiful sound. "I am not tired of this one yet." How good it felt to speak whenever she wanted!

"And I'll fight you for her," her mate told Slide, latching his arms around her. "I'll keep her a long time. You'll see."

Their tribe watched, egging them on with laughs and jests. Her mate set to gnawing at her neck, a rough but delicious sensation. She held onto him with all four limbs. Through the dancing goblin feet she caught a glimpse of the human liaison, still lying bound and gagged on his side, his gaze locked on the pair of them. A tear ran down over his nose, and he closed his eyes. Flowerwatch touched his head gently, then crawled to the railing and peeked over, as if standing guard against intruders.

None of it mattered to Skye. She hadn't a care in the world. She rolled with her mate and enjoyed the music and watched the lanterns swing in the cold wind, tiny snowflakes tumbling down through their beams.

Livy shed actual tears of relief when the underwater path began sloping upward again. "Here I was thinking it was a good idea to stay on the island tonight," she muttered. "Jesus."

A glowing jellyfish bobbed up next to her. It morphed into a gnome-like blob, and opened a gelatinous mouth to speak. "No matter where you started, there would have been a water path. It is built into the magic."

"Yeah. Okay." Fae rules didn't make sense. She'd been reminding herself of that, with a serious serving of resentment, all through this wet, creepy slog.

To her best understanding, the goblins had set up their lair such that the only easy way into it was through their own path; and the only other way in, the hard way, was this one: several layers of defenses that had to be opened for you by the other fae, one element at a time. Or maybe that wasn't the goblins' plan at all, but it was the only way the locals could help her do it. Or maybe the locals wanted to test her courage: no magic sword or monster to slay, just a scary path to take. At its end, a magic ring to grab hold of, which a monster of sorts happened to be wearing.

Madness. Still two more elements to go before she even got to that end.

All taken into account, she completely understood why no one had managed to break this curse in several generations so far. As solutions went, this was complicated, frightening, and nonsensical. Not many people would attempt it, and that was assuming the locals even showed up for them, which she gathered they rarely did. She was lucky; they "liked" her.

The slope climbed, steep again, so that now when her knees slipped she slid backward. She fought on. Barnacle-covered rocks poking through the seaweed served as handholds. She was thankful she'd worn ski gloves, though the barnacles' sharp edges were cutting dozens of slits in their outer layer. Creatures both fae and ordinary glided past her bubble, but she'd become determined about ignoring them and keeping her eyes on the path.

The slimy green gave way to mud, then to rocks. She switched back to walking, though as soon as she stood, her spine seized up in pain from the prolonged crawling. Wincing, she pressed her hands to her lower back and kept forward, her legs stiff.

Cold poured down over her. She jolted with a gasp, thinking she'd broken her bubble again. But looking up she found sky: dark, cloudy, night sky, welcome and gorgeous. The frigid air washed down around her, smelling of fresh snow, colder than the water by probably twenty degrees.

She sucked it in and let out a long breath. "Oh, thank God." A few yards up, she dragged her weary feet past the last two glowing sand dollars on the beach and stood on dry land again, shaking. She looked back at the island where she had started. Such an innocent body of water between here and there, a calm little stretch of black. She knew she'd never look at it again without a vivid recollection of its dark depths and the creatures that swam there.

She turned toward the forest, and barely had time to wonder what her next element would be when a lightning bolt zapped a tree with a deafening crack. The force of it smacked through her body. Orange flames erupted in the branches. Though the trees stood at least forty feet from her, she felt the blast of heat. All the snow on the beach melted within seconds. Flames licked the fir, madrone, and cedar trunks, searing them black. The fire spread up the trees and out to both sides, leaving a ribbon of dark air between two patches of inferno.

The fire path.

Livy could hardly breathe. Fear rooted her to the beach.

She'd been near forest fires before, never this close, but close enough to be afraid she wouldn't get out in time. Part of her job in the dry summer months was to assist with dispatch for wildfire-fighting crews, and sometimes she had to go help flush out citizens in the affected area, or take up a station on a nearby road to keep people from entering. There had been a couple of times when the fire had changed direction unexpectedly and roared toward her, and…she still suffered nightmares from it.

Livy had written papers in college about how wildfires were a normal and necessary part of the forest ecosystem. She got that. But they killed firefighters and trees and animals, and she detested and feared them for it. Now she had to walk through one? It wasn't just some illusion—or if it was, it was a hell of a convincing illusion, because she could feel the heat, smell the smoke, hear the sap crackling.

The path was safe. She had just crawled beneath the earth and under a hundred feet of water. She could face this. Skye lay on the other side, in the hands of beings about to take her away forever.

Livy told her feet to move, and a moment later they obeyed. She walked forward.

The fire made its own hot wind, blowing her hair back. Steam rose from her clothes, eliciting a fleeting smell of seaweed baking under a summer sun. The stench of smoke obliterated the odor within seconds. Her eyes watered and the back of her throat stung even before she stepped onto the path.

No particular glowing lines defined the path, but it remained unmistakable, a stripe of blackened ground in the midst of a fire that was consuming what looked to be at least an acre. Livy hesitated at its threshold. The path was less than three feet wide, but the flames did seem to be holding back from crossing into it. Her face, her only exposed skin, had already thawed from its damp chill and felt dried out, like she was looking into the open door of a hot oven.

She walked in.

Five steps in and her eyes were streaming from the smoke and heat. Ten steps and she had to tuck her chin down and cover her mouth and nose with her coat collar to keep from coughing. She kept going. The flames roared like a storm, gusting hot wind at her. She caught a whiff of burning hair, and realized the ends of her long ponytail were blowing out of bounds and getting singed off. Choking on a sob, she twisted up her hair and stuffed it down the back of her coat.

If she had stretched out an arm on either side, her fingers would have caught fire. Sparks and tiny airborne embers sometimes flew past, any one of which could set her aflame if it landed on her. Her tear-blurred vision seized upon each one that came near, keeping watch on it.

One of the sparks hovered, rose, stretched into a star-like white ball, and…smiled at her.

Fire fae.

"Hi," she croaked in greeting, the word muffled in her collar.

It whistled in answer, a sound like a campfire igniting a vein of sap in a fresh log, but the sound did strike her as friendly somehow. As she continued staggering forward, the faery swirled around, staying just ahead of her, and soon three other sparks joined it. They danced in loops, like sparklers being waved by children.

A voice called out, a human cry slicing through the crackling roar of the fire. Livy looked to her left, startled. She gasped, stopped on the path, and kept staring even though her eyes streamed in the smoke.

"Skye?" she cried back.

For there stood Skye, maybe ten feet away, in a dark space between two burning trees, looking at Livy through the flames. Heat made her shimmer and ripple, but the pale face, the dark eyes, the hand lifting to catch Livy's attention—it was undeniably her.

Skye called out again: "Hurry!"

It couldn't be her. A fae illusion, a face in the fire, the way you could see if you stared into any burning hearth long enough, but enhanced with magic.

But she looked so real. Livy stood still, staring at her in agony. Skye was out here somewhere. What if she'd escaped the goblins and was trying to find her way back, and had been caught in the fire?

"Hurry," Skye implored again.

What if by "hurry" she meant "save me"?

Livy sucked in a huge breath and dove off the path, running through flames as fast as she could, hoping with all her courage that the remaining dampness of her clothes would keep her alive for this requisite twenty seconds. Her feet crashed through the burning layer of underbrush and into the mushy moss beneath, but she kept moving until she reached the spot where Skye stood.

The image of Skye broke apart into ripples of smoke and rose into the air.

And Livy realized what a horrible mistake she'd made.

Already coughing and choking, half-blind with smoke-borne tears, she spun and raced back toward the path. Her boot plunged deeper into a patch of fallen twigs, and she tripped. She fell against a burning tree, shielding her face with both arms, but screamed when the fire found its insidious way between her clothes, or burned right through them. Searing pain lashed her forearms and ribs.

She yanked herself away from the trunk, landed on her back, and looked up for a second into the hellscape of orange and red flame curling high up into the canopy. Then she rolled frantically back and forth to put out the fires that had caught on her clothes.

The spark-shaped fae squealed and swirled in the edge of her vision. She guessed they were right over the path, so she rolled toward them, crashing through burning trees, choking, feeling new sizzling pains on her cheek, her legs, her sides.

She tumbled straight into the relative coolness of the path and landed on her back, weeping softly.

"Hurry." This time it came from one of the squeaking sparks, bobbing around in her face.

Had they shown her Skye saying "Hurry" as a way to encourage her onward? Had they meant well? Or had it been mischief, meant to lure her off the path like a will o' the wisp luring people into the swamp to drown?

No time to ask, and it didn't matter. She wouldn't leave the path again.

Though her burns still throbbed—the ones she could see were second-degree—she couldn't do a thing to treat them right now. She certainly couldn't go on lying here. So, she got up, and limped onward.

The bright white sparks looped along in front of her, keeping her company.

A minute later she glanced over her shoulder, and blinked in surprise. The forest fire was dying in her wake, though it still blazed ahead of her and around her. Fireweed shot up behind her, green leaf blades unfurling from stalks topped with magenta spikes of flowers. The blossoms bobbed at her like a curtsey, then the plants hopped off the path and vanished in miniature flashes of lightning.

She turned forward again. The heat and smoke and pain still threatened to overcome her, but trusting the path was her only option.

Her trust was rewarded with one more visitation: a scurrying shape on a tree trunk caught her eye, and she looked up to see a foot-long orange salamander clinging to the burning tree; the fire didn't bother it at all. It unfolded a pair of leathery wings, leaped into the air, and soared away.

Livy watched it vanish into the shimmering heat waves. Did she just see a small dragon?, she wondered, astounded. Then again, why not? Faery creatures apparently came in no end of shapes.

One of the living sparks flew up beside her. "Quick. They have transformed your tribemates."

Livy sucked in a breath in alarm, and immediately began coughing. "Okay," she rasped out, and began running down the path.

Sweat dripped down her ribs under her clothes, stinging her burns. Everything on the outside of her clothes was seared dry. The fire continued to rage around her, though another swift glance back proved it was still dying out a few yards behind her. Spark-creatures and other orbs of light zipped about like fireflies.

Finally the path opened into a cool gray-and-white world: the snowy forest, untouched by flame. The last few feet of the path turned out to be glowing red embers—a walk on coals—even though the surrounding trees weren't on fire here. Livy didn't slow to think about it. She put on an extra burst of speed and ran straight over the embers. In five seconds she was across, and came to a gasping stop on the snow-dusted forest floor, the soles of her boots smoking slightly.

She bent over, hands on her knees, coughing up sooty phlegm and spitting it out. The firelight faded away. The air turned cold again. Her whole body felt sunburned. She picked up a handful of snow and dabbed it against her face and arms. Where it touched her burns, the pain faded. In surprise, she packed more fresh snow onto the blistering burn between her glove and coat sleeve, where some of the fabric had been singed and warped. When the snow melted away, her skin had been healed, though the fabric was still gone.

"Oh, thank God." Livy flopped down into the snow and rolled gently from front to back, letting the cold erase the damage.

Magic. How bizarre, how terrible, how fortunate.

She stood back up. Spark-sized creatures glimmered in the air. "Got to say," she told them, "after earth, water, and fire, air cannot be that bad."

Then, squinting above, she realized that one of the light-clusters she had taken for glowing fae in the treetops was actually a collection of lightbulbs and lanterns. Music, screeches, and cackles drifted down from it, audible now that the fire's roar was gone.

A small white shape zoomed up to her and hovered: a hummingbird, an all-white one, a type she had never seen. "The goblins' lair," it told her.

"Oh. Wow."

The lair wasn't directly overhead; it was still fifty yards deeper into the forest, but now it seemed frighteningly close.

"Wouldn't they have seen that fire?" Livy said. "Won't they see me?"

"No. We cloaked it from them, as we have cloaked you. Until you touch their dwellings or their trees, they will not see you. But dawn approaches. You must climb to them. That is your air path."

"But…" Livy's gaze stayed locked on the lights of the goblin tree-houses. "That's got to be a hundred feet up. Is there a ladder, or…"

"You must take your path."

Livy spotted a line of glowing shelf-shaped mushrooms climbing the trunk of a big cedar nearby. She picked through the snowy ferns to the cedar, laid her hand on the bark, and frowned up at the mushrooms. "But the goblins aren't even in this tree." There wasn't a ladder, just lots of small branches someone could, in theory, grab onto and climb.

"If you climb their trees directly, they will sense you. Your path must go through other trees, and thence to their dwellings."

"What?" Livy swung to stare at the hummingbird. "I have to climb *through the canopy*? Like, jump from one tree to another, way up *there*? Without even a safety rope or anything?"

"Your path," it said again, calmly. "The air fae will guide you."

"Oh, for the love of God." Livy ran her gaze up the path, following it until the glow of the mushrooms faded in the dizzying height of the trees. "Okay, I take it back. Air is going to be just as bad."

She gripped a small branch in each hand, found footholds, and began to climb.

CHAPTER THIRTY-THREE

KIT DIDN'T BOTHER STRUGGLING ANYMORE. He lay on his side on the mossy deck, not even caring that the dancing, thumping feet of the goblins were rattling the boards against his skull.

Livy hadn't come. Chances were good she was trapped, hurt, stuck in an enchantment, or even dead. Any number of fates could have befallen her. Goblin scouts could have snuck out and waylaid her. The dangers of the fae path could have ensnared her—some of the other fae sounded nearly as treacherous as the goblins, if legends were true. She could be lying alive but insane, maddened by a spell, never to return to the human world. If she didn't come back…his heart felt like it was tearing itself through his chest at the thought. He wouldn't dwell on it, not yet. She might still arrive.

But if she did, she'd be too late. Grady and Skye had changed into goblins; it was done. Soon the tribe would probably throw Kit off this treehouse and let him die slowly in the snow from his injuries and hypothermia. He hardly even cared about that, except then they'd go latch onto some new liaison. One of Grady's siblings, maybe; another perfectly nice cousin whose life he'd be destroying. He'd rather keep the burden himself than let it fall on anyone else.

If he could go on living after tonight, and if he had Livy, maybe that'd be enough. At least she knew the truth about his messed-up life.

If she and he, both of them bereaved, had each other to lean on, maybe they could get through…though really, she might not love him anymore once she'd lost her sister to his family curse. He couldn't blame her if that was how she felt.

Grady and Skye lay beneath a table, making out, or whatever exactly you'd call that tangle in a pair of goblins. He tried not to look at them. They'd become gargoyles, hideous.

The rest of the tribe had mostly ignored Kit. Now a scratchy hand touched his shoulder, and a small goblin crouched before him. Her necklace dangled into his line of sight: an ancient pocket watch with a flower etched on it.

"Their new forms are not permanent until dawn," Flowerwatch said. "So if anyone were to interfere before then…the locals, perhaps…they could yet save your friends." She held his gaze, anxious.

Kit glowered back.

Flowerwatch glanced over her shoulder, then hooked a finger into his fabric gag and tugged it down so he could speak.

He smacked his tongue, shuddered, and glared at her again. "You know I can't talk to the locals. Lot of good this information does me. Why are you nice to me, anyhow?"

Though her gray-blue eyes were too round and big for her face, they looked more human than most of the goblins'. She had only sparse hairs on her head, but the way they curled around her ears to chin length reminded him of a young woman with long bangs. He could almost picture what she used to look like, maybe. "Do you know who I was?" she said.

He softened a little. "Françoise. Or such is the rumor."

She nodded, lowering her gaze. "Most forget their old lives. But I've made a point of remembering." She clicked a latch at the side of the pocket watch, and it opened. A tiny square of paper fell into her hand, folded and stained and falling apart at the creases. After another fearful glance back at the reveling tribe, she unfolded the paper to show him. Pencil handwriting covered it.

He made out *Je m'appelle Françoise Gourcuff* before giving up with a sigh. "I don't really know French."

She refolded it and tucked it back into the watch. "It says, 'My name is Françoise Gourcuff. I was enchanted and taken away by the goblins when I was twenty, just before I would have married. I would have been a wife and a mother, and my human life was taken from me. I do not ever want to forget.' I have kept it all these years. One's name-token is sacred; no one dares touch it. I read it whenever I can, so that I always remember and never truly become one of them."

He studied her downcast face. "Has it worked?"

She nodded. "The others assimilate. But I have never completely let myself belong."

"Shouldn't you hate me, though? It's my great-grandma who dragged you into all this."

"She, not you. Even her I did not hate. She didn't know what they would do to me."

"That's true. I don't think she would've done it if she knew."

"She told me so once, years ago. I have forgiven her. But I am still here, of course, and am always looking for ways to lessen the cruelties we commit. I'm usually powerless to stop them. If anyone is coming tonight to save your tribemates…" She waited for Kit to confirm it. He didn't move, still not daring to give anything away. Flowerwatch let her head droop. "I would be glad to see your two friends get away, that's all. Glad for you, and for them."

"What could the locals even do to you guys? I thought you were immortal."

"Yes, but if we transgress, they can steal property from us. Some of our gold. Or they can take one of us and transform us into their kind, so that we will not be goblin-kind again."

"Isn't that exactly what you want?"

"Me, yes. Most of my tribe, though, they would hate it. Or at least, they would choose not to be transformed, but once they were, they would become tranquil enough. Therefore I do wish it...if help were coming tonight, perhaps..."

"Yeah, well. That isn't looking too likely. But thanks for trying."

Flowerwatch nodded unhappily.

"Flowerwatch!" Redring's voice sliced through the noise.

Flowerwatch jumped, pushed the gag back into Kit's mouth, and looked up.

Redring scrambled over. "Why do you linger over this useless lump? Come celebrate."

"Yes. Yes." Flowerwatch hunched down, hands splayed on the deck. "I was merely making sure his bonds were tight. So he will not disturb our revels."

"If he does, we'll kill him." Redring honestly sounded like she didn't care one way or the other, like these years of liaison interaction meant nothing to her. It chilled Kit's blood. "He's so nasty and rude, I wouldn't mind an excuse." She smiled at him, baring her pointed teeth.

Kit glared back, then recalled his desired future of staying alive alongside Livy, and dropped his gaze.

Redring sneered in triumph, kicked him in the thigh, and pulled Flowerwatch away toward the dancing tribe.

Climbing a hundred-foot-tall tree without any safety gear would be hard enough. Climbing a frozen tree, Livy found, was even harder. Frost and ice clung to the bark, making her boots slip on the skinny branches. She had managed not to fall, hanging on to branches with her gloved hands, but she squeaked in alarm at every slip, and shook from exertion and that special fear she got when she looked over the railings of high bridges.

She didn't look down often on this ascent. She had made that mistake once so far, and it had felt like all her insides plummeted back to the ground. The snow made it worse, because she could see the whitened ground, and how far away it was, too clearly. Much better to only look upward, at the line of glowing blue mushrooms guiding her.

She estimated she was halfway up by now. The tree remained thick in circumference, the handhold branches still solid enough even if they did bend more than she liked when she hung her weight from them. The higher she climbed, the more the wind buffeted her and made the tree sway.

Air fae, meanwhile, swished by as fast as the wind, ghostly wisps that changed shape like puffs of mist, hovering for a second now and then to look at her. Some took the forms of birds or other flying creatures: she spotted a raven, a white owl, and a brown spotted moth, all of which she would have taken for ordinary animals except that they dissolved into clouds and blew away among the snowflakes.

She reached the canopy, or at least its underlayers. Here the cedar stretched out wide branches with scaly green needles. The path of glowing mushrooms ventured off the trunk and out along a branch as thick around as her waist. Livy climbed until the branch was at chest level, wrapped both hands around it, and with a whimper of reluctance, pulled her knees up on top of it.

Now she had no choice; she had to look down. It was practically impossible not to when you crawled along a horizontal branch. Her gaze locked onto the forest floor so far below, past the hundreds of dark branches she had climbed. Snowflakes tumbled in the vast space between her and the earth, their motion making her so dizzy that she dropped to her belly and twined all four limbs around the branch.

She squeezed her eyes shut. "I'm going to fall. If I fall, I'm off the path, and that's it."

"Keep going." The whisper was aloof, but soothing. "Our path is safe."

Livy opened her eyes to find the hummingbird hovering next to her. It darted back and forth, hanging in mid-air like any hummingbird, but when it moved it left a temporary sparkling trail in the air. "How long till dawn?" she asked it.

"Not long. You can still get there if you keep going."

She turned her head forward. The mushroom path led along the branch, disappearing several yards ahead under the hanging green fingers of the branch above. The canopy blocked most of her view of the goblin hideout, but through gaps between branches, she caught sight of the lanterns. The wind blew laughter and guttural voices to her.

Skye was there. In their hands.

Livy began inching along the branch on her belly. "I sure hope you have a plan for getting us down, that's all."

"The way will depend on the outcome." Having delivered that enigmatic pronouncement, the hummingbird zoomed away.

Moss and lichen carpeted the top side of the branch; a soft surface to crawl on, at least. It was also frosty, and thus more slippery. Soon came a dreadful moment: the branch narrowed, and the path hopped down onto a different branch, a Douglas-fir this time, some five feet below Livy's branch. It was time to switch trees.

"No," she begged.

But she couldn't crawl back down this branch, descend the tree, and leave Skye to an endless fate as a goblin. So although every part of her body trembled, she lowered her legs into the air, hanging onto the cedar branch. It felt like she was dangling above the Earth from a satellite. Her shaking feet touched the fir branch, which sagged alarmingly under her.

"Oh God. Please don't let me fall."

Snowflakes and air fae flitted past her face. The goblins caroused loudly, a few trees away.

The fir branch steadied. Livy settled her feet, let go of the cedar branch, and let herself drop onto the new branch on her front. She flung both arms around it. Christmas-tree scent from its crushed needles engulfed her face.

"Okay, tree. Don't drop me." After her trembling had subsided a little, she focused on the glowing mushroom path, and started scooting along, ankles locked around the branch.

The transfer to the next tree a few minutes later, a western hemlock, went more smoothly. She got to stand and hoist herself up onto the new branch this time, which felt less frightening than dropping down.

Now she could see more of the goblin village. It reminded her of one of Kit's sculptures, except evil instead of lovely: a junkyard's worth of boards, scrap metal, and lights, probably held together more by magic than by nails. The things bouncing around on it and screeching at each other emphasized the ghoulish atmosphere. This was her first look at the goblins in person, and though she was still too far off to see them clearly, she could tell Skye's drawing had accurately captured their repulsiveness.

One more tree to transfer onto, then the next move after that would be the drop onto the goblins' decks. Livy kept glancing at the lair as she scooted along. Though it made her want to scream in agony, she was trying to decide which of those knobby creatures was Skye. The tribe did seem to pay special attention to a pair who was rolling around and rutting against each other, snarling at anyone who tried to join in. Grady and Skye, quite likely. A nauseating thought. Although not as nauseating as the idea of it being Skye and some *other* goblin.

Livy forced her aching thighs and bruised knees to speed up. Soon it came time for the drop onto the next tree, a spruce. In her hastiness to reach Skye, she dropped onto the branch without bracing her feet properly, and they slipped on the icy, curved bark. With a shriek, she plummeted under the spruce branch. She held onto it with her hands, but not securely enough; she hadn't had time to find an ideal grip, and the moss was peeling off, crumbling away, under her gloves.

"Oh God, oh no no no," she sobbed.

A powerful gust of wind surged through the forest. The trees swayed and sighed; tiny ice pellets struck her cheek. The wind lifted another branch just under her feet, holding it there long enough for her to shove her boots against it and push herself higher, wrapping her hands in a stronger grasp around the spruce branch. She hauled herself up onto it and clung to it, gasping. "Thank you. If that was you, air fae, thank you so much."

Maybe they honestly wouldn't let her fall, then. But she wouldn't count on it. She crawled the rest of the path with extra caution, testing each patch for ice before shifting her weight onto it.

Finally she reached the end of her path, three or four feet above the outer railing of the goblins' decks. The section below looked deserted at the moment, as most of the tribe was frolicking in the large central deck some twenty yards along, to her left. But other goblins could lurk in one of these huts atop the decks. She couldn't see inside them, beyond a few glimpses through cracked, mismatched windows. Some huts were dark, while firelight glowed in others. On the outside walls, the goblins had strapped machetes, axes, bows and arrows, and other lethal tools, the way normal people hung kayaks and paddles upon garage walls.

So many ways they could kill her.

The golden frog zoomed into view. "Well done, Olivia Darwen. Dawn is in mere minutes. Remember, they will sense you as soon as you touch their dwellings, but we will do what we can to keep them from harming you."

She swallowed. "I'm supposed to get Redring's ring?"

"Yes. When you arrive, say to them, 'I claim these three humans back, for they were wrongly stolen from my tribe.' Then when you have the ring, give it to me, and we will use its magic to disband the goblins if we can."

"If you *can*? Wait, *three* humans?"

"They have the liaison as well. He came to them."

"What? Kit did? Oh my God."

"He has not been transformed. They cannot do that to him. But they have tied him up and may hurt him further. So go, Olivia Darwen."

"But how? How am I supposed to walk up to this deadly, strong goblin leader and just take her most treasured possession from around her neck?"

The frog looked somber. "Any way you can."

Livy felt like she was ripping up all her hopes and tossing them into the winter wind. "Well, this is…this is just insanity." But then, it had been insanity to think she could survive the path through earth, water, fire, and air, yet she had.

Joining her ripped-up hopes, she jumped through the wind, and landed on the goblins' lair.

CHAPTER THIRTY-FOUR

SKYE HAD TO THINK A MOMENT TO REMEMBER HER NAME, AND SHE ONLY BOTHERED TRYING BECAUSE IT PIQUED HER curiosity. She recovered it, but it didn't matter. She'd soon take a new one, after whatever item she stole from the first person she'd lure onto an enchanted path.

"I'll make sure to steal something fun," she told her mate, who held her across his legs, running his hands up and down her leathery body. "Something with a name I like."

He laughed. "Good idea. I'll do the same."

Then they both tensed, along with the rest of the tribe. Everyone looked toward the huts on the northern side of the village. Skye looked too, from instinct, before she even knew why. A moment later her tribe-mates sent up the alarm.

"Intruder!"

"Someone upon our home!"

"Get the intruder!"

Skye and her mate stayed dazed upon the deck floor while the tribe dashed around, seizing weapons off walls and screeching commands to each other. Other than Skye and her mate, only Flowerwatch remained where she was, crouched over the chained-up liaison to shield him from being trampled. Ridiculously soft-hearted, that Flowerwatch.

"We have her! We have her!"

Seconds later, the tribe hauled in a woman by the arms and threw her down in the middle of the central deck, not far from Skye. The woman landed on her knees and lifted her arms in surrender, her gaze snapping around from the tip of one weapon to another. A circle of blades and arrows trapped her. By happenstance, Skye and her mate formed part of the circle, the only ones unarmed in it. Fear and resolute courage took turns on the intruder's face. She was a mess, coated with mud and soot.

The liaison thrashed and emitted a muffled roar when he saw the woman, and something flailed in pain deep in Skye's heart too. To soothe herself, she turned her face away and nuzzled her mate's shoulder. He purred in satisfaction.

"What is this?" Redring sounded delighted. Skye looked up, encouraged by her leader's voice. Redring pushed to the front of the circle and examined the intruder. "How in the world could you have gotten here, hmm? I suspect *someone gave you help*?" She amplified the last four words and directed them outward to the forest.

Gleams lit up in the surrounding trees—the hateful, stupid, weak locals. Skye and the rest of the tribe snarled at them.

"I claim these three humans back." The intruder's voice rasped as if she was exhausted, or ill. "They were wrongfully stolen from my tribe."

"Oh indeed? Some fat frog has coached you well."

A gold-colored gleam drew closer. Skye recognized it as a local leader, whom her tribe always just called the Fat Frog.

"You know this claim is valid, Redring," the Fat Frog said. "It is magical law. We will retaliate on her behalf if you refuse."

"Yet magical law *also* lets us kill anyone who enters our dwellings without our invitation. Hmm, how to resolve this?" Redring tapped her lip, pretending to be thoughtful, while the tribe jeered at the locals, and prodded weapons at the intruder.

The woman shot a startled look at the Fat Frog, then back at Redring—probably the frog hadn't told her that part. "Please," she said.

"Just return these people to me. That's all I want. We'll leave you alone. No retaliation."

"Oh, but I'd like to think about it a little longer," Redring said. "Because dawn is so close now. Then your claim would become worthless, for their forms will be permanent. Or at least, I could turn them back into humans, but they'd never be the same again. Their minds..." Redring shook her head in mock regret, and the tribe shrieked with laughter.

"Please." The woman's voice broke. "A deal, then? Anything to change them back and let me take them home."

The liaison roared again in furious protest, but no one paid him any attention. Even Flowerwatch had drawn away from him, creeping into the inner edge of the circle to observe the action.

Redring beckoned Skye and her mate forward. They obediently disentangled and crawled over. "Let me show you," Redring told the woman, almost gently. "New tribemates, do you want to return to being human? Do you want to go back to that sad little town with this woman?"

Skye turned to look into the woman's eyes. The woman locked gazes with her, and caught her breath. Tears filled her green eyes.

"Skye," she whispered. "Come back. Please."

The whole tribe hushed, watching.

The agony in Skye's heart kicked harder, tortured. Strangely, she wanted to say yes. But that made no sense. Why say yes to something that caused so much pain?

Her mate grumbled behind her. She sensed uncertainty in his scent.

Skye looked away. Too much unhappiness in that life. Never again. She'd be foolish to accept.

"No," she said.

"No," her mate echoed.

"Skye," the woman sobbed. Tears made wet, pale tracks in the soot on her face.

The sound tore into Skye's heart, and she shrank away, wanting to escape that emotion. She turned her back on the woman, hooking her arm into her mate's.

"You have your answer," Redring told the intruder.

"Redring," the Fat Frog warned, bobbing just outside the railings.

"She doesn't know her mind anymore!" The woman's voice grew strong again. "Change her back, change them both back, and I'll—I'll make a new deal with you."

The liaison growled and writhed, louder than ever. Slide stomped on his head, hard enough to knock him half-unconscious, and he fell silent.

Redring smiled at the woman. "I am listening. Amuse me. What kind of deal?"

The human glanced in fear at the liaison, then looked Redring in the eyes again. "Gold. That's what you want, right? I'll get you more. For my whole lifetime. More than he's getting for you—in addition to what he brings you."

An interesting tug-of-war of feelings battled in Skye: gold-lust combined with a strange abhorrence, a desire to keep the woman from agreeing to this deal. The abhorrence came only from that surviving kernel of humanity. It would fade before much longer; she only had to ride it out.

Redring edged between weapon points to draw out the intruder's necklace on her fingertip. "Starting with this little piece?" She snapped the yarn and clutched the gold ring in her palm.

The woman gasped, darted a look around, then held still, watching Redring.

"Ugh." Redring flung it aside. It bounced between the feet of other goblins, some of whom scrabbled for it, then grunted in disgust and let it fall again. "It's foul," Redring said. "It's local. It will take extra magic just to cleanse it. So that's how you got here." She bared her teeth in a menacing grin as the woman stared at her. "Thought you'd vanish if I stole that, did you? No, not once you stepped onto our lair. *We* hold you now. You will leave when we wish it."

"Then—then yes, take that gold, and more. How much more do you want, in exchange for letting us go, all four of us, unharmed, tonight?"

Above, the Fat Frog and other fae zipped back and forth, whispering in frantic consultation.

Redring considered the human. "Fifty times the weight of my ring. Every month."

The woman's gaze dropped to the talisman. "What does it weigh? Can I…" She reached out a hand toward it.

"Why, yes, weigh it in your hand and see. It is but a little trinket."

The woman cupped the ring in her palm, testing its weight. Then with a move she probably thought was fast—but pitifully clumsy to the eye of a goblin—she yanked at the chain.

Everyone shrieked. Redring leaped back, the ring still safe on its chain. Knives and arrows lunged at the woman, but the locals plunged in and blasted them back with a wall of air, a whirlwind knocking weapons asunder and keeping the intruder safe, temporarily. Skye knew her tribe would soon scatter the pests like a cloud of gnats. Indeed, seconds later they did, but Redring held up her palm to stop the tribe from attacking the woman.

The intruder crouched on hands and knees, cringing up at her. Redring swung her ring back and forth. "A sad attempt. As if *you* could break this chain, little mortal. Only a goblin is strong enough."

"Please." The woman's voice was low and serious. "I apologize. The deal, then."

"No, Olivia Darwen!" the Fat Frog insisted overhead.

"I'll do it, really I will," the woman continued. "If it'll save her…"

"I think not." Redring turned away and addressed Slide. "Escort these two humans off the premises. The fast way."

"No!" the woman begged.

Slide and another goblin stepped forward and grabbed her arms and legs. Two more did the same with the dazed liaison.

Flowerwatch scurried back and forth, mad with excitement. Skye and her mate stayed still, though she felt oddly agitated inside.

"We warn you for the last time, Redring," the Fat Frog said. "Put them down and do not harm them."

"You haven't the power to get rid of us," Redring told the frog. "You'd have done so by now if you could. You're weak." She turned to her goblins and barked, "Over the edge."

"No, please, no!" the woman said.

They lifted her and the liaison over the railings.

Redring watched, along with the rest of the frenzied tribe. Skye huddled with her mate, frozen.

Flowerwatch leaped. She tore the necklace from Redring's neck, spun, and flung it straight toward the frog.

The Fat Frog caught it, zoomed up out of reach, and hovered there.

"You stinking worm!" Redring picked up Flowerwatch and threw her against a wall. Flowerwatch yelped and slid down, and huddled on the deck. Redring rounded on Slide and the others. "Drop them! Kill them!"

"Olivia Darwen," the Fat Frog said, "do not fear—"

Whatever the frog was about to say, the humans wouldn't hear it, for the goblins dropped them both off the treehouse. A thin shriek from the woman, then Skye heard nothing but the tribe's yelps and shouts.

The pain locked in that tiny human dungeon cell inside her burst open like an explosion and broke the jail door off its hinges. She raced to the railing, her mate running beside her. Together they clutched the top rail and looked over. But from that height the ground was hidden by lacy layers of evergreen branches, swaying in the winter wind. The humans had fallen. They were gone.

A keening whimper escaped Skye's throat. Her mate echoed it. They looked at one another, shocked and confused.

CHAPTER THIRTY-FIVE

IT SHOULD HAVE BEEN DEATH. ONE COULDN'T FALL FROM THAT HIGH AND NOT DIE.

Livy plummeted, so terrified she couldn't even scream anymore after one brief wail. She and Kit crashed through conifer branches; needles and twigs lashed at her on the way before whipping back up. The next layer of branches had more heft to it; some of them bent and slowed their descent for a second before giving way.

Then another layer, maybe halfway down: this time the branches curled tangibly around their bodies, and Livy and Kit slowed considerably. She grabbed at the branches and began to hope. Then those branches creaked and broke too, and they plunged again.

Lights zipped above and around them, impossibly fast. Their fall slowed once more, and when Livy flailed to seize anything within reach, she found her arms stuck to something. She and Kit were sagging in some kind of net. She turned her head, and met his astonished gaze some ten feet away. He seemed to be shaking off the blow to the head. They were both caught in filmy white stuff that spun out between trees and was stretching down to accommodate them as they sank into it. Snow-covered branches? No, a spiderweb. The biggest, strongest, fastest-built spiderweb she had ever seen. Then the web tore and they fell again.

And landed with a thump on the ground, a foot below, safe and whole.

"Oh my God." Livy sat up, her clothes dusted with snow and webs. She crawled to Kit. She yanked the gag off him and cupped her hands around his face. "Hey."

He drank in the sight of her, blinking fiercely. "I thought…oh God, I thought you were dead, I thought we were both about to die, and that I'd never…"

She hugged him close, feeling him press against her with all his might, though his limbs were still tied and he couldn't embrace her. "You shouldn't have come," she said. Her eyes filled with fresh tears. "We failed." She looked toward the east, where the sky was lightening to gray in an open strip between tree trunks. "Dawn's almost here. We failed."

"Olivia Darwen." The frog zoomed down, still holding the ring with the red stone. Livy and Kit looked up. "We have just enough time," it said. "But the contract bound up in this ring involves powerful blood magic. To undo it and disband them will require a sacrifice."

"What kind?" Livy asked.

"Either something from each of the four of you, or the life blood of one of you."

"Take mine," Kit said at once.

Livy clapped her hand over his mouth. "No!" She looked the frog in the eyes. "Each of us. No one dies tonight." She glared down at Kit.

She could tell from his eyes that he smiled. He acquiesced with a nod.

"I will do my best to make it painless," the frog said. "But it will be permanent. Do you choose mind or body?"

"Permanent? Wait—what do you mean, mind or body?"

"To lose a piece of, from each of you."

Livy felt queasy, and drew in a breath to steady herself, but answered without hesitation. "Body." She thought of Skye and Grady, their minds compromised all this time; of Kit's mother, her memory lost toward the end of her life. No more losing any parts of their minds. She glanced down at Kit, and dropped her hand from his mouth.

He nodded. "Definitely."

"Then so be it." The frog flew up again, fast as a rocket.

Livy set about untangling Kit from his chains. "I thought this was over."

"I thought so too."

She shook off the last chain and they held each other tightly.

At that moment the fireworks began.

One second Grady was looking into the eyes of his mate, trying to comprehend the war of strange feelings inside him. The next second, the treehouses started falling apart. Sparks flashed on the dwellings and in the air all around. The magic holding up the village collapsed; boards, furniture, weapons, and everything else that had been transformed began turning back into gold and falling out of the trees. And the goblins started to fall too.

The tribe screeched, clawed, cursed, and hung onto branches and dangling boards. Redring yowled loudest of all, but she already looked smaller and weaker, and Grady felt the change deep in himself. The tribe's center was collapsing, all because the humans had finally found a way to work with those horrid locals—of which there were now hundreds, flitting around too fast to get a fix on them.

Grady and his mate leaped onto a board nailed to a branch. Just after they jumped, the central deck they'd left behind creaked, snapped, and went tumbling to the forest floor, carrying several screaming goblins. His mate clung to him. Their board wobbled. A whirlwind of locals bashed into them, tipping them and the board over. They squealed, but there was nothing they could do. They fell, smashing through branches, whipping through cold air, and hit the ground with a painful blow.

Everything in his body hurt. But they were immortal now, and healed almost at once. Two breaths after landing, he rose up on his knees, and caught his mate, who jumped into his arms. They knelt on the ground in the snow, staring around in amazement. Debris rained from the treetops, mostly gold trinkets that glittered bright in the icy blue of the forest, but also all the items that hadn't started out as gold: dried fruits, kitchen gadgets, blankets, shoes, bottles, cans, anything the goblins had stolen or been given by their liaisons.

Half the tribe scampered around grabbing gold and fighting each other over it. The other half, including Redring, formed a snarling circle around the intruder and the liaison, who crouched, unhurt, on the forest floor, staring at the tribe.

Fae sparks swirled down among them, and a second later a ring of fire whooshed up between goblins and humans. Both parties yelped and drew back from the flames, but no one seemed hurt. The fire stayed in its perfect circle.

Then a wind—a wind with hands and talons all over it—surrounded Grady and his mate. It picked them up, flew them over the flames, and deposited them at the feet of the two humans. It all happened so swiftly he hardly had time to take a single breath.

Though the drop was short, the landing made everything hurt again, and this time the pain lingered. He curled up on the ground, groaning, as his body underwent a flood of pins and needles and cramps and burns.

"Grady!" It was Kit's voice. A second later his cousin threw a coat over his back.

The pain eased, at least partly, and Grady found he was shaking like a leaf, cold beyond endurance, naked in the snow. His skin was pale and soft and human again. Kit's thick black winter coat was draped around him. He clutched it shut, staggered to his feet, and looked in horror and remorse at his cousin. Grady had stood by and done nothing while they tried to kill Kit and Livy.

"Oh my God," Grady said. "Oh my God, I'm so sorry."

Kit was bloodied, bruised, and dirty, but he beamed and clapped a hand on Grady's shoulder. "Not your fault. It's good to see you back."

Around them the ring of fire still held off the furiously screaming goblins.

Next to them, Skye and Livy sat on their knees, locked in a tight hug, tears running down their cheeks. Skye was bare-legged and bundled in Livy's mud-smeared coat, her hair a disheveled mess. Still beautiful.

Tears stung Grady's eyes. His stomach churned. Everything he'd done with her, *to* her, all the things she'd never have wanted from him if it hadn't been for magic…it was unforgivable. So many things he'd done in the past month just shouldn't be forgiven.

The frog faery darted over, and addressed the goblins. "These humans have been returned to their rightful tribe, and your contract with this man's bloodline has been broken, paid for in blood by these four."

Livy and Skye rose. The four of them exchanged a bewildered glance. Paid for in blood?

"You have no right!" Redring yelled from the other side of the fire.

"We have every right," the frog said. "Furthermore, your unjust actions against this tribe, and against all of ours numerous times, give us the right to take permanent action against you. Goblin tribe, you are disbanded and transformed, and shall never be goblin again."

"You cannot!"

Redring's howl was lost in a wave of whistling, sizzling, splashing, and cracking. Sparks and lightning flashed. Snow evaporated to steam. The ground rumbled and bits of earth and moss landed upon Grady and the others from some minor explosion nearby.

The ring of fire fluttered down and became a circle of magenta fireweed blossoms, which hopped away and vanished.

Grady, Kit, Skye, and Livy stood in a stunned cluster and watched the vanquished tribe get apportioned out to the four elements. Some became seals, jellyfish, or other swimming creatures; an impromptu stream formed from the snow's meltwater, and they dove into it and splashed out of the forest in the direction of the Sound. Others took the shapes of mushrooms or gnomes, and burrowed into the ground and disappeared under beds of moss. Another quadrant flashed away as sparks and tiny dragons, leaving a whiff of smoke in the air. The rest became moths or birds or bats, and twirled into the sky on transparent wings.

The last to be turned was Flowerwatch. She cowered alone, trembling. The frog descended to almost ground level, and spoke to her kindly. "For your assistance, I am pleased to let you choose your tribe. I only regret I cannot any longer return you to humankind, for it has been too long and surely you would die."

Flowerwatch nodded, stunned. "Then…air. Becoming a flying creature is one of my few joys. Thank you."

The frog gave her a nod, and the white cloudy forms of air fae swirled around her and obscured her form. A second later, a new moth arose, pale blue and decorated with marks on its wings that reminded Grady of flowers. She and her new tribe soared upward into the dawn sky, and flickered out of sight.

A startled gasp from Skye drew Grady's attention. She splayed her left hand in front of her. "My finger!"

Livy lifted her own hands. "Oh!"

Kit and Grady checked theirs out too.

"Well, shit." Kit sounded shaken.

His ears ringing in shock, Grady stared at his right hand, on which his smallest finger was completely missing, as if it had never existed. He turned to compare with Kit's: same deal. Livy and Skye stretched theirs out, the four of them in a huddle, hands in the center. Missing pinkies all around, healed and totally painless, just gone.

"Blood payment," Livy said.

"Guess that counts," Kit said.

"Left hand for me," Skye said. "Right for the rest of you. Our dominant hands."

"How are we going to explain this to our families?" Grady asked.

Skye met his gaze for a second. She had spoken freely, and her features looked mobile rather than spell-fettered—all of which was a dream come true. But she looked ill, probably mired in remorse and disgust, just as he was. That is, he was only disgusted at having had sex in front of the goblins, not at having had sex with her—never that, not even with the spell finally torn out of his head. What if she was disgusted at having been with him? God, she would hate him once she thought about everything for a few seconds. She should hate him.

Sure enough, her gaze slid down after a moment, and she looked more nauseated than before. He felt like he'd been quietly stabbed. He looked away.

"Your families will already know," the frog said. Grady looked up, through his shivers and heartbreak, and focused on the golden creature. "It is part of the spell. It will be as if your fingers never existed, in everyone else's memories."

"Even in photos and things?" Livy asked.

"The spell should affect all records. Brave humans, you have done well. You are free of the goblins, as are we, and we thank you for helping us forge a path to them."

"What happened to Redring?" Kit asked. "I didn't see."

"We sent her to the water fae," the frog said. "It was merciful of us. Her mate was turned to water-nix, long ago, far away. There is always the chance she might yet find him. Even if she does not, her angry soul can be healed in the seas, and her vengefulness turned to better cause. Now we must return you to your tribe, as well."

"Wait," Livy said. "What if we need you again? Can I summon you?"

"You may try." The frog flicked its wing. The four-element gold ring flew through the air from somewhere in the forest and bounced at Livy's feet. She picked it up. "But we only answer if there is reason," the frog added, "and I doubt you will have reason. Nonetheless, Olivia Darwen, our protection will always extend over you in thanks for your kindness to our home. It will extend over you all, so long as you keep showing our woods and waters such respect."

They all nodded at once in agreement.

"I'm free?" Kit sounded stunned. "The liaison contract, it's really gone?"

"You are free," the frog said. "I am sure none of you will enter lightly into any agreement with the fae again."

"Hell, no," Skye said, speaking quite well for all of them.

"Before you go, you are free to take any gold you wish, or other goods." The frog turned, drawing back to look at the wreckage of the lair scattered all over the ground. "We have no use of it, and it belongs rightfully to humans."

"Seriously?" Now Kit sounded as delighted as a mega-lottery winner.

"Indeed. It will only lie here to be found by other humans."

"I promise you," Kit said, already stepping forward toward the loot, "I'm going to return as much of it as I can to the people it came from."

"Or donate the money to environmental charities, if we can't find the rightful owners." Livy waded in and crouched to scoop up jewelry. "That'd be a fitting use, right?"

"For sure." Kit found a tin box and began filling it with treasure.

After another tentative glance at Skye that once again left her looking upset, Grady wandered into the debris, wretched, and started picking stuff up. So did Skye. Before long they had both found the clothes they'd been wearing, crumpled on the ground and damp with melted snow, and put them back on. He was still shivering so hard his teeth clattered together.

"Dawn is upon us," the frog said. "Rest well today."

"Thank you," Livy said. Kit and Skye echoed the words, fervently.

Grady glanced up to add his thanks, but the creature had already vanished. Gray-blue sky lightened the spaces between trees. The darkness was evaporating; he could see deeper now into the snowy woods. The forest looked ordinary again, though he couldn't pinpoint what had changed exactly, other than the disappearance of the glowing frog and the passing of the night.

God, he was exhausted.

"You guys ready?" Kit tucked his box of gold under his arm, holding a bulging sack in the other hand. "I left the truck on the road right over there."

"Thank God." Livy wrapped up the bundle of gold she had piled in an old curtain. "I think we all need to shower and then sleep for, like, a day and a half."

"For sure." Skye shuffled up next to her, holding a coffee can full of treasure. She and Livy turned toward the truck.

Grady followed, his pajama pockets stuffed with jewelry.

Kit fell into step beside him and tapped his elbow against Grady's. "You all right?"

Grady nodded, though his head still ached, along with most of his joints. "Just...have to process all this."

They came out onto the road, where the prosaic sight of Kit's dented truck was the most comforting thing Grady had seen in a long time. Kit opened the passenger door for Skye and Livy. He frowned at Livy's clothes, which looked even filthier in the brightening light of dawn. "Liv, what did they make you do, anyway? What happened to you?"

"Oh…" She clambered into the cab with a grunt. "Nature."

Grady got in last, squished between Livy and the door. Skye sat on one of Livy's legs, to give Kit enough room to drive. It should've been Grady's lap she sat on. Now she barely looked at him. Grady shut his eyes and rested his head against the cold window.

"Nature how?" Kit started the truck, and began driving down the bumpy road.

"Well, first," Livy said, "I crawled through a tunnel of dirt under the island. Then I crawled an underwater path across the bottom of the inlet. *Then* I had to walk through a forest fire. And *then* I had to climb into the canopy, like a hundred feet off the ground, and jump from tree to tree to get to the goblins' lair."

Amazed silence from everyone for a second. Grady opened his eyes and blinked at her.

"Damn," Kit said.

"I suppose you think you're so bad-ass now." Skye employed the skeptically teasing tone that could only come from a sister. Grady knew it well from his own siblings, but he'd never had the opportunity to hear it from Skye.

"I kind of do, yeah," Livy informed her, loftily.

Skye leaned her shoulder against Livy's. "That's because you completely are."

She was *smiling*. Only for Livy. It made Grady's heart hurt in a weird mix of happiness and sorrow.

"You are," Grady murmured to Livy, because even in the middle of his turmoil he couldn't forget the immense thanks he owed her.

Livy acknowledged him with a smile, then tipped her head back and closed her eyes.

Skye yawned loudly and did the same. "So. Tired."

They re-entered Bellwater, and soon pulled up at Skye and Livy's house. Grady hopped down to let them out. While Livy slid over to kiss Kit goodbye, Skye and Grady stood in their pajamas in the ankle-deep snow in the cul-de-sac, shivering and gazing unhappily at each other.

"You must hate me," Grady said. "Just…everything. I'm so sorry."

She pulled her eyebrows together. "What? No. You must hate *me*. What I did to you…" She shuddered, a level above her cold shivers, and looked away.

"How could you even—no. Of course I don't."

Livy climbed down. "Laundry," she said, running her glance over

Skye's clothes and her own. "After sleep and shower. God, what a night. You ready to warm up?"

Skye nodded. She met Grady's glance again, but kept her arms folded tight; no hug on offer. "We'll be in touch. After…sleeping, and everything."

"Yeah."

She was probably right. No use trying to sort this out until they'd rested and recovered. Still, he ached for some word of reassurance as he watched them shamble toward their house. Receiving none, he climbed back into the truck.

"Well." Kit rolled toward Shore Avenue. "Back to the world of the living." Even through Kit's exhaustion, happiness bubbled up in his words. He was suddenly free of what had been a lifelong obligation.

Grady was pleased for him. In a cerebral sense, at least. He was also, in theory, pleased to be unshackled from his own curse, and back among the ordinary human world. But now what? Get busy again searching for jobs and an apartment, off in Seattle?

He'd do it, he supposed, but the plan didn't carry much sparkle anymore. Nothing did, not if Skye didn't want to be with him.

Grady wasn't sure at all that he wasn't still under some kind of spell.

CHAPTER THIRTY-SIX

SLEEP. SO MUCH SLEEP. A BRIEF AWAKENING, THEN A CRASH BACK INTO SLEEP. THEN ANOTHER FAILED ATTEMPT TO keep her eyes open, and more sleep after that. In Livy's brief glance at the room, she registered it was still daylight, and therefore she and Skye and the Sylvain cousins were safe, just in case any goblins still existed.

The smell of fresh coffee finally woke her properly. It drifted into her room from the kitchen, where she heard the clink of utensils. She glanced at the window—still light out. The alarm clock said it was a little after three p.m. She got out of bed.

Skye sat at the kitchen table, drawing in her sketchbook. She was wrapped in hoodie and sweatpants, hair held back in a bandanna. A mug of coffee and a half-eaten piece of toast with cheddar cheese melted on top of it sat next to her. Hip-hop played from Skye's phone through the small speakers on the kitchen counter.

Livy hesitated in the door frame. "Hey," she said. The music and the food were good signs, but what if her sister answered in only echoes again? What if the smiles from last night had vanished?

Skye looked up, flashed her a brief smile, and said in a tired voice, "Hey. Have some coffee. I made a whole pot."

Livy's tension washed away. She took a moment just to breathe, and to thank the local fae in her mind, over and over. Then she shuffled forward, ready at last for coffee. "Awesome. Wow, how did I sleep longer than you?"

Skye's pencil scraped and swished as she shaded part of her sketch. "From the sound of it, you worked way harder than the rest of us last night. Still, I only got up fifteen minutes ago myself."

Livy poured a mug of coffee and sat across from Skye. She peeled a cheese-coated crust off Skye's toast and ate it. "Are you drawing stuff from last night?" She could make out what looked to be a ring of flames and a bunch of spark-like things.

"Yeah. As much as I can." Skye winced, squeezed her eyes shut, then opened them wide and blinked a few times. "Ugh. I still feel like crap. But I wanted to get it down before I forgot. I'll want details on all the things you saw, too."

"I know, I should've taken pictures. I wasn't sure it was allowed. I wonder if you even can take pictures of them."

"Doubt it. I tried to take a photo of the glowing mushroom path that got me into all this shit, and it only turned out looking like ordinary mushrooms." Skye kept sketching, her hand dashing back and forth. "Anyway, I bet I could make a graphic novel out of this. It's fairly epic. Argh." The pencil slipped under her thumb and went rolling across the table. She wiped graphite off the side of her hand, and picked the pencil back up. "Trying to draw without your pinky takes some getting used to."

Livy's face hurt from smiling so wide. "You have no idea how good it is to hear you babbling like a freak again."

Skye smirked. "Yeah, well. I still don't want any fruit desserts."

"Fair enough. I'm starving, now that you mention it." Livy got up, wincing as all her muscles protested. She staggered to the fridge and examined the food inside. "I could make eggs. Would you eat eggs?"

"Sure."

"I guess today we can't force Grady to come cook for us." Livy took out the egg carton.

Skye didn't answer.

Livy found skillet and spatula, and bowl and whisk. "Have you heard from the guys?"

"No." Skye kept her back turned, still sketching.

Livy picked up her own phone, plugged into the charger beside Skye's, and checked messages. "Me neither. They must still be asleep."

Skye didn't answer that either.

Livy sent a text to Kit, for whenever he woke up: *Hey, all ok here I think. How are you guys?*

Then she navigated to email. "Message from Mom. Seeing how we're doing after the snowstorm. Sounds like it hit Portland too."

"Mm. Already melting here, though."

Livy glanced out the window to find Skye was right; holes and slumped edges had appeared in the blanket of snow, and a drizzle was falling, eroding away the white. "Typical western Washington." Livy put down the phone and set about making scrambled eggs.

She waited until she and Skye had eaten them, along with more toast and leftover salad, before bringing up what was seemingly the most sensitive topic.

"So. With Grady. Was that only a spell?"

Skye sighed a ponderous, drawn-out sigh. She slumped back in her chair and spent a while folding the dishtowel that lay across her lap. "Well, it *was*, but…I don't know. Mainly I just hope he doesn't hate me." She leaned forward to rest her forehead in both hands.

"I really don't think he hates you."

"I almost ruined his life! And I molested him, like, constantly."

"He looked to be enjoying the molesting just fine."

"He was enchanted."

"Exactly," Livy said. "So were you. So no hard feelings on either side, right?"

Skye groaned, keeping her face hidden.

"Okay, it's awkward," Livy said. "I get that."

"So awkward."

"Well, what do you want to have happen?"

Skye massaged her forehead and scalp. "I'm still not sure I can trust my wants."

"Of course you can. The spell is off you, I can tell."

"I don't believe it yet." Skye stayed slumped over, face covered.

"It's okay, no rush." Livy picked up her plate and Skye's, and rose. "You guys'll sort it out."

"Eventually. Ugh. I feel awful, like I have the flu. Everything aches. Walking is hard."

"I bet. Well, take it easy. Rest up." Livy took the plates to the dishwasher, then washed out the skillet in the sink. She glanced back at the table as she dried the spatula with a towel.

Skye had turned to a page covered with sketches of Grady: his profile, his back, his hand holding a kitchen knife, his foot in a sock. Leaning her temple on her knuckles, Skye drank in the drawings, her face naked with sadness and longing.

Hey. We're alive, doing ok, Kit texted back to Livy, after waking up enough to function. He limped down the stairs and into the kitchen, opened the fridge, and swigged some milk from the carton. He leaned against the island counter and glanced at Grady, who was still in bed but awake, blinking at the ceiling.

"Think the bastards twisted my ankle throwing me around," Kit told him.

Grady raked his hand through his hair. "Yeah. Sore all over here. Nothing broken, I don't think. Just…missing." He splayed his fingers above his face. His voice sounded husky and tired, but at least he was talking.

"Uh-huh. Already dropped my phone the first time I picked it up. Just because of one little finger gone. Who knew."

A text buzzed in from Livy. *Good. How's Grady? Back to himself?*

Grady got out of bed and staggered into the bathroom, and shut the door.

More or less I guess, Kit answered. *Skye?*

He set the phone down and started scouting for food. He decided on a box of freezer waffles and took it out.

Livy's answer came back. *Talking, drawing, sometimes smiling! Still... I think it's serious. The relationship drama I mean ;)*

Grady came out of the bathroom, slumped onto one of the bar stools, and scowled at the box of waffles.

Kit held the box up. "I was going to toast some of these. Want one?"

Grady met his gaze, his blue eyes accusatory and offended. He shoved up from the stool and came around into the kitchen. "Out. Go. I'm making crepes."

Kit backed off, grinning.

Grady picked up the box of waffles and deposited it back into the freezer with a derogatory twist of his lips. When he glanced at Kit again, Kit gave him a big exaggerated double thumbs-up, just to make sure he could get him to smile.

It was a brief smile, accompanied by a soft snort, but there it was.

While Grady pulled out eggs, milk, flour, and mixing bowls, Kit perched on a stool and responded to Livy's text: *I got him to smile and he's cooking crepes, so, score. But yeah I think you're right. Those two have shit to sort out.*

Sitting in bed with her multicolored comforter tucked around her, Skye finally dared to text Grady. *Hey. The sun's set and I have no wish to go*

into the woods. So, that's good. How are you?

She chewed her lip and wiggled her toes for the interminable three minutes it took him to answer.

Nice, yeah, me neither. Feeling ok then?

I guess. Super tired. Going back to bed, just wanted to check in with you.

Yeah, I'm worn out too, he answered. *We should get together and talk tomorrow if you're up to it.*

Definitely. She drew in a stabilizing breath and added, *What you said this morning…honestly I don't hold anything against you. I still think it's you who should be pissed at me.*

Again it took him too long to respond, and she clenched her sweaty four-fingered hand in the edge of the comforter as she waited.

Well I'm not, he said. *It wasn't your fault.*

I knew they were watching us in the woods. And I did it anyway, all those times. Now aren't you pissed?

That's…creepy but still not your fault.

Still, he didn't elaborate. She sat weighing options about what to say, wondering what he was thinking, picturing him frowning over his phone screen in the cabin on the island. This was all so awkward. So mixed-up.

A new message from him finally appeared: *Sorry, I'm just really beat. I'll be able to make more sense tomorrow. I hope.*

He was exhausted. So was she. But it didn't stop her from wishing they could jump over all the explanations and land on the space marked *Happy.*

Happy and dating, though? Or happy and just friends? Which did he want? Which did she want?

Of course, sorry, she typed back. *We'll meet up tomorrow.*

She tried to think of more to say, maybe something about how it would be good to speak to him, to see him smile. But she got the impression he wasn't ready to process any more sentiment tonight.

Goodnight, see you then, he texted while she deliberated.

Night, she responded.

Great. Echoing again.

Chapter Thirty-Seven

LYING ON HIS SIDE ON THE SOFA-BED, GRADY GAZED AT THE LEAPING FLAMES IN THE FIREPLACE. HE AND KIT HAD KEPT it burning all day to thaw themselves out, and by now his bed a couple of yards away from the hearth had gotten quite toasty. Still, he didn't feel particularly comforted.

He brought up the messages from Skye again to review them. *We'll meet up tomorrow. I don't hold anything against you.* Could be encouraging, looking at it one way. Could be the groundwork to breaking up with him, looking at it another. Hard to know.

Was there really anything to break off, though? Their relationship had all been a magical illusion. Sure, the sex had really happened, but maybe it didn't count under those circumstances. She'd be completely within her rights to tell him it didn't, and to declare she'd rather not pretend there was anything between them.

So if it had all been illusion, and the spell had been lifted, why did he hurt so much?

He looked at his four-fingered hand. No getting out of this situation without a few lasting scars, apparently.

He sat up, tapped the contacts in his phone, and dialed home.

His mom answered, over in Moses Lake. "Hello, Grady!" Her cheerful sing-song greeting made his eyes sting with tears again.

"Hey, Mom."

"How's Bellwater? All covered in snow like we are?"

He blinked the tears back, sniffled, and steadied his voice. "Yeah. Or at least, it was. It's melting now."

"We got over a foot and it's not going anywhere. So what's new, other than that?"

"Not a lot. Hey, I just wondered…you know how, um…I have four fingers on one hand?" He held his breath.

She chuckled. "Yeeees, I've been aware of that since the minute you were born. We said, 'Hurray, ten toes, and, oh, *nine* fingers.' As we've told you."

He lifted his eyebrows, astonished. "Right. Uh. I was just…trying to remember what you used to tell people. When I was a kid. If they asked about it."

"Oh, lots of things. We called it your 'lucky hand.' We said, 'Who needs a pinky anyway, what's that good for?' And so on. You remember this."

Wow. Magic. Kind of scary, actually.

"Right. A kid was asking me, and I…somehow couldn't remember exactly. Anyway. What's up with you guys?"

As she chatted about her latest recipes, his dad trying to sell one of the cars, and his siblings' tests and social lives, Grady drew up his knees and watched the fire, listening and murmuring, "Uh-huh." He still suffered a Skye-shaped wound inside him, but he felt a little less desolate now. His life did contain reason enough for him to go on living, he supposed. Or close enough.

From the stash of gold he'd gathered in the woods, Kit took at least $5,000 worth of jewelry and other pieces, and dumped them into a manila envelope. All of them were items he couldn't remember obtaining himself and therefore wouldn't be able to find a rightful owner for. After sunset, while Grady was on the phone with his parents, Kit told him from across the cabin, "Going out for a bit."

Grady nodded to him, then glanced away, talking to his folks.

Kit drove to the forest, to his customary spot below the former site of the goblin dwellings. With the envelope full of treasure, he trudged through the leaf litter, wiggled between trunks, and stopped in the tight clump of trees. The smell of wet ashes hung in the air, possibly left behind by last night's ring of fire. He'd have to go looking for scorch marks during daylight sometime.

He whistled a few notes upward.

No one answered.

He whistled more of the song. Still nothing. He tried singing it aloud, only the notes, since he didn't know any words for it—"Da da da doooo, dadada da daaaa…"—like a complete lunatic.

Whole song. Still no answer.

"Aren't you guys going to show?" Kit called to the darkness. He was grinning. "Check it out! Whole huge bag of gold here." He grabbed a fistful of it and held it up. "Don't you want it?" His heart beat swiftly; his instincts still expected that sinister laughter, those twiggy arms appearing out of nowhere to snatch away the gold.

Nothing happened.

He tipped his head back and laughed, almost as maniacally as the goblins used to. "You sure?" he shouted to the forest. "You're done with me, for real?"

The wind gusted, and a few fir needles sprinkled down onto him, along with something a bit heavier that slid past his wrist and landed on his boot. He crouched to pick it up, and recognized the slender gold chain with three hearts on it. The one he'd brought in December, that had served as the inadequate monthly payment that caused them to enchant Skye in retribution.

Maybe the necklace had gotten caught on the branches when everything fell down last night, and was just now shaking loose. But Kit didn't think the timing could be quite that coincidental. He tucked it into the envelope along with the rest of the loot, and glanced up into the trees. "Thanks, locals."

He strolled to the truck, leaned against it, and stood breathing the rich mossy air for a minute, appreciating being out here and being left alone.

Then he texted Livy.

I'm free. Tried to summon them with a huge pile of gold, and nothing happened. They're just gone. I'm free. Holy shit, I'm really free.

Free as that whale on your back :) , she answered a minute later. *I am so happy for you.*

All thanks to you, babe. Don't think I'll forget it.

You can thank me tomorrow. I'm going to bed. Goodnight, lucky man.

CHAPTER THIRTY-EIGHT

I HAVE SOME FREE TIME BEFORE MY WORK SHIFT, Skye's text said the next morning. *Say around 11. Can you meet up?*

It was a little after ten. Grady was already at the auto shop with Kit and Justin, doing a brisk trade in scheduling repairs for people who had dented their cars on the icy roads over the last couple of days. He texted back, *Yeah sure, that'd be good. Where?*, without checking with Kit first.

Kit wouldn't be mad. He seemed incapable of being mad today. He'd been joking with everyone and bopping around the garage like he hadn't been chained up and thrown out of a tree the other night.

Dock behind Green Fox, Skye answered. *See you there.*

Cool, I'll be there. Grady bolted out of the office and buttonholed Kit on his way past. "I need to take off at eleven for a little while. I have to… talk to her," he admitted.

Kit beamed, and thumped him on the arm. "'Course you do. Go for it." He looked past Grady, and strolled onward. "Edna, hey! Good to see you in town, m'lady."

At 10:55, Grady rushed down Shore Avenue on foot, and turned between the kayak rental shop and Green Fox Espresso, following the gravel driveway that led to a small dock.

The snow had melted overnight under a steady rain. Today the sun shone, drawing vapors of mist up from the wet dock boards and the surface of the Sound. The air was calm, and for early February it felt almost warm.

One side of the dock was open to the water, to allow for kayak launching. A wooden railing bordered the other side. Skye leaned her elbows on it, looking out at the water. She wore skinny jeans, a slouchy maroon knit hat, rain boots, and her thigh-length dark wool coat, buttoned tight around her middle. Grady approached, his legs weakening. The lining of that coat was silver-colored and smooth; she'd worn it into the woods with him lots of times, and he knew exactly how it felt on the backs of his hands when he reached under her clothes.

His insides felt like they were shredding themselves apart.

She noticed him. Her face was solemn and apprehensive, the way she had looked that day he'd walked into her kitchen the first time. So many firsts, so many memories, all in a single month.

"Hey," she said.

He walked onto the dock and settled his elbows beside hers on the railing, not quite touching her. "Hey."

"How are you and Kit doing?"

"Pretty good. Kit especially. He's basically thrilled." He smiled for a second.

He caught a smile in response, though only briefly. "I bet." She rolled her lips together and looked out across the shining water again. "So. Seriously, listen, I am really, really sorry. I almost destroyed your life. I was shameless about it. I mean, I regretted it, even at the time, but I couldn't stop, and—I'm just so sorry. I can't say that enough."

Grady breathed in and out. The air smelled of cold saltwater, fresh but somehow lonely. "No, look, I'm the one who's sorry. I completely took advantage of you when you were…not yourself. I can't stand it. I can't believe I did that."

"You wouldn't have done it, though, not normally. You were under a spell. And I'm the one who dragged you into it."

"You were under a spell too. It wasn't your choice." He exchanged a cautious glance with her. She didn't look offended, only worried. "So," he added, "we're both sorry. I forgive you, though I really don't think you did anything wrong."

"I forgive you too," she said. "Though, likewise."

That encouraged him a little. "Then we can stop talking about being sorry and how we should hate each other?"

She nodded, turning her face outward again. "Definitely. No hate. So now what? Back to normal?"

He let his gaze float down the shore to the white masts at the marina. "Finding jobs. Guess we have to do that."

"You were going to move to Seattle maybe."

"Yeah. Don't know yet. You had graphic-design leads?"

"A few. I'll look around. I don't know where I'll live yet, either. Maybe here, maybe somewhere else." She lifted her chin and set her shoulders back. "Which is all really stressful. But hey, not as stressful as being under a curse."

"Right. Well." Unhappiness dragged at him like an anchor. He surrendered and let himself slip under. He cradled his forehead in his hands, staring unfocused at the water. "I'm still scared, though. I don't think the spell is totally gone. I'm thinking about you all the time. I still…love you. So doesn't that mean I'm still enchanted?"

He couldn't look at her, and it took her a few seconds to answer. When she did, he heard kindness in her voice. "I don't think so. I think maybe that's the natural thing to feel after you go through a major experience with someone."

He sent her a sideways glance. Though he was afraid to ask, he pushed the words out. "Is that how *you* feel?"

"Yeah. It is."

This time he held her gaze, letting his hands lower again, settling them along the railing. The prettiest pink color had bloomed in her cheeks, and she wore a tender smile. "I don't feel enchanted," she added. "But I do love you."

A grin broke across his face, unstoppable as sunrise. "It's so good to see you smile. You have no idea."

Skye closed the space between them, fitting herself into his arms, against his body, in the way that had become habit for them. "You too, stranger."

He shut his eyes and held her, breathing in the smell of her shampoo, feeling he might break into pieces from the sheer force of being in love. She lifted her face and kissed him, and he sank into that happy occupation for several long breaths.

When they pulled back an inch, she looked at him, her gaze sharpening with amazement. "Was it just me, or was the sex incredible? Even though it seems like it should be all wrong to think that."

"Oh my God, it was fantastic," he said with fervent sincerity.

She laughed—and hearing her laugh was ten times better than seeing her smile, and he had to kiss her again for another minute or two solid.

Then he relaxed his hold on her, and looked toward the marina with a hopeless head-shake. "So I mean, do I stay in Bellwater just to be near you? Work at the auto shop? I guess I'd find my own place to live so I wouldn't drive Kit crazy, but…"

"No." She poked her finger into the middle of his chest. "No auto shop for you, Awesome Chef. Don't you dare. Go find somewhere that appreciates your skills."

"But that's…almost certainly not going to be around here."

"I know." She sighed. "I hate it, but, look. Go find a job you love. Go there, to it. It'll probably be in another city, but we'll manage. And I'll look for something too, and maybe it'll be near you, if we're lucky, and maybe it won't, but that's how we have to do it. We have to prove we aren't codependent. We aren't enchanted. We're responsible adults who *can* live in separate towns if we have to, without wasting away. We have to give it time and see what we think about…you know. An actual relationship."

The mere idea of living in a different city from her made Grady feel like pouting and whining, if not outright wasting away. But he did grasp her point. He summoned up the maturity to nod. "You're right. We ought to be responsible. It's important."

She looked sad for a second, then smiled again. "Do you have time to get coffee and have a real conversation? One where I actually talk? See if we can stand each other in real life."

He turned toward the cafe, sliding an arm around her. "Yeah. Let's."

"Hey, Livy," her boss at the Forest Service said over the phone. "You live in Bellwater, right?"

She had pulled over to take the call, on her way to the Quilcene office. "Yeah, why?"

"We heard from DNR that someone reported fire damage in the national forest just west of there." The state's Department of Natural Resources was often the first agency to receive reports of forest fires, and passed along word to the Forest Service. "They checked on it and said it's out," he continued, "but an acre or so got burned, probably from lightning. Did you hear about it? When could that have happened? I mean, jeez, it's been so wet, not to mention frozen. Did you guys have lightning with that storm the other night?"

Livy's mouth fell open. Her mind temporarily relived the walk through the roaring fire, trees blackening all around her. She hadn't been back there in daylight to look; she had assumed it was all fire-fae illusion. "Um," she said, "maybe? It was kind of a crazy night. You know what, is it okay if I go back there right now and have a look?"

"Yeah, could you, actually? That'll get us a head start on mapping any damage. I'll email you the location."

"Thanks." Not that she'd need it. She had a pretty good idea where that fire damage would be. "Talk to you soon. Bye."

She hung up, flipped a U-turn on the quiet two-lane highway, and sped back toward Bellwater.

Within half an hour, she stood staring at a swath of blackened trunks and scorched undergrowth. She snapped a few photos, and sent one to Kit with the text, *Wow. Guess those fire fae were for real.*

Whoa, he responded. *Thought I smelled something burned last night, but couldn't see much in the dark. You still over there?*

Yeah, checking it out to report on it for work, ha, she answered.

Stay there. I'll come.

In a little while, his truck growled up the Forest Service road and stopped, its roof just visible through the bushes. He swung the creaky door shut and tromped through the forest to her, where he stood with hands on hips, surveying the burn.

"Damn," he said.

"Yeah, I'm surprised. But it's all right, actually." She touched the charred bark of a giant cedar. "Most of these trees'll be fine. They can survive a certain amount of fire, especially one that burns through quick like that. It's good for them, even."

"Huh. What are you going to tell work?"

"That we had some freak lightning, I guess. Which is true. Caused by fire fae, but I'll leave that part out."

"Good call."

His gaze drifted down to her, and he smiled. Leaning back on his boot heels, hands in his jacket pockets, he looked utterly content.

"Listen," she said, "you finally get to be free now. I know you're grateful to me, and I was happy to do it, and I would have done it all for Skye anyway, even without you and Grady mixed up in it. So you don't have to feel tied to me. I swear I'll understand, if you want to be—well, free. Like you deserve."

He drew his eyebrows down, puzzled. "What are you talking about? You think I was lying the other night?"

"Not lying, just…under certain stresses. As we all were."

He lowered his face, and scuffed at ashes with his boot. "Ah. So *you* want your freedom. Well, I get that, but I'll tell you now, I'm not thrilled. I intend to argue with you about it."

"No, no. I…come on. I love you. But…you want to roam the world. You'll have money; you'll get to do that. And you should. Me, I like it here and I'm staying, but why would you stay?"

Kit's smile rekindled. He sauntered two steps closer. "A, because I like it here too, as we've discussed. B, because you're here, and I love you. So C—should this be C?—yes, I want to enjoy not having to steal, and getting to save money, and doing things with it I've been meaning to do. Travel, restore cars, fix up the cabin, hire extra help at the garage. But can't I do all that and also have a girlfriend?" He took one more step, and hovered within reach. "Do I have a girlfriend?" he added, husky and vulnerable now.

Everything had gone blurry through the happy tears in Livy's eyes. She jumped forward and hugged him. "Yes. Definitely, yes. Okay, you've convinced me, no need to argue."

When they kissed, Livy wondered if fae disguised as ferns or mushrooms or crows were watching.

They'd always been watching. She could live with that. Just part of the local color.

CHAPTER THIRTY-NINE

SKYE DROVE DOWN THE WINDING HIGHWAY ON A FRIDAY MORNING, HER VOLKSWAGEN PACKED TO THE ROOF WITH boxes. Sprays of white and pink glimmered in the greening forest that lined the road: Indian plum, red currant, and salmonberry in bloom. Spring had arrived. Not everyone knew the names of those plants, but when you had a sister in the Forest Service, you learned that kind of thing.

Her chest ached at the thought of Livy, and her eyes still felt tender from the tears she'd shed this morning upon hugging her goodbye and moving out of their house. But happiness swept back in like a spring breeze at the reminder of where she was heading: an hour and a half south, to Olympia. To Grady.

Grady had taken a cooking job at an upscale bistro in Olympia, and found an apartment there. He and Skye had continued liking each other in real life just fine, it turned out. They'd lasted almost two months living in separate towns, driving to see each other every weekend or whenever they had days off. Then Skye found a position with a graphic design firm in Olympia, where she would start work on Monday. So it only made sense to move in with him.

In her spare time she was also hard at work on her graphic novel, tentatively titled *The Goblins of Bellwater*. A small press was already interested, having loved the first few pages she sent them.

Besides, she'd still see her sister a lot. She and Grady vowed to get together with Kit and Livy as often as they could. In the meantime, she'd left Livy a little present to find when she got back from work today.

Skye smiled.

❧

Livy read the text from Skye as she walked to the front door after work.

Arrived and moved in! Btw, look behind the winter coats in the front closet ;)

"Hmm." The intrigue lightened Livy's melancholy at coming home to an empty house. She leaped up the front steps and unlocked the door.

Against the closet wall behind the coats she found a two-foot-tall framed picture wrapped in brown paper—no, four framed pictures stacked together, she realized as she tugged them out.

Kneeling on the front hall tiles among dried muddy boot-tracks, Livy unwrapped the framed paintings, and laughed aloud even as tears rose in her eyes.

Skye's art took vintage-travel-poster style this time, and featured an intrepid Livy in each frame.

In the first, she wriggled through a black and brown tunnel of dirt with roots stretching into it and spotted red mushrooms sprouting above. *THE EARTH LOVES YOU IN OLYMPIC NATIONAL FOREST*, said the all-caps hand-lettering.

In the second, a shining blue sea-star path led her into the Sound with the green water parting magically around her boots. Skye had lettered *DIVE INTO BEAUTIFUL PUGET SOUND* in the night sky above.

The third showed Livy dashing through red and orange flames with her coat pulled over her nose and a dragon soaring past, with the title *WESTERN WASHINGTON, THE HOT PLACE TO BE!*

The fourth, captioned *CLIMB HIGH IN THE PACIFIC NORTH-WEST*, featured her ascent into the dark green tree canopy, her hair streaming in the wind, white snowflakes and ice-colored hummingbirds hovering around her.

Livy sniffled, still laughing, and dialed Skye.

"Oh my God, I love them!" she said in lieu of "Hello" when Skye answered.

"Yay!" Skye said. "It was so hard to keep them hidden from you while I was working on them. Jamie let me keep them in her house and do the painting in her garage."

"I am *so* hanging these in the hallway. But you kept copies for your portfolio, right? You've got to."

"Definitely. I took scans. In fact, during my job interview I showed them those, and they were some of their favorites. I kind of think those pieces got me the job."

Livy laughed again, tracing her fingers across the air-poster lettering with pride. "They must think you have one weird-ass imagination."

"Eh, artists. We're like that. Plus I told them we have a family tradition of some pretty crazy stories about the woods."

"Yeah. Don't we, though."

It was summer in Bellwater—or nearly, since it was late June, and everyone knew summer in western Washington didn't truly start till the 5th of July. A layer of clouds hovered over the Sound, but the air had warmed, sunsets lingered until ten p.m., the town had filled with vacationers hauling speedboats, and in the evenings Livy frequently heard the whistle and crack of fireworks.

Today Livy finished work early and showed up at the garage to hang out with Kit until it closed. She helped bring in wind chimes and movable sculptures. He had finished the mermaid months ago and it had sold, and so had the dragon, the mushroom gnome, and the oversized hummingbird he had followed it up with.

"How's she coming along?" Livy asked, running her hand along the rust-speckled green hood of the 1967 Barracuda he was restoring.

"Slow, but I'm loving every minute. I finally found the tires I wanted, and ordered them. I'll show you the picture over dinner."

"Sweet. I've got travel ideas to show you."

After he had anonymously returned as many of the gold pieces to their proper owners as possible, the value of the remaining gold, cashed in, had still come to almost half a million dollars. Livy had insisted he set aside enough to fund his house, shop, and vacation dreams, then helped him choose environmental charities for the rest. One of his dreams had been to buy this battered muscle car and restore it to prime condition. A car of that vintage, she noted dubiously, did not possess an environmentally friendly engine, but he promised with a grin that it wasn't really for driving around much anyway. It was all about the joy of making it look pretty and run smooth.

As for vacation dreams, they were planning to go to Hawaii together in the fall. And from there, on to Japan perhaps, or New Zealand, or elsewhere in the South Pacific—Livy had bookmarked several options to discuss with him tonight.

"Oh, and check this out," he said as he locked the garage office. He fished out his phone and swiped to his texts, and handed it to her. "Grady's latest creations."

Livy stepped into the shade of Carol's Diner to view the screen, and examined the three photos Grady had sent: clams arranged on greens with some sort of lovely red garnish, a delicate dish of ravioli, and a pork slider with an artful zigzag splash of sauce around it on the plate. "Oh my God, can't he just FedEx us the food instead of torturing us with pictures?" she said.

"I know, right? We've got to learn to cook. Meanwhile—shall we?" He tilted his head toward Carol's.

She handed him back his phone. "Yeah. I'm starving."

They'd been fulfilling their promise to get together often with Grady and Skye. The four of them met for dinner each month. On the evening of every full moon, Kit and Livy drove to Olympia to see them, so they could celebrate Kit not having any goblin obligations that night. Grady cooked for them, and Livy always got to choose the menu. It made her self-conscious, but the other three insisted, and she'd come to enjoy browsing ambitious recipes and emailing them to Grady. So far he was never daunted and turned out all the dishes fabulously.

She tried not to choose recipes involving sweetened fruit, though. Neither Grady nor Skye wanted to eat them, even though Grady had the skill and willingness to make them. "But we've worked our way back up to eating fresh fruit," Skye told her brightly, "so that's something."

Livy didn't blame them. She still had the occasional nightmare about cave trolls and centipedes, kelp tangling her legs underwater, a forest fire trapping someone she loved, or a fall from a stratosphere-high tree branch. At least when she did have those dreams, she now usually woke up next to Kit, and snuggled into his warmth and remembered she had been sufficiently brave after all.

Carol brought Kit and Livy their menus. "Dang, Sylvain," she boomed, "good to see you sticking with the same woman for so long, though I'm hearing lots of weeping and wailing from all the others who had their eye on you."

"Stop." Kit smirked, scanning the menu.

"I've had death threats," Livy confided to Carol.

Carol laughed. "Bet you have. It is cute how your hands match up. Shows you're meant for each other. Even though you and Skye were born that way, and he lost his finger being careless with a chainsaw."

Kit scowled. "It's just insulting how you all believe that."

"Like we don't remember it, Sylvain? Nice try." Carol winked at Livy. "What'd you do to get him to settle down, anyhow? Put a spell on him?"

Livy and Kit's gazes met, and they smiled.

"Actually," she said, "I took a spell off him."

AFTERWORD

"Nature is awesome, but be careful, that shit'll kill you." So said cartoonist (and my friend from high school) Astrid Lydia Johannsen to me a few years ago via Twitter. Her sentiment is the basic philosophy I worked under for this story. Like Livy, I love the natural world and want to preserve and help it, but like most pampered city dwellers, I'm also kind of scared of the gazillion ways nature can kill us. Humankind has always felt that way in general, I suppose, thus all the legends, faery tales, and myths involving gorgeous yet dangerous forces of nature. These forces became the stars of our longest-lasting stories, personified as gods and faeries and goblins and other beings, dressed up by human imagination (i.e., the wilderness inside our heads rather than outside).

In writing this, I also operated under the notion that even in our urban society, fae and spirits could be hiding in the scraps of the natural world that do remain, and we wouldn't know, because we rarely even notice the natural world. How often do we really look at the tops of trees? Or ponder the bottoms of rivers and lakes and oceans? Or notice whether exotic invasive plants are growing in our own gardens?

My original inspiration for this story was, of course, the poem "Goblin Market" by Christina Rossetti, published in 1862. I became aware of it in 2011 when a longtime online friend of mine named Aaron brought it up in a blog comment, in which he related a story from his high school years. In his words:

...an English Lit teacher (let's call her Judith) announced to her room full of sixteen-year-old charges, including me, that each of us would have to memorize and recite a poem to the class; she suggested "anything from the Oxford Book of English Verse." Some of my classmates raced to find the shortest and easiest to memorize. (Should you ever need to do this, it's "Twinkle, Twinkle, Little Star.") Meanwhile I took a moment to make sure I was awake and had really been handed such a blank check, then sat down to memorize "Goblin Market." I was looking forward to my classmates' reactions to:

> *She cried 'Laura,' up the garden,*
> *'Did you miss me?*
> *Come and kiss me.*
> *Never mind my bruises,*
> *Hug me, kiss me, suck my juices*
> *Squeezed from goblin fruits for you,*
> *Goblin pulp and goblin dew.*
> *Eat me, drink me, love me...'*

Came the day, and alas I had got no farther than "Clearer than water flowed that juice/She never tasted such before" when Judith woke up, realized what was coming next, and stopped me in my tracks with a frosty "Thank you, that *WILL* be all."

Much amused by this story, I Googled the poem, read it, and commented back to Aaron:

Ooooh la la! This poem is gold to the paranormal romance writer! And um, yeah, surely even the Victorians noticed the overt biting and sucking going on. Still, I may actually have to stick this in my "story idea file" and use it sometime. For a modern paranormal romance, however, I'd need more

nuance than "maiden good, goblin evil." This day and age, after all, it's
"maiden conflicted, goblin sparkly and heartthrobby."

As it turned out, of course, I did more or less go with "maiden good, goblin evil." By the time I got around to writing this novel, I had just come off a long, epic trilogy about Greek gods (*Persephone's Orchard* and its sequels), and was tiring of immortality and special powers being the goal. Ordinary human life appealed to me this time around.

But I also didn't want the fae to be *only* troublesome; that would imply forces of nature were inherently sinister, which isn't my opinion at all. For that matter, it would be unfair to the larger body of faery lore, in which the fae are all kinds of things, ranging from benevolent to lethal. So I invented some local fae, the native species, to balance out those invasive species, the goblins. All of them, in keeping with ancient faery tales, live by very different rules and morals than we humans, so their behavior is never going to make perfect sense to us. Glimpsing them and their ways would be fascinating, but all things considered, most of us (as Livy, Skye, Kit, and Grady would agree) would prefer to live in the human world.

Bellwater and Crabapple Island are fictional locales, but lots of small towns and islands in the Puget Sound area could stand in for them, including some I've vacationed at my whole life. My grandparents bought property in Mason County that my family still visits, and everyone who goes there sees the alluring mystique of the area—the tall evergreens, the calm water slipping in and out with the tides, the little islands, the modest marinas and one-lane bridges, the smell of forests and saltwater. My sisters and I loved our visits there (and still do), wading in the cold shallows, rowing boats around, eating huckleberries in the woods, building bonfires on the beach, and examining the mossy stumps with their fantastical shapes. My grandmother told us those were the houses of Teenyweenies, which became the inspiration for Livy and Skye's Teeny-tinies.

I decided Bellwater stood on the shore of Hood Canal—which despite its name isn't a human-dug canal at all, but merely one of the many long segments of the Sound. That way their backs could be right up against Olympic National Forest, in which, of course, "Here be goblins!," as I wrote on my homemade badly-drawn map of the area.

To find out the depth of Hood Canal—something Livy has to experience firsthand—I talked to my husband Steve, who's an environmental scientist. He gamely consulted official maps to find out some numbers for me. I was guessing the Canal would be maybe twenty or even fifty feet deep, but apparently most of it, in spite of its narrowness, is more like four hundred to five hundred feet deep. Yikes! Daunting indeed. However, if there was an island right offshore, as is the case for my imaginary Crabapple Island just across from Bellwater, then probably the water in between would be somewhat shallower than all that. So I settled for "around a hundred feet," which is still plenty daunting enough, thank you.

ACKNOWLEDGMENTS

In the writing of this novel, I must thank:

My husband, Steve, for fun geography tasks, for answering "what would this character drive" queries because I know nothing about cars, and for generally tolerating my "creative temperament" moodiness.

My kids for tolerating same, and for making me laugh, and for having fabulous imaginations that make this story look tame.

My editor, Michelle Halket, for handling this book and many others of mine with complete professional care, and for supporting me and cheering me on with each new story. She's created a group of true friends out of her stable of authors, and I'm proud to be part of it.

My beta readers! Dean Mayes and Abbie Williams provided expert back-and-forth email discussions about all kinds of plot points, and didn't bat an eyelash when I was all, "Here's a longer sex scene I wrote; what do you think of it?" Fellow writers are tolerant that way. Tracey Batt wrote me up a superb and pro-level outline of detail issues she caught and questions for me to consider, and even treated me to tea in person under the Space Needle—a great day! Melanie Carey brought her own vivid imagination and keen eye to the draft, and made me see aspects of it in a whole new light; and of course shared lots of in-person tea with me as well—conversations which will always be cherished. Ray Warner and Beth Willis lent their delightful enthusiasm to this story, as they have for many others of mine, and I always treasure their feedback.

And of course my parents and grandparents for securing and taking care of that odd little cabin on the beautiful Puget Sound, which has been our family's favorite spot for decades now. May its magic never fade.

The Chrysomelia Stories